# Table of Contents

The Mountain Man's Unexpected Family

- Disclaimer & Copyright .................. 2
- Table of Contents .................. 3
- Let's connect! .................. 5
- Letter from Lydia Olson .................. 6

Prologue .................. 7

Chapter One .................. 17

Chapter Two .................. 23

Chapter Three .................. 30

Chapter Four .................. 36

Chapter Five .................. 42

Chapter Six .................. 50

Chapter Seven .................. 53

Chapter Eight .................. 59

Chapter Eight .................. 70

Chapter Nine .................. 78

Chapter Ten .................. 85

Chapter Eleven .................. 92

Chapter Twelve .................. 99

Chapter Thirteen .................. 106

Chapter Fourteen .................. 115

Chapter Fifteen .................. 123

Chapter Sixteen .................. 130

Chapter Seventeen ................................................. 138
Chapter Sixteen ..................................................... 143
Chapter Eighteen ................................................... 151
Chapter Nineteen .................................................. 161
Chapter Twenty ..................................................... 167
Chapter Twenty-One .............................................. 174
Chapter Twenty-Two .............................................. 181
Chapter Twenty-Three ........................................... 185
Chapter Twenty-Four ............................................. 193
Chapter Twenty-Five .............................................. 200
Chapter Twenty-Six ............................................... 206
Chapter Twenty-Seven ........................................... 212
Chapter Twenty-Eight ............................................ 219
Chapter Twenty-Eight ............................................ 226
Chapter Twenty-Nine ............................................. 233
Chapter Thirty ...................................................... 239
Chapter Thirty-One ............................................... 249
Epilogue .............................................................. 264
  Also by Lydia Olson .......................................... 279

# Let's connect!

**Impact my upcoming stories!**

My passionate readers influenced the core soul of the book you are holding in your hands! The title, the cover, the essence of the book as a whole was affected by them!

Their support on my publishing journey is paramount! I devote this book to them!

If you are not a member yet, join now! As a FREE BONUS, you will receive my Novella "A Race to Save His Childhood Love":

**FREE EXCLUSIVE GIFT
(available only to my subscribers)**

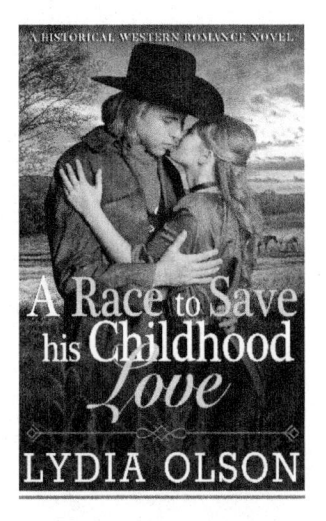

**Go to this link:**
https://avawinters.com/novella-amazon

# Letter from Lydia Olson

***"There is no better place to heal a broken heart than on the back of a horse"***

This is my moto; this is how I grew up.

My name is Lydia and when I am not baking cookies with my daughter or riding the bike with my son, I am a Western Historical Romance writer. It is my passion, my hobby and my career.

After I received my BA in Psychology I realized that this would help me create believable characters. Characters that are based on real people. I want my readers to feel as if they have lived themselves in the West.

Growing up myself in a ranch I have a lot of tales to share. Stories that will help you not escape reality, but rather navigate you through reality. You will feel what it would feel to go through situations that make your heart pound and your palms sweat. You will access the depths of someone else's mind; you will open yourselves to new experiences and different point of views.

What do you say? Do you want to take a vacation with me?

**Lots of hugs,**

*Lydia Olson*

# Prologue

*Great Bend, Kansas*

*1880*

Eva Hall swept a hand through her chestnut brown hair and sighed, her eyes scanning the room for anything she might deem a necessity. Her chest was tight as she took stock of the items in the small home. The shelves her husband had made, his boots by the door. Things she wished with all her heart to bring with her but to which she couldn't afford. She had her wedding ring on, and that was the only sentimental thing she could carry along; besides the pocket watch she was keeping for their son to have when he grew older.

She had always been pretty, or so people had told her. She was a small woman, petite and mannerly, and when she'd met Jim he had treated her like porcelain. At least at first. They'd had a storybook romance when they were teenagers, and she had always pictured a beautiful life together with him. He had been a dream come true to her, especially after her parents had passed away. Meeting him had felt like fate. She'd lost her family when she was so young, then met a man who wanted to do nothing but take care of her. The last thing she had ever expected was to be a widow at 22.

Jim had been young, healthy, and strong, but he still hadn't managed to survive to see their son grow up. He'd changed a lot over the years, growing cynical and bitter the deeper into drink he got. He stopped treating her like porcelain and sometimes she was certain that he hated her; the way he spoke to her and handled her. He'd died just over eight months ago, and although she grieved the man he once was, it hadn't hit her the way it might have if she had still been in love with him.

Jim's death was an unexpected tragedy that had left her penniless. He was murdered in cold blood one night after drowning himself in booze, and it had changed everything. He had gone off drinking with his friends, but before he made it home, he was shot behind the saloon and no one had seen who had done it or how it had happened. Worse still, Jim's friends could barely look his widow, Eva in the eye anymore. They felt responsible for being out with him that night and none of them would speak to her about what had happened.

Eva and Jim had already been behind on all of their bills. He had been out of work for a while; his fondness for drink becoming the focal point of his life. Eva had been doing her best to make ends meet without his help, but with their son, Charlie at home it hadn't been nearly enough, and now, without Jim there at all, their debts had snowballed.

He might not have been killed if he hadn't taken to the bottle. The alcohol made him irritable and mean, and Eva's last years with him had been awful. She'd suffered at his hands more than once, and grieved the loss of the man she loved long before his actual death. Still, it had hit her hard, especially with their son to look after on her own.

It was hard enough emotionally to lose her husband and her son his father, but there had been another unforeseen consequence to his death. They were s also losing the house, the only bit of stability in their lives, and they had to leave. Now.

"Mama, he fell down!" Charlie exclaimed with a giggle.

Eva managed a smile for her three-year-old son, who was sitting on the floor with a small collection of soldiers his father had carved and painted for him to play with. The soldiers would be coming, of course, and it was time to pack everything up they could carry.

"Well, that's okay," Eva said. "It's time to put them back in their bag anyway. Will you be a good boy for me and do that?"

"Why?" Charlie asked, his beautiful golden eyes fixing upon hers. They were her own shade, not his father's, though everything else about him reminded her of Jim, as far as his appearance went anyway. In temperament, he was more like Eva.

"We have to go on a trip," Eva said, struggling to keep the emotion from her voice. She didn't want her son to see her break down. She would save her tears for a better time. They wouldn't do either of them any good right now, that was for sure.

"Where are we going, ma?" Charlie asked in his soft, innocent voice, obeying his mother by placing the soldiers into the pouch she'd sewn him to keep them safe. Even as an infant, he had been a good-natured child. He had cried so rarely that at times she had been worried that something wasn't quite right with him. Once he got a little older though, he had so far developed into a perfectly perfect little boy. His looks favored hers as far as complexion, as well as his light brown hair and golden eyes, and most of her physical features, but there was also an unmistakable look of his father about him. She saw it mostly in his serious eyes and the thoughtful expressions he made as he was learning or working something over in his mind. He was a very bright little boy and had learned to speak fast. He'd been painfully shy when he was younger, but he was growing more extroverted every day, especially without the looming, irritable figure of his father around.

She considered telling him the truth briefly, but she didn't want to scare him. "You'll have to wait and see!" she replied.

The truth was, she didn't know where they were going. But they had to go somewhere. If they stayed in that house one more day, she'd be dealing with the sheriff, and she'd risk losing Charlie to the orphanage. She'd do anything to keep that from happening.

She'd done everything she could to find somewhere to go, but with no work, no one would take her. Worse yet, she couldn't make nearly enough money to support them on her own. There was no one to look after Charlie if she took a job, and although she had managed to make a little bit of money doing mending for people here and there, it hadn't been enough. They were homeless, and Eva was terrified.

But she wouldn't let herself lose hope. She took stock of her possessions; a large potato sack filled with food that she had sewn a strap to so she could carry it on her back with her rifle, two thermoses full of water, and a suitcase with a spare outfit for each of them, several blankets, and some other necessities. The food would last them around two weeks. She could only pray it would be enough.

*People survive on far less for far longer. We'll be okay.*

It would give Eva enough time to try and figure something out, no matter what that something may have to be. Charlie collected the remainder of his toy soldiers and Eva held the suitcase with his little pouch hanging around her wrist, reaching for Charlie's little hand with the other. They gave their home one last, long look before Eva took a deep breath and headed for the door.

They were hit with a gust of frigid wind that carried the scent of the nearby trees. They were nearing the end of autumn and had only one more week until the chill of October began. Winter in Great Bend was cold and unforgiving, and she could already see and feel the signs of its return. It was going to be a harsh one, and she fully anticipated another blizzard that year. She would have to figure something out quickly so that she and her son would be all right.

Great Bend was a comfortable town that had been established along the Santa Fe trail. All kinds came and went, and a lot of them brought trouble right along with them. She wondered often if some rowdy cowboys riding through had been the cause of her husband's fate. Either way, what was done was done, and she had to keep moving forward.

Eva braced herself against the icy wind and bent down to make sure Charlie's coat was buttoned and secured before continuing. She felt anxiety welling up in her chest as they began down the road, knowing that they had no set destination.

Eva's swirling thoughts were interrupted by the gentle tugging of the little hand in hers. Charlie looked up at her with his bright eyes, so gentle and unaware of just how much trouble they were in.

"Can I carry my soldiers, ma?" Eva felt a heartbreaking pain in her chest.

"Of course, darling," she said, ignoring the stinging tears in her eyes as she handed the little pouch to her son.

He took it with a dimpled smile, holding them dutifully in his other hand. She cleared her throat, willing herself once more not to cry as they continued their walk. She could head to town and see if there was something she could find.

But she was afraid if she did that, some busybody would know that they were homeless and insist on taking Charlie, separating them before she'd had a chance to figure out what to do. No, what she needed was a place where she could keep him safe, just for a little while, until something better worked out. Somewhere secluded.

A jolt of hope came rushing through her and she let out an audible gasp. An idea had come to her as if sent from heaven. Something that might allow them the opportunity they needed to get back on their feet. The lodge.

Several times she had gone on walks with Jim through the woods. He had always enjoyed nature and hunting and she had pointed out to him the old hunter's lodge, sharing with him fond stories of the fun times she'd had with her friends there when they were children, playing in that very lodge. It had been abandoned for several years at this point, and hardly what you'd call a home anymore, but it was better than sleeping out in the cold, she hoped. Regardless of whether or not the wood was rotting and the weeds were overtaking its floor, it was still a sound shelter; a better option, anyway, than risking losing her son.

Filled with momentary relief, Eva looked down at Charlie with a smile. "I just realized that we're going the wrong way," she exclaimed. "Come on, darling. Let's turn around. It isn't too far to go."

"That's okay, ma, it's hard to remember where things are sometimes," he replied comfortingly, stroking her hand with his tiny thumb; a reassuring gesture that she had always done to his own little hand. She realized then that it didn't matter whether or not she had tried to hide how she was feeling from him. He had noticed her worries anyway, and he thought it was because she couldn't remember where exactly they were supposed to head. A surge of tenderness and that special kind of excitement only shown in a child's innocent joy for life overtook him as they forged ahead.

"It sure can be hard to remember sometimes," she agreed, smiling down to him. "Thank you for being so kind to your silly old ma. I don't know what I would do without you."

Charlie smiled shyly at the ground and shrugged his shoulders as they continued on toward the hunter's lodge. Now that she was beginning to formulate something of a plan, a lot of the pressure was lifted from her tense shoulders. The abandoned lodge wasn't ideal, obviously, but it gave her hope.

They walked quietly for a while, shivering as the sun began to set and the chilling winds grew even colder. She did her best to ignore the discomfort in her tired arm, keeping her small son nearby until they finally approached the old hunter's lodge. It was still standing, set deep in the forest, and surrounded by tall trees whose leaves had piled up on the ground at their feet, leaving the air perfumed with all that surrounded them as they dissolved back into the earth. She felt a twinge of nostalgia remembering the times she used to play here as a child of Charlie's age. It was much different now, of course, neglected over time and finally forgotten, but it hadn't disappeared altogether and remained a stable fixture. It was far from a home, but it was shelter.

Because of how far away the lodge was from town, there was rarely anyone passing by, which made Eva feel a bit safer. The whole situation was so shameful to her. She didn't want anyone to know how dire her situation was, or to think that she couldn't take care of her son. People were aware of the lodge, but it was clear that nobody had used it in years, based on its dilapidated state. It was nowhere near good enough for her son, long-term, but it was the best she could do in an emergency.

They stood outside for several long moments as the weight of the situation pressed down once again on Eva's shoulders.

She felt reluctant to go inside. She knew it could be dangerous inside, even though it had weathered the test of time. Still, it appeared just as she had seen it the last time she had been through the area with Jim. Its door was closed tight, the shingled roof a little less shingled than before. But still, it was a roof. She had no idea if she would be able to light a fire in the old place safely, but it was a darn sight better than sleeping on the ground.

"Wow!" Charlie exclaimed, in awe of what stood in front of them. "This place looks old! And fun!"

"I used to think the same thing when I was a little girl," Eva said with a soft chuckle. "Hey, I have an idea. How about the two of us use it like a secret hideaway? We can pretend this is our home for a little while and have an adventure out here together. Doesn't that sound fun?"

The little boy's eyes lit up with excitement and he nodded enthusiastically, charging ahead to the rickety front porch. "Yeah! Let's go inside!"

Eva laughed and followed her son, stopping him before he opened the door. "Now, I'm glad you're excited, but first we need to make sure it's safe inside, all right?"

Charlie nodded, holding very still. "Okay, ma."

"Good boy. Now just stand here for a moment while your ma takes a look inside. I'll make sure that it's safe to stay here."

Charlie nodded, making sure to not move a muscle while Eva pushed the door open with a loud creak, and stepped inside. "Stay where you are, all right? I just want to take a look around."

"I will, ma."

***

It took Eva's eyes a few seconds to adjust to the darkness inside. The windows were shuttered closed and the last remaining bit of sunlight was fading fast, peaking through gaps in the shutters and through the opened door, casting the room in deep shadows. Once Eva's eyes adjusted, however, all the familiar furniture came into focus. There was the same old table sitting off to the side of the room, and the little fireplace. The cast iron wood stove was still there too, but she could tell it was in bad shape and she wouldn't be using it. Hopefully, they wouldn't be here long enough to need it anyway. Winter was well on its way, and in a matter of weeks, the snow would settle in.

If she could just use the time until then to figure out her next step. She would take care of her son, no matter what.

"Look!" Charlie shouted, pointing at the gun rack on the opposite wall. "It's just like pa's at home! Hang the rifle up on it!"

He was so excited that Eva couldn't help but laugh. She was satisfied enough that there weren't any other people staying there, or animals that had nested inside, so she reluctantly sat her suitcase and the bag of food down, surprised by the relief she felt. "Come on in son" she requested. "It's getting mighty cold out there." Her back ached, but she had hardly registered it until now. Her concerns had been elsewhere and her emotional pain had clouded the physical ones.

Eva surveyed their new surroundings. It was filthy, full of cobwebs, dust and dirt tracked in by a great many muddied boots passing through on their adventures. She immediately opened the dusty shutters to quickly air the place out before the biting wind would require them to be closed again, wishing that she had thought to pack some cleaning supplies. But she would make do, just as she always did.

"It's perfect," Charlie said with an approving nod as Eva placed the rifle on the gun rack. "Just like home."

Eva felt another twinge in her chest, but she wouldn't let her smile falter. "Just like home," she agreed, despite being inwardly ashamed that Charlie thought this filthy place even compared. She had always prided herself on keeping a tidy home for her husband and son. But it was a silly reaction, she knew that. He was just a small boy optimistically viewing the world through rose-tinted glasses, and that was for the best. "Now, what do you say we have some supper? That was a long walk and I bet you're as hungry as a horse."

Charlie nodded enthusiastically and soon she was busying herself, getting the small lodge as clean as possible before preparing their meal. She made some sandwiches for them both, and then set to work trying to clean the old fireplace so that they would be able to rest in its warmth. But when she peered up the chimney, her heart sank on discovering that it had collapsed and the smoke would have nowhere to escape. A fire was out of the question, too. She would have to set up a campfire outside to cook on. It would be all right for now, as long as she and Charlie found a place to go before the snow arrived.

Their first evening in the lodge passed by like a blur, and when it finally came time for her to blow out the solitary candle lighting up the room and say good night to her son, tucking him in with the one warm blanket she managed to pack along with a pair of long johns, she was relieved to find that he was already sound asleep.

Eva kissed him on the forehead and smoothed the hair back from his face, finally giving herself permission to softly let out the stream of tears that she had been holding back for days. She was grateful for the lodge. She was, truly, but to see her small son, the boy who depended upon her for everything and deserved the world, to see him lying in this decrepit old place with nothing but one warm blanket thrown on top of a musty mattress worn out decades ago, well, she couldn't help but feel like a complete failure.

But she wouldn't dwell on it. No, Eva was made of stronger stuff than that. And she would prove it to everyone. She was going to get herself and her son out of this mess and get him the life that he deserved. Just as soon as she figured out how.

# Chapter One

"One more?" Charlie asked, for what was the fifth time. Eva had felt bad enough to give in to his requests for several extra bedtime stories, but she was beginning to sense that he was simply seeing how long he could get away with managing it before falling asleep.

"That's quite enough for tonight, darling. I want you to get nice and comfortable and go to sleep now. Ma's got some things to do." She brushed the light brown hair from his forehead and kissed it before stepping away from the bed and blowing out the candle nearest to him.

Charlie snuggled into his blanket and was soon asleep. Eva did her best not to look over him, her chest tight with worry. They had been living out at the old hunter's lodge for the past two weeks, and as of that evening, they were officially out of food.

She had been trying to work something out but nowhere that would have been willing to hire her would allow her to bring Charlie with too. She had been asking around town to see if anyone needed mending done, and she had found a couple of people who wanted her help, but they were small tasks and hardly enough to keep them going. She needed a place to live with her son. Once the mending was done, she planned to buy flour and butter. It would be something in their bellies until she was able to get something more for them.

Once it was daylight, she thought she might take Charlie hunting with her, but the truth was that she was a terrible shot and she was worried about wasting the few bullets she had been able to bring along with her. Still, maybe if she could get some meat on the table, it would help them both feel a little better. They were starving.

Charlie had a bad cold and she didn't want to leave his side, but the reason he wasn't well had a lot to do with being cold and hungry. She'd been with him all day long, sitting on the icy floor next to his mattress and trying to console him and keep him calm, so she hadn't had a chance to go out and forage for food, and bringing him with her was out of the question.

He had finally grown quiet and had stayed that way for the past several minutes. The sun would be setting soon, and Eva checked to make sure Charlie was asleep, realizing this would be her only opportunity to head outside to forage for berries before nightfall. She knew there were some blackberry bushes nearby, so she walked there carefully in the twilight with a potato sack, hoping she would find enough to help until she could figure something else out. She shivered as an unforgiving wind ripped through her. It was November now, and things were looking grim. She had to do something soon, this wasn't sustainable for them. During those days, she had been working at trying to get the old wood stove to work properly, but she had never been much good with that. Charlie was relying on her though and she knew she needed to get them warmer or he would suffer even more than he already was.

Once she got to the bushes, she scoured the area for several minutes, growing increasingly desperate as she quickly realized that there were no berries left.

"That's okay, Eva," she said, trying to talk herself out of the panic that was building in her chest. It would do no good now. "There are some nuts. The squirrels have to eat too, right?"

She set to work, hunting for anything remotely edible, but finding nothing. She felt hot tears stinging her cheeks before she could stop them, and a wave of hopelessness crashed down on her. How could she get enough food to feed her son? He needed a hot meal, anyway, not just nuts and berries. She was going to try hunting, but that would still be no guarantee. She'd never been a good shot, and with Charlie with her she wasn't sure she would even be able to keep an animal close enough to shoot if she tried.

She began the trek back to the cabin, surprised by how far she had walked in her desperation. She made her way to the roadside so she wouldn't get lost in the woods, rubbing a cold spot growing in her chest. It felt tight and constricting.

Eva suddenly heard the clopping of hooves and a deep lowing, and glanced to her left, realizing that she was passing by the ranch where her husband had worked before he had been killed. She'd been there once before for a Christmas party with him. She'd been so impressed by the place. They wanted for nothing, and even had an outdoor cellar where they kept their excess harvest stored away for harder months.

An outdoor cellar. Full of food.

An idea began to form in her mind. She hated the thought, but what choice did she have? There were rocks in the pit of her stomach as she made her way cautiously toward the cellar. The ranch was quiet now, all except the livestock settling down for the night, and she made sure not to make a sound as she crept toward the house from the roadside. It was a longer walk than she remembered, likely due to the fact that she was terrified.

After what felt like an eternity of jumping out of her skin at every sound, she arrived. She stood, hesitating at the cellar doors for a moment as she realized what she was about to do. She had never stolen a thing in her life. It felt wrong. It was wrong. Even if the people here were wealthy, they deserved better than to be robbed.

But Charlie also deserved better, and she couldn't let him starve. She was certain that if she could just get a little more time, they would figure something out, something that would be enough to finally feel secure.

Eva sucked in a deep breath and carefully opened the cellar doors, then made her way inside, carefully lowering her foot until it caught the top rung of the ladder leading down. When she was inside, her survival instincts took over. She began grabbing food frantically, eager to get out of there as quickly as she could so that she could get back to her son and put this shameful act behind her. Eva worked until the sack was full to bursting and then made her way out of the cellar, her heart thudding hard in her chest. She closed the doors as quietly as she could, letting out a little gasp when one of them fell from her shaking hands and thudded closed.

She froze in terror; sure she was about to be caught in the act and. Charlie would be left stranded while she was carted off to jail. The panic in her mind clouded all her thoughts until finally she realized she was already safe.

No one had heard the door bang closed, and she had immediately taken off running with all the energy she could muster, 'til she was finally back at the lodge. She sat the potato sack down, feeling exhausted and sick to her stomach. Even though she was grateful she would be able to continue feeding her son for a while, the grim reality of their situation was toppling down on her shoulders.

Things weren't getting any better, and no matter how hard she tried, she wasn't going to magically fix the situation they found themselves in. Eva needed something she could rely on, something stable. Charlie deserved that and she wasn't going to deprive him of it for much longer. If nothing turned up by the time this newly acquired food was gone, she knew what she would have to do, even though it would break her heart. She just didn't want to let it come to that. She would keep doing her best until there was absolutely no other option than to part with her son. She couldn't allow Charlie to suffer.

She thought about eating but quickly decided against it. They would need to save their food, and besides, her stomach was upset from the stress of the situation. So, she curled up on the bed beside Charlie and tried to get some sleep.

Her sleep was fitful, and morning came too soon. But when it did, she couldn't help but smile at the sound of Charlie's gasp of wonder.

"Look, ma! The angels brought us breakfast!" He ran toward the table, where she had set out a small meal of fruit for him the night before, in case he woke up hungry. He gaped at it before running to the bag that was overflowing with food. "It's a miracle!"

Eva didn't correct her son. If he felt it was a gift from God, then maybe for him it truly was. She wouldn't take that away from him by telling him that his mom was a thief. She already felt terrible about the whole thing. It was nice that some good was coming of it outside of simply feeding them both. Her son's faith in miracles was being restored.

"Have some breakfast, darling," Eva said gently. "There's plenty here for you to enjoy."

The bright smile on the little boy's face lit up the room. "Eat with me, ma! They brought it for you too!"

Eva felt a guilt-ridden gnawing in her chest at the words, but also an odd sense of relief. Charlie was right. God had blessed them with this food, and she was just as worthy as anyone else, even if she had stolen it to keep her child alive. And herself.

"Yes, and let's say grace before we begin, okay? That way the angels know we got their wonderful gift."

Charlie nodded enthusiastically, and they held hands at the old table and gave thanks for the meal that had come from the open cellar on the ranch where his father once worked. She hoped he would never have to know anything about what she had done, but she knew that he might one day understand. Right now, though, she was happy to let him have his miracle, and the smile on his face was enough to fill her with hope of her own. If God could do this for them, then maybe God would help get them through the hardest parts of what was yet to come.

# Chapter Two

"This isn't adding up, Gregory. Think about it," Carl sighed. He ran his hand through his coal-black curls in annoyance. "We're missing food. I need to know exactly how it happened. I was checking the inventory and the eggs are entirely gone. Did I miss a meal somehow?"

He already knew that he was being overbearing, especially considering this wasn't his normal cook. Maggie had come down with a cold earlier in the week and Gregory had the training to fill in for her during times when she wasn't available. Maggie was the one who usually kept things together, so Carl found it even more frustrating that things were unraveling without her there. Not that he blamed Gregory, but he wanted to know what was going on.

He knew that he was being heavy handed, but his staff were used to his ways. Carl liked to maintain full control over everything that went on at his ranch, and when things didn't add up, he had to find out why and correct it. Missing food could either be a sign of carelessness, or something more sinister. Both ways, he needed to deal with it, and he couldn't wait until Maggie was feeling better before things would get back to normal. Maggie had worked for Carl's family her whole life and had stepped in as a mother figure for him when he didn't have one of his own. She was like family, and she knew exactly how he liked things to be done. He felt far more secure with her there.

"No, Mr. Spencer, you haven't made a mistake. But I don't know where the food went," Gregory said. Carl sighed again. He believed his cook. The man had been working for him for years at this point and there was no reason for him to lie about something like this. It could only mean one thing. A thief had been in his cellar. And Carl didn't like thieves.

"Someone's been stealing from us," Carl said. Gregory nodded in agreement. "Do you think they will try it again?"

Gregory gave another slight nod. "If they think the cellar is an easy target and they want the free food, then they will probably be back."

Carl narrowed his eyes pensively in thought. He didn't like the idea of his hard work being disrupted, and his inventories suffering because of someone else. Whether it was incompetent record keeping or a thief, both were an offense to his business, and he had to sort it out. "Well, then I will just have to deal with it myself."

Gregory nodded but knew better than to ask any questions. Carl left the kitchen, already forming a plan in his mind. He didn't like being made a fool of, and if someone who was working for him thought it was okay to go to his stores and rob him of his hard-earned resources, they had another thing coming. No, he wasn't just going to lie down and take it. He was going to make sure they were caught and dealt with. Thieving was a serious crime, and once he knew who was responsible, they would be going directly to the sheriff for a nice little chat.

That night, Carl set up camp in the cellar. He placed a coin between the doors so that, in case he fell asleep, if he heard it drop, he would know someone was there. Once he was satisfied with his trap, he made himself a cot in the far back corner behind a shelf and crouched down in hiding. He didn't want to scare them off before he even had a chance to identify them and address the issue. He brought a block of wood and a knife so he could whittle as he waited, knowing his eyes would adjust enough to the dark for him to do at least something while he waited, since he didn't want to light a candle to read. So, in the dark he remained, hidden throughout the night, only resting lightly enough that he would be awakened if he heard his trap go off.

The next morning, Carl was annoyed to have wasted his time down there without anything occurring. He was a light sleeper, so he was confident that he hadn't missed the crook, but regardless, he was meticulous about his inventories and took stock of his stores just to be sure. Nothing was missing, so he went to clean himself up and get ready for the day.

"Mr. Spencer, may I have a word with you please?"

Carl was surprised when his housekeeper, Anna, stopped him on the way out the door. Anna was a young woman with copper hair and a fair complexion. She spoke with a light Irish accent and often entertained him with her stories about the large family she had left back in New York so that she could travel with the man she loved and settle down in Great Bend with him.

"Of course," he said, straightening his clothing. "Is everything all right, Anna?"

"Yes, sir - well. No, sir, actually." Anna looked down at her hands and sighed, clearly uneasy.

Carl waited patiently for her to speak. He was alarmed to hear that something was wrong, and his mind went in a thousand different directions as he tried to puzzle together what might be going on at the ranch to upset her. Anna took a long, shuddering breath before finally continuing.

"I just got word that my mother has fallen ill, and they want me to travel back home to help look after things. It isn't looking good for her and as it's my mother, well... I feel an obligation. I hope you can understand." Anna's voice trembled as she spoke, and Carl felt his sympathy ignite.

Anna looked genuinely distraught, and just like his cook, Carl was quick to believe that she wouldn't have approached him if she had only just wanted some time off work. He had exacting standards for the way his ranch was run, and those standards were usually only met by exceptional help. If someone didn't live up to his expectations, he usually spoke with them and gave them a chance to correct themselves, and, depending, he might even give them several chances, whether it put him out or not.

"That's terrible news, I'm so very sorry to hear that," Carl said with a frown. "How far away do you have to travel?"

"Well, sir, they live up in New York, so it will be several weeks I suspect."

"Weeks?" Carl asked, furrowing his brow. It sounded like her mother's illness was a matter of urgency. A long journey like that would mean she might not even make it home in time to care for her mother or see her if she were expected to pass. Time had already advanced since she'd gotten the telegraph, yet here she was, still showing up to work to ask his permission to leave. "You're going by horse?"

Anna nodded, already looking exhausted by the prospect but keeping her shoulders square and her face composed, despite the puffy, red rings around her eyes that told him that she had been crying. "Yes, sir. The sooner the better, of course. I just wanted to let you know and ask for permission to take leave and... resume my position when I return."

Her voice quavered as she asked, and Carl's heart went out to her. He could imagine what she was going through, having experienced similar difficulties with his own father during the end of his life. He hadn't had to travel to him like this, fortunately, the first heart attack had debilitated him before the second took his life several weeks later, but the stress of it all on top of such a long trip, not even knowing if Anna would make it before her mother passed away... It was horrible to imagine having to go through something like that.

"Are you traveling alone?" he asked, now suddenly feeling concerned with the trip himself.

"No, sir, just with my husband."

"And you two don't have children, right?"

Anna sighed and looked down at the ground, her expression almost ashamed. "No, sir. God didn't see fit to make me a mother."

"I tell you what," Carl said, reaching for his wallet. "I want you to take this and buy two train tickets. Right now. And when you're back in Kentucky, just come and let me know and we will get you back to work, all right?"

Anna flinched as he retrieved the money from his wallet. Southern pride at its best. She shook her head quickly. "No, sir! That's far too generous. I couldn't accept it!"

"You'll accept it, or I'll go down to the station myself. Consider this a holiday bonus, all right? Your work here has always been exceptional, and I know what it's like when a parent is ill. The last thing you need is a grueling journey 'cross country. You hear me?" Carl spoke firmly, but in a gentle voice, finding Anna's hand with the wad of money he had pulled from his wallet. "I would really like to do this. I fear God wouldn't forgive a man of means if he didn't use it with his heart once in a while."

Anna's red-rimmed eyes filled with fresh tears, and she clutched the money with a curtsey. "Thank you so much, Mr. Spencer."

"You're welcome, Anna. Now get on off to the train station, would you? Time isn't gonna stop for no one."

"You're truly wonderful, Mr. Spencer. I'll get in touch when I'm back home."

Carl smiled at Anna with a quick nod, and she hurried out of the house. He watched her go, glad he was able to do something meaningful for someone who had been loyal to him and his ranch for so long. It was truly a shame about her family, though, and he let out a low sigh before heading off to get his work done, thoughts of the thief far from his mind until night began to fall.

Whoever had stolen from him had taken enough food to last a while if they were alone. But he wouldn't count on waiting for them to get hungry again. He would remain at his post every night until the thief was caught, and he could move on with his life. At dusk, he took his position back in the cellar, turning the wooden block in his hands as he whittled and waited to make his move.

He was starting to grow attached to this carving. At first it had begun as a meaningless block, but as he whittled away, he realized that it was intended to be a horse. A specific horse, in fact, as it reminded him of one he had on the ranch when he was just a boy. His name was Smokey, and he had come to the ranch a wild thing that couldn't be tamed. His father had done his best to and was furious that he had wasted his money. Smokey was a beautiful stallion, but he wasn't proving useful.

One night, Carl had walked over to the stables and Smokey didn't run away or act ornery. Carl decided he was going to try and get to know the horse, and before long, they were riding together through the fields during Carl's free time.

Carl's father had always been strict with his son, and often made him feel like he was good for nothing, but when Carl and that horse had bonded, even his father couldn't deny it. He'd given him a nod of approval and then he had given that horse to him. It was the first time he'd felt like his father cared about him, even respected him. The feeling didn't last. His father was back to his old ways soon enough, but it was a moment that Carl cherished, and his relationship with Smokey had always been special to him.

Now, he found himself carving the likeness of that horse as he waited in the cellar for the thief to come back to the ranch. It took several more nights before the sudden sound of a coin hitting the floor woke him from a dead sleep. Whomever had opened the cellar doors hadn't seemed to notice, and Carl sat up fast, readying himself to step out from his hiding place. They crept down to the shelves, and he peeked around the corner. All he could see was a silhouette with a large sack, and the sight made his blood boil.

Once they were occupied with filling the sack with *his* food, Carl rounded the corner and gripped what was a surprisingly small shoulder. He turned the thief around and was shocked by the beautiful face staring at him in terror. He released her, startled by the unforeseen twist in his plan, his eyes roaming her up and down. She looked worn out and painfully thin, and a surge of compassion stilled the powerful anger that had risen unbridled in his chest.

He found himself lost for words, but knew he had to be stern. She was trespassing on his property. Stealing from him. So, he hardened his gaze and folded his arms across his chest, knowing that there was no need to use force with someone so slight, so... *defenseless.*

"All right," he said, trying to keep his tone cold, despite the feeling that there was something about this woman that he just wanted to protect. "You have some explainin' to do."

# Chapter Three

Eva's heart dropped when she felt a strong hand on her shoulder, and all she could think about was how she had failed her son. Charlie would suffer for this, and she had to act fast to try and make sure that she could get back home to him that night. Well, it wasn't really home, but it was all they had. The idea of not being able to make it back to him before he woke up, and how confused and scared he would be if someone else came and took him to the orphanage… She didn't want to put her son through all that.

"Well?"

The man's voice was low and stern. When she finally had the courage to look up at him, Eva was surprised to find a handsome man's face, with dark, curly hair and a well-groomed beard trimmed neatly along his strong jawline. His eyes, although steady on her, did not seem unkind, and even in the dim light of the cellar, she could see that they were a piercing gunmetal blue. He was like a work of art, and she felt a sense of wonder and attraction that, under different circumstances, might have turned their conversation in a different direction. But he was here to punish her, and she was terrified. Eva looked back down quickly. His severe tone scared her when he spoke. Even though he wasn't yelling, she could tell he was a powerful man.

"Just what on earth are you doing down here?" he asked, his deep voice piercing into her. "I'm going to get the sheriff."

"No! Please. I'm sorry, I can explain…" Eva trailed off, unsure of whether or not the man's silence was an invitation to continue or a stubbornness to do exactly as he said he would. Just in case she had a chance though, for Charlie's sake, she let the words spill from her lips, hoping that there would be a way out of this mess. "I have a son…"

"A son?" the man asked, his voice still even. It was a warm voice, really, though under the circumstances, Eva still felt threatened. He could take away everything she cared about with just one word to the sheriff. Her lungs constricted, and her hands were shaking so badly she was certain she was going to drop the sack. She clutched it tighter as she tried to form the right words.

"Yes. Charlie. My boy, well, he's four now, and he lost his pa - my husband. We weren't left with anything, and we were evicted. So, it's just been him and me, and nobody to help take care of him if I go to work. I've been doing my best to keep him fed and all, while I try and sort out what to do, but since I'm alone and he needs someone with him, it just ain't easy for us. We're barely making it out there. We found somewhere to stay, a little bit of shelter, but... My son is still growing. He needs proper meals. I never would have taken a thing from you if I weren't worried about my boy."

She spoke quickly, every word running into the next. It was hard to admit to this perfect stranger just how bad her situation was, but it felt like the most natural thing in the world as if it were somehow safe for her to expose every shameful thing about her life to this man. He listened carefully.

Mr. Spencer, of course, now she remembered his name, her husband's boss at the ranch. This was his home, his cellar, and he was the one who had taken the time to catch the villain stealing his food. How was he going to deal with her now that she had been caught red-handed? Would he yell at her? Strike her? Drag her by the arm down to the sheriff's station?

"Slow down, ma'am," Mr. Spencer said, holding his hand up before running it through his beard in complete exhaustion. He had been biding his time in the cellar for who could say how long, waiting to catch the invader. There was no other reason for him to be down there in the dark at an hour like this. "You're telling me you lost your husband and your home, is that right?"

Eva nodded, tears of shame burning hot in her eyes. "Yes. And my son is starving. I just want to take care of him the best I can, he's so small and so hungry. I've done the best I can to ration everything we have but I know I've got to work something else out, and I will. But if you tell the sheriff about this, they will take him away from me. He's all I have. The thought of him losing his father and me, it's just too much for me to bear.."

Eva stopped, embarrassed by her actions. She felt vulnerable, ashamed, but more than that, confused. She never would have felt comfortable sharing these feelings to her own husband, let alone a complete stranger, and a man to boot.

It was because she had been isolated for so long with only her small son to talk to. Or she was becoming delirious from starvation. Perhaps still, she was feeling panicked and afraid, and her nerves were to blame for the way she was speaking. She would have said or done anything to make sure that Charlie was okay, and that was what she was hoping for now. The last thing she could handle was losing her son.

Mr. Spencer was quiet for several moments and then, finally, let out a sigh. "I don't suppose it will hurt me all that much to lose a few things for now. You should run along home and feed your boy. Sounds like he needs it." He was quiet again before adding, "I know I never sleep well on an empty stomach."

Eva stared at the man in utter astonishment. "Really? You mean that?"

The man sighed with a slight nod of the head and Eva could see that he truly did. She couldn't have been more grateful if he had hand delivered the food to their doorstep. She was overwhelmed, but also afraid that if she didn't get out of his sight soon, he may change his mind.

"Thank you so much, you don't know what this means to me," she said, choking back the tears tightening her throat. "I'll find some way to repay you for all of this, I promise. When I'm back on my feet I will—"

Mr. Spencer raised his hand, gesturing he didn't want to hear another word on the matter, and Eva felt he genuinely had nothing more to say. She had heard her husband speak of him often, especially back when Joe had been doing well. Before his alcoholism had changed everything. He would come home from the ranch after a long day's work and praise Mr. Spencer, saying he was a kind and fair man, but that he didn't talk much. But the deeper into drink he got, the more Jim's opinion of the man altered. Soon, she heard nothing about him except that he was a tyrant and a bully. A man who didn't let anything go and ran his ranch like a dictator.

She supposed it must be different to be around a man of few words, she certainly wouldn't know. Her husband had always been a talker and got meaner and meaner over time as he succumbed to the bottle. She could see now that some of what he'd said was true. He certainly had a generous nature, and he wasn't overly talkative, but he had dismissed her, and she was still lingering there in front of him like a fool. What was wrong with her?

"Thank you, again," she mumbled with a clumsy curtsy before she took off running from the cellar doors. She could feel him watching her as she ran into the dusk, eager to get the food back to her son and herself out of sight.

She hated to leave Charlie alone at all, but it seemed easier when he was sleeping. He had been falling asleep earlier and earlier of late, likely because the boy wasn't getting nearly enough to eat. At least tonight he would have something to enjoy for supper. She would have liked to feed him sooner, but she couldn't risk leaving him awake in the house by himself.

Eva opened the door to the cabin and closed it quickly again with a shiver. The weather was biting, the ice-cold snow and wind seemed to cut right through her and leave her wishing more than anything for some way to rid her bones of it. November was here, and soon they would be in true danger. The seasons had been harsh, and she knew they were in for another bad winter. She'd overheard the farmers talking while she had been running errands in town before she'd lost the house.

The days were growing shorter and colder, and without could the means to heat the cabin properly, Eva and her son could freeze to death. She could still see her breath when she got inside, and she searched the room for Charlie, who was still lying on his little bed, huddled under his blanket. The poor child had been through so much, and she couldn't stand it to get any worse.

"Mama, where did you go?" Charlie asked, his tiny voice soft under the covers. "I missed you."

"Oh, darling. I missed you too, but I had to make sure that we had enough food for supper."

Charlie's little eyes brightened and wandered to the window. "It's dark outside. And I'm really cold, ma."

"I know, sweetheart, but we're going to get this place nice and cozy, soon. Just wait and see. And in the meantime, I will make you something real nice and yummy to eat. What do you say to that?"

Charlie nodded, a small smile creeping across his face. He wasn't looking nearly as healthy as he had when they first arrived, but he was doing okay. Eva had always made sure to give whatever she could of her meals to her small boy. He needed to eat more, but even then, it didn't seem to be enough to keep either of them healthy. It would only be a matter of time before they both wasted away if Eva didn't figure out a real plan to keep them fed and warm.

"Can we make the fire now?" Charlie asked, shivering under the blanket. He hadn't moved a muscle from when she had left him, and she wondered whether or not to be further concerned. Boys Charlie's age were known for running around and getting into things, and part of her wished that he had gotten up to some mischief while she was gone, instead of lying there.

It was time to admit defeat. Take him somewhere that he could truly be taken care of. She would know he was eating, drinking and warm, if nothing else. That was more than what Eva could provide for him. She felt like a failure.

She sat the bag of food down and went promptly outside to gather up some wood for a fire. She had been avoiding making one, but knew that if she didn't soon, her son might catch pneumonia, and that would be the only thing worse than leaving him at the orphanage.

When she had finished collecting outside, Eva did her best to set the sticks up in the fireplace and get them lit. She tried over and over again to ignite the kindling, increasingly frustrated by the fact it wasn't working. The wood was too cold and wet to catch and she was close to tears when she heard a sudden knock at the door. Her heart leapt into her throat and Charlie looked at her in surprise, not making a sound. He only watched the door from under his blanket with his tired eyes held desperately open.

Eva's heart was pounding as she stood up from the fireplace. She took a deep breath and nervously composed herself, bracing for whatever might meet her on the other side of the door.

# Chapter Four

After the young woman left, Carl was quiet for a long time. He lit his lantern and sat back down on his little cot in the cellar, his mind pouring over what had just occurred. He had had the strangest feeling when he saw her, as if he had met her before. And it was taking everything he had not to kick himself for not even asking for her name.

She was a devoted mother. He could see it in the way she spoke about her son, and by the sheer fact that she had risked stealing from his cellar. Everyone knew that thievery was a punishable crime, but she was just doing her best to survive. There had to be something that he could do?

He contemplated this for a long time before grabbing the little horse figurine and placing it in his pocket. There were always things that could be done around the ranch, he had even hired staff to come and check on things during the evenings. He caught sight of one of them, a balding man in his forties who everyone called Teddy and motioned him over. "You know these parts pretty well, don't you, Teddy?"

Teddy smiled, rubbing the top of his bald head in thought. "Yessir, Mr. Spencer, I sure do."

Carl nodded. "Did you happen to see a young woman around recently, really delicate looking, on her own? She's living nearby with her young son, he's about four. Would you have any idea where they might be?"

"I saw a woman last night, now that you mention it. She was walking down the road looking spooked and I asked if she was all right. I don't reckon she heard me and she just kept on walking, but I haven't seen her on your property before. I thought it was strange for her to be walking past that time of night." Teddy said. "Why do you ask, Mr. Spencer?"

Carl sighed. "I think she's in trouble."

Teddy was quiet for several moments before speaking again. "When she didn't answer, I walked along behind her, not letting her see me or anything. I was worried she was lost. I wanted to see her home safely. But I was kind of surprised when I saw where she was headed."

"Really? I'd like to know, Teddy. It's important." Carl couldn't get this weight off his chest. He wanted to know what exactly was going on with this woman. It felt wrong just to let her leave that way, knowing she was struggling. He shivered as they stood outside in the cold, his mind rolling over the whole strange situation until he felt like he could hardly stand it anymore.

"She's at the old hunting lodge, Mr. Spencer. You know the abandoned spot south of the old dirt road? I've seen her coming and going from there for a few weeks now."

The old hunting lodge. Carl frowned. That was hardly a home. "Right. Thanks, Teddy."

"My pleasure, Mr. Spencer."

Teddy left to resume his chores. Carl was feeling too restless to go inside, so he set to work doing some tasks around the ranch, frowning as the temperatures dropped lower and lower. He felt a churning in the pit of his stomach. It was blizzard weather, and they were likely to get hit hard.

After making preparations to ensure the safety of his livestock, Carl saddled up his horse. He couldn't just leave them out there. Not on a night like this one. It would be far too dangerous, and he would never be able to live with himself if something happened to them. He believed that sometimes God worked in mysterious ways, and if the Lord had sent that woman to him, he wasn't going to ignore that.

He rode out quickly. He could have walked, but it was already getting late, and the sun had already fully set. Normally, he would have been ready for bed by now, resting for the next morning's early rise, but tonight he had a job to do.

When he finally reached the old hunting lodge, he looked around the place with his stomach still in knots. This was no place to stay for a night, let alone weeks. He dismounted and made his way to the door, knocking firmly on it. It took a good minute before the door opened, and the same young woman stood before him n, clearer in view now that they were no longer in his cellar.

She was even more beautiful, despite looking like she had been missing meals for longer than he cared to think about. He felt a pang of guilt as her face clouded over with horror at the sight of him. She stepped out onto the porch and shielded the doorway with her slight frame, forcing him to take a step back.

"Have you come to take me to the sheriff?" she whispered. Again, the nagging thought that he had met her before tugged at him. He tried to ignore it, but it wouldn't be chased away until he could figure it out.

"No, I'm not here to get you in trouble," Carl said with a quick smile. "There's a blizzard coming, and I just wanted to see to it that you and your boy are safe. It's only right."

"Thank you for your concern, but we're fine," she replied, avoiding his eyes. "I'm just getting the fire lit."

Carl peered at the woman, seeing the red rims around her eyes. She looked like she had been crying, and he looked over her shoulder to where a pile of firewood lay in a heap. "That wood of yours doesn't look fit to burn," he stated firmly. Carl had spent much of his time out in the mountains. He knew exactly what wet wood looked like, something this poor woman knew little about.

"I said we'll be fine, thank you," she murmured again, her gaze still facing the ground at his feet.

Carl caught a pair of little eyes looking at him from the far end of the room. The boy was small, even for his age, and looked gaunt and tired. He was a pretty cute little fellow besides. Seeing him made Carl sigh.

He took a small step toward the young woman and lowered his voice. "I don't want anything happening to the two of you. You and I both know it would be better if y'all stayed at the ranch tonight. You and the boy can ride my horse there and I'll follow along. But we've got to get a move on before the weather gets real bad."

"I'm just not sure it's a good idea," she whispered, her voice distressed. Carl imagined there were several reasons for this, but he didn't have a chance to speak again. A small figure appeared and an even smaller voice interrupted him.

"Mama?"

They were both surprised when Charlie's voice reached them. He had his mother's skirt by the hand and was tugging on it trying to get her attention. "Mama, who's this man? I'm hungry. And cold. When can we have supper?"

Carl couldn't bear to watch. He gazed at the young woman, hoping that she hadn't taken offense at his sudden arrival. She was scared. After all, they were in the middle of nowhere, and he could do just about anything, if he were the kind of man to do that sort of thing. It was likely terrifying for a woman like herself to be out there alone with her young son. Why hadn't he thought to bring one of the female workers along to make her feel more comfortable? He had been in such a hurry to beat the blizzard that he hadn't even considered her saying no to his offer. It seemed like common sense to take it. Where else was she going to go?

"I know you're hungry, sweetheart. But this nice man is here to help us. There's is going to be a snowstorm and he was hoping we might like to spend some time with him at his ranch until it's all blown over. That way, we can stay warm. How does that sound?"

"It sounds real good, ma," the small boy answered, huddling against his mother's leg. "Can I have an apple?"

"We don't have any more apples sweet-"

"Once we get to my house, you can have all the apples you want," Carl interrupted, eager to get these two away from this place before the weight of the coming storm brought the cabin roof down around them. "How do you feel about riding my horse? Your ma is going to take you to my ranch right away."

Charlie's eyes looked past Carl and settled on the stallion waiting outside. "What's its name?"

"Smokey, the third," Carl said with a chuckle.

"Where's the first one?" Charlie asked, looking up at Carl with eyes almost as pretty as his mother's. Carl couldn't help but grin at the small boy and he pulled the whittled horse from his pocket.

"Right here," Carl replied. "And if you're a brave boy while you ride with your mom to the ranch, I'll even let you play with him. Sound good?"

The little boy nodded eagerly. "Yeah!"

"All right," Carl said, turning to Eva and studying the delicate features of her face. He couldn't get over how pretty she was, despite her dirty gown. The urge to take care of her was overwhelming. "I know this isn't quite what you had planned for the evening, but please get on the horse and ride. If I wanted to kidnap y'all, I would have done it by now."

A glimmer crossed Eva's lips and she nodded, finally looking into his eyes. Carl's heart pounded in his chest as he found himself powerless. "Thank you." She said. "I guess we will be seeing you there, then."

"That's right. I'll catch up, don't you worry."

Carl walked with them over to Smokey and gave his muzzle a quick but affectionate pat. He watched with a light frown as the young woman did her best to pull herself up on the saddle, but she just didn't have the strength. She was weak, and if she didn't get a proper meal into her soon, Carl was afraid she might just faint right in front of him. He wanted to make sure she was okay, to see to it that she was nursed back to health, but when everything was said and done, he had no idea how he would convince her to stay.

Besides, he couldn't go taking in every stray he found. He was a generous man, surely, but he had to draw the line somewhere. He wasn't stupid. He would help them through the storm and then see if there was someone he knew who would know what to do with the woman and her boy, so that they could get out of that wretched place once and for all.

Once Carl had helped Eva onto the saddle, she gave him a beautiful, haunting smile before he lifted Charlie up into her arms. Securing him against herself, Eva began at a trot toward the ranch as Carl followed behind them with his icy hands shoved deep in his pockets, wondering just what on earth he had gotten himself into.

# Chapter Five

Eva and Charlie arrived at the ranch before Carl did, but he wasn't far behind. She had ridden slowly to make sure the little boy wouldn't topple off the horse, and it had been a while since she had been on one herself. She also didn't have a lot of strength in her arms to keep him steady and she didn't want to take any chances. She led the horse to the stables where a kindly man nodded and helped them both down before taking the reins and leading Smokey off to stable him for the night.

Eva took Charlie by the hand, and they walked together toward the house just as Carl was heading up to the porch. "Come on in, I'll show you around."

Eva nodded, not sure what to say, and followed him in. He moved quickly, not seeming at all bothered by the long walk from the hunting lodge to the ranch. He had gotten there almost as soon as they had. She was impressed, although embarrassed that she was taking note of his muscular form and the self-assured way he held himself. A widowed woman shouldn't do such a thing, and a mother at that. It was improper. Besides, she felt beneath him in a way, relying on him and his pity for food and shelter. The whole situation was shameful and she loathed herself for even considering that a man like Carl Spencer would be interested in her. There was no way he could be. She was just a charity case.

"I sent my staff home for the night, most of them anyway. Some live out in the ranch quarters, but they won't be a bother to you or the boy." Mr. Spencer stopped in front of a door and smiled at her, opening it. "In here is where you two can stay for the night. I have to make sure everything is secured for the blizzard; I raced out there after y'all and didn't quite get everything I needed to done. I'd have my cook prepare something for you, but I let him go home early. It's going to be too dangerous to be out in this weather, but feel free to use the kitchen and make whatever you'd like. I'm sure you could use a hot meal."

And with that, he offered her a quick, gentle smile and walked away, almost embarrassed looking.

Charlie looked up at her, his little face full of wonder. "It's so big here," he whispered. "There's so many rooms!"

Eva couldn't help chuckle at the small boy as she ruffled his hair. "That's right. Mr. Spencer is a truly kind man for letting us stay with him tonight. It's getting cold out."

"I don't want to go back," Charlie said, making a beeline for the bed. He hopped into it and immediately pulled the covers up to his shoulders. He was still frozen from the biting-cold ride over. The wind had gone right to his bones. "It's nicer here."

Eva's shame was magnified but she smiled at her son in understanding. "It is nice, yes. And we won't have to go back tonight. Let's try and have a really fun time here until the weather clears up."

"Okay, mama."

"Good boy. Now, I'm going to make us both some supper, all right? You stay here for now and get warmed up. I will be back soon to fetch you to the table."

"Yes, mama."

Eva left, shutting the door firmly behind her and walking back down the hallway. She hadn't been given a tour of the place, so she walked around in search of the kitchen, feeling in awe as her son had. It *was* big, as he had stated, and she had only been here once before, during that Christmas party years ago.

It took several minutes of wrong turns, but she finally made the right one and breathed a sigh of relief. She had never cooked in a kitchen like this before. It had all the most modern appliances, and she felt a little bit overwhelmed. So, she took her time as she moved through the space, finding the cutlery and selecting from the food stores.

Once she had an idea of what ingredients she could work with, she began to fumble with the stovetop until she was confident that she wouldn't burn the food or herself. When she was satisfied, she prepared her ingredients.

She decided to stick with something simple for the night, something comforting. A hearty beef stew. And she would make enough for Mr. Spencer to enjoy himself as much as he wanted, should he wish to join them.

She was feeling a little more at ease now and went to go check on Charlie before she started to cook. To her surprise, he wasn't asleep. He was playing under the bed with his little wooden soldiers. She smiled at him and called his name softly, not wanting to surprise him into bumping his head on the bedframe.

"Mama, is supper ready?"

"Not yet, darling, but why don't you bring your little soldiers with you, and you can play in the kitchen while I cook? Mr. Spencer was right, too, there are some apples if you'd like one now to tide you over until the supper is ready."

Charlie's eyes gleamed with excitement, and he gathered up his toys quickly and followed his mother down to the kitchen.

"Wow, mama! Look at all this stuff!" Charlie exclaimed, running over to the stove. Neither of them had ever been so close to this kind of affluence before. Eva couldn't imagine how much work she would be spared by not having to ignite the fire for herself, should she ever manage to get a stove like this in her own home.

She had always wondered what it might be like to cook in a kitchen like this one, and now that she finally was, it seemed too good to be true. She sliced up the apple for Charlie and he sat on the floor with his snack and his toys, eating and singing softly to himself as he played at her feet.

Eva was mesmerized by the fancy appliances, and once she was done preparing the ingredients for the stew, she walked around examining everything until she had to return to stir the food.

"The fire stops by itself!" Charlie exclaimed when Eva turned the stove off. She laughed and nodded.

"It's really amazing, isn't it? I never thought I would be able to cook like this!"

"It's going to taste really yummy, too," Charlie said, scrambling to his feet. "Is it time to eat now?"

"We've got to let it cool down, sweetheart, and while it does, I want you to go and wash your hands. We're eating at a proper table. There is a basin in our room. Let's go, okay?"

Charlie nodded and she led him to the bedroom and oversaw him washing his hands. When she was satisfied, she sat him at the dining room table and began setting the table. Just as she was finishing, she heard the front door shut and felt a pang of anxiety in her chest.

She still had no idea what to make of Mr. Spencer. It was kind of him to have allowed her to go back to the lodge, to keep the food, to keep the sheriff out of everything that was going on. Of course, it was so, so kind of him. But what if he wanted something in return; something that she wasn't comfortable giving? Or there was some other reason that he was being so nice to them? Whatever it was, she felt uneasy about the whole situation.

But she had to calm herself. If there was anything she had learned from being married to an alcoholic, one who got real mean when he drank, it was to take things moment by moment and to enjoy the peace while it lasted. She would try to enjoy all of this to the fullest while she was here and deal with any issues if they happened to arise. There was no point in wasting her time and energy on worries before they came about.

"Whatever you made smells delicious," Carl said when he entered the dining room. "I've got everything set outside, so hopefully once the blizzard has passed, there won't be too much damage done."

"Come sit down and eat with us," Eva said quickly, pulling out a chair for him. He hesitated at the doorway for a moment but came along soon enough and sat down at the table. Eva took her seat across from him and bowed her head, praying softly over the food, aware that he may not be a religious man. He waited until she was finished though, before serving himself. Eva dished up some stew in a bowl for Charlie, who was practically bouncing with excitement.

"We haven't gotten to eat warm food in so long!" he exclaimed.

"That's right." Eva added, blushing in embarrassment. "And we haven't had company during meals in a long time either, so try and remember to mind your manners, darling."

"Yes, mama."

Eva shot a glance at Carl, who was smiling at the exchange. It warmed her heart and set her at ease to know that he wasn't entirely serious, and she decided she was going to enjoy herself, even if they had to leave the next day.

"I realize I've been quite rude. I haven't introduced myself properly yet. My name is Carl Spencer. I own this ranch and a good deal of land beyond the fence line here. It's nice to meet you both."

He looked both of them in the eyes with a smile and Charlie paused to watch him talk, his eyes wide. "I don't think you've been rude. The circumstances of us being here are a little... unique," Eva said with a soft laugh. "I'm Eva Hall, and this is my son, Charlie. And we're both incredibly pleased to meet you, Mr. Spencer."

Carl made a face and shook his head. "No, please. Mr. Spencer was my father. Please just call me Carl. Both of you. It would make me far more comfortable."

"Carl," Eva said, testing the name out. All her time of knowing this man and she had only thought of him as Mr. Spencer. It might be a strange change for her, but she would try. She was a guest here and she didn't feel right about making a man feel uncomfortable in his own home.

"That's right. And you're Eva."

Eva smiled involuntarily. "That's right."

Carl returned her smile with warmth, and she couldn't help feeling butterflies in the pit of her stomach. She quickly dropped her gaze down to her plate, hesitant to begin eating. It had been so long since she had been able to enjoy a meal like this that she worried she couldn't even manage it anymore. She would try to eat slowly, even though everything in her was screaming for her to shovel in the whole bowl right there and then. But she had already scolded her son on his table manners, and she was definitely not going to be seen eating like a pig in front of Mr. Spencer. Well, Carl.

"So, Eva, why don't you tell me a little bit more about yourself?" He was looking at her strangely. She was sure she wasn't imagining it. He didn't recognize her from their brief meeting at the Christmas party.

Of course, it had been quite some time ago, why would he have ever remembered something like that? A man like Carl probably had people coming in and out of the place all the time. There was nothing remarkable that stood out about her.

"Well, I'm not really sure where to begin," she admitted with a smile. "I'm busy most of the time, trying to keep up with things and take care of Charlie. It's my favorite job," she said, smiling over at her son, who was so absorbed in his dinner that it didn't seem like he was listening to a word out of her mouth.

"I see," Carl said with a nod. "Well, he seems like a fine young man. Does he take after his father?"

This time, Charlie seemed to hear them, and looked between Carl and his mother curiously. She felt sad for him, knowing that although he was still young, he had memories of his father as a cruel man.

"He takes after the best parts of both of us," she said with a little wink to her son, who smiled back and continued eating his stew. "The truth is, Mr. Spenc- Carl - that my husband had a problem with liquor. He drank too much of it, and he drank it too often.." Eva looked surprised after she said this to him and glanced down at her plate with a flush reddening her cheeks. "I'm sorry, I didn't mean to blurt that out. It's been a long day."

Carl studied Eva for several long moments, wishing he could take her in his arms and comfort her. The last thing he wanted her to do was apologize. It did make him feel a fierce pang of anger though, even though the man was dead. He hated the thought of Eva being treated poorly. He considered saying something but chose the safe road instead.

"I'm sorry to hear that," Carl replied, his brow furrowing. "That had to have been hard for the two of you."

"It wasn't easy," Eva admitted. She was surprised once again by how easy it was to talk to Carl. He watched her with a steady gaze, one that made her feel safe somehow, no matter what types of concerns she may be facing.

"If it's not too difficult to answer, may I ask if it had to do with, uh, why he died?" Carl cast a glance to Charlie, worried that the question might not be appropriate in the presence of the little boy. Another shot of warmth wound its way through Eva's chest. He was truly a remarkable man if all of this was sincere.

"Yes, in a way," Eva admitted. "He was killed, actually. Murdered in cold blood behind the saloon. They never did figure out who did it though. No one has ever fessed up to it. It doesn't seem right, does it? To do something like that without even giving the man's family some closure. I can't even imagine who thought it was their right to steal a man's life like that…"

Eva looked up to Carl, who was staring at her. She frowned at him, completely bewildered. He looked as if he had seen a ghost, but she got the feeling that it had nothing to do with Carl. It reminded her of the way he looked at her before, as if he were trying to place her. She hadn't told him that Jim had worked for him.

She sat her spoon down in her bowl and pursed her lips, wondering whether or not she had just cost herself and her son their safe place away from the blizzard.

# Chapter Six

The sudden and horrifying truth struck Carl like a damned lightning bolt. This was Eva *Glass,* or she was if she hadn't gone back to her given name. Her husband, Jim, had worked for him, and he had fired him. That also meant that he was indirectly responsible for a widow and her small son being homeless.

It felt like all of the air was sucked out of the room around him. Carl took a drink of water quickly as his throat dried out. He had no idea what to say to her. Of course, she would have known exactly who he was the whole time. And he had met her before, once, at a Christmas party that he'd held back when Jim was still a dependable worker. She'd had such a charming smile that he had been drawn to her right away, but of course, he had never thought of her inappropriately, no matter how pretty she was.

He was sickened again by just how much weight she had lost since the last time he had seen her. Her cheeks had been rosy and full then, and her figure healthy and voluptuous. Now, she looked like even the smallest gust of wind might carry her away with it. So did her little boy. And it was all his fault.

"I'm sorry to hear about all of that happening to you," he finally managed to say, still frantically searching his mind for the next best move to make. He wanted to fix it. But how? He couldn't just give her a wad of money and some property, could he? What would people think? No, he would try and work something else out, something she wouldn't be able to refuse. The one thing he did know for certain was that she and Charlie would not be returning to the hunting lodge. He was grateful that she'd had somewhere to take her little boy besides the orphanage, but really, that place should have been torn down by now.

"Your husband worked for me," he said, more direct than he would have liked. But he was in shock, and he didn't want to hide anything from Eva. He wanted everything out on the table between them if it were able to be, and he had every intention of making sure that she was taken care of if he could make it so. They would stay with him. An idea formed quickly in his mind, and he smiled at her.

"Yes, Jim worked for you. But he was doing real bad," Eva said quietly. "I didn't expect you to keep him around as long as you did. You gave him a lot of chances to do right by you."

Carl shook his head. "That's irrelevant. What I do want to do now is offer you a position."

"A position?" Eva asked, looking at him in confusion. "What do you mean?"

"My housekeeper has had a family emergency and is heading to New York. I would like you to replace her while she's gone. You and Charlie can stay here at the house, and you can earn a little bit of money. That way, you can save up for something more stable. She will be gone for a while, a couple of months if I had to guess, if she even comes back at all."

Eva was quiet for several long moments, her beautiful brow creased in thought. "A housekeeper? For you?"

"Yes, that's right. Is that something you think you might like to do? You two would have somewhere to stay together, and you wouldn't have to worry about the winter weather... You can't go back to that cabin, Eva. It's no place for a woman, let alone a woman with a little boy. Hell, I don't even know if it will still be standing after the blizzard."

When Carl cursed, the little boy's eyes shot at him in fear and Carl pursed his mouth shut, realizing that Charlie was reminded of his father. He looked apologetically at Eva, who wasn't as upset by her son's reaction and laughed lightheartedly. "It isn't anything he hasn't heard before. He's just being dramatic because he's been learning his manners."

Carl couldn't hide his relief and Eva chuckled. "Good. I don't wanna shock the boy, do I, boss?"

Charlie looked up at Carl with a small, shy smile. The nickname had had its intended effect. It felt nice being able to make him smile that way. He remembered how much he wanted to hear things like that from his own father. He would wager that this little guy hadn't had much in the way of affection from Jim during his last years as a father. The man had been decent and kind when he was first working for him, but over time that all seemed to change. But Carl had never stopped hoping he would get his act together and go back to being the man he once was. It had pained him to see things go so downhill for him.

"So, what do you think, Eva? Will you take the job? I could really use someone here right now; you'd be doing me a favor."

Eva was quiet and Carl felt himself tense up. Finally, she looked up at him and he held his breath, hanging on her every word.

# Chapter Seven

The job offer made Eva pause. She had heard good things about Carl from Jim, when he had first started working at the Spencer Ranch. She had heard about his generosity and goodwill, and of course she was experiencing so much of it for herself; from the gift of food and shelter, to an actual job offer. But she also remembered other things that Jim had told her.

Carl Spencer had a reputation for being strict and unyielding with his workers. Jim would have work friends over from time to time and they would often complain about the way things were done on the ranch. He was strict and controlling, and paid attention to every single task. It was no wonder that he had noticed the missing food and done his due diligence in figuring out who was behind it.

To Eva, the idea of working for someone like him was terrifying. She had never had a real job before, besides her mending. She married Jim right after school, and then she became a mother. Jim had chosen to take care of the family, as most men did under the circumstances. He had done well enough at it until the alcohol had started to become an issue.

But that meant that Eva's work ethic would be called into question. Especially considering she wasn't entirely sure if she even had one.

"You mean we can live here, mama?" Charlie asked, his eyes fixed upon her. She glanced at him, furrowing her brow. What on earth was she going to do if she didn't take this offer? It would give her everything she and Charlie needed. And more than that, her son would be able to have somewhere safe to stay as she worked and did her best to make the money she would need to embark out on her own.

But it wouldn't be a permanent solution. Even if she got comfortable there and she wasn't fired by the boss, it would only last for a few short months. Then again, if she did well, perhaps he could recommend her to someone else, someone with a nice house like Carl's, and who would let her live there with her son until he was old enough to start school. Maybe even while he was attending school too.

"Mama?"

Her son's voice broke into her thoughts, and she looked at Carl, her internal debate weighing heavily upon her.

"I've never done any type of housework before, Carl. I feel like you should know that before you just go and hire someone out of the blue."

She watched his face turn from expectation to surprise. He offered her a reassuring smile. "I don't expect you to do it all right at first," he told her. "I do like things done a certain way, but you're a smart enough woman to catch on to the details pretty quick, I'm sure. I like to have people working for me that I don't have to worry about too much. Who can follow instructions, so I don't have to manage everything on my own."

If there was anything that Eva had learned from her husband and his friends talking about Carl Spencer, it was that he was a taskmaster. She feared being responsible for the most intimate details of his home life. It was intimidating.

"Ma's really good at knowing what to do," Charlie chimed in with an eager nod.

"I believe you, boss. It sounds like she's still trying to make up her mind though, so we should let her ask all her questions. We don't want to miss anything." Carl winked at Charlie, who nodded seriously as if they were having a man-to-man powwow. She couldn't help but smile at the exchange. Her son had missed having a man around, and she had to admit, she had too, although it felt strange to be sitting down with him like this at the table.

The last man she had dined with was her husband, yet somehow it felt more intimate with this man.

"What would you expect of me here?" Eva continued, feeling nervous to hear the answer.

High expectations came to mind. If the men her husband had worked with were any indication, Carl had a temper when things weren't done his way. She couldn't pretend that wouldn't bother her as she might not do well at first because she had never had to work at it before.

But she needed to stay positive. There was no way she could take Charlie back to the lodge, she knew that. She couldn't risk her son's life because of her own hubris. No matter what difficulties or trials Carl Spencer threw her way, she could rise above them for the sake of her son.

"Is there any sort of training I'd need to do?" Eva asked reluctantly.

"I want you and Charlie to rest and get comfortable here, then we can talk about your responsibilities once you're acquainted with the place. How does that sound?"

"I suppose it sounds good. Thank you so much for the opportunity," Eva said, offering a hand to Carl. He chuckled and took it with a firm pump.

Electricity traveled from his fingertips to hers, sending a shockwave through her body. It took every ounce of willpower she had not to jerk her hand away. When he released her grip hand, she dropped it her hand to her lap and looked down at her stew, unable to prevent the rush of heat that spilled over her cheeks and formed into an infuriating blush.

She took in a deep breath before bringing her spoon to her mouth, forcing herself to focus on eating and avoiding the eyes of the man she had just contracted herself to.

"Does that mean we get to stay?" Charlie exclaimed from his seat. Eva ventured a nod to him with a light smile.

"For now, darling, until mommy's done working for Mr. Spencer."

"You know he can call me Carl too, right?" Carl stated, his eyes grasping for hers from across the table. Like a magnet, hers connected with his and she shook her head with a wry smile.

"Maybe when he's older. But for now, he has to refer to adults with the proper respect. I don't want anyone thinking hist manners are poor. He's a good boy and I want everyone to know it. Right, Charlie?"

Charlie nodded, looking down at the table. "Yes, ma."

There was a short silence among them before Carl cleared his throat. "I'm sorry if I overstepped there, Eva."

She was surprised by the uncertainty in his voice, and she looked to Carl. "No need to apologize. I appreciate that you want us both to feel comfortable."

A look of relief washed over Carl's face, and she felt a quiet tenderness towards him. Jim had wanted to take care of her after her parents had died, and here Carl was, actually doing it. She knew he had never married, but why was that?

Thinking back to her late husband, Eva wondered if she'd have to see the men he used to work with. She hoped she wouldn't have to. The men were ranch hands and wouldn't be spending a lot of time indoors, so she figured she had nothing to worry about.

"Whether my housekeeper is ready to return or not in the coming months, I'd like you and Charlie to stay here through the winter. So, you can save some money, take care of things, and leave in the spring, okay?"

It was as if he could read her mind and knew just how uncomfortable she was with the situation. She felt reassured that she would be able to be in a better position once winter was over. "Thank you, Carl. For everything."

Carl fixed a broad, genuine smile on her and nodded. "My pleasure, ma'am. Now finish up that stew. You're living on a ranch now. Time to put some meat on those bones. That's my first order of business, for the both of you."

Eva couldn't stop the grin that lengthened her lips, and she nodded. "Yes, Mr. Spencer."

After dinner was cleared away, a very sleepy Charlie lay in the big bed beside his mother, sleeping soundly. He was warm and well-fed. She gazed at him, her heart feeling full. It was nice to see him so comfortable, with no complaints about a cold bed or gnawing hunger in his belly. All she wanted was to give him the best life possible and take care of him the way he deserved. And somehow, the so-called mean Mr. Spencer was making that all possible. He was a curious man, really, and it made Eva eager to learn more about him. Who was he, really?

She was safe and sound here, content, full, and warm. Even if Carl was an absolute tyrant like some seemed to think, there had to be more to him than that. She was sure of it.

Eva snuggled under the covers, feeling entirely at peace for the first time in months. She was so grateful she had met a man who was full of compassion. And those eyes...

Eva shifted in the bed and closed her own, willing the thoughts away. They wouldn't do her any good. The last thing she needed was to jeopardize her new position, so she fell asleep, blocking out any thoughts about Carl Spencer that could do so.

# Chapter Eight

"Morning, Jeff," Carl greeted, nodding pleasantly at one of the ranch hands. Jeff was a little younger than Carl, tall and reedy but with a handsome smile and contagious laugh. His straw-colored hair was slicked back, and he greeted Carl with a grin.

"Morning, boss!"

"How are things looking?" Carl asked.

"We're clearing things out, but all the buildings are okay. We lost a sheep. Other than that, it wasn't as bad as the last one."

Carl nodded. He hated to hear about the sheep, but he was glad that the buildings were intact.

"Good work out here," he said, looking around. He saw that he would have to clear a path to the cellar. It was all covered with snow. That would be his next task. He was reminded once again of Eva and her son, and he felt a gnawing curiosity about the little family. He knew that Jeff had been friends when Jim when he was working on the ranch, so he decided to see if he could find out more about them all.

"Do you remember the guy who worked here a while ago; Jim Glass?" Carl asked.

Jeff nodded. "Of course, we were good friends, Mr. Spencer."

"Yes, I thought so. I just gave his wife a job until she can get back on her feet. She and her boy are having a rough time, you know, since his passing."

"Oh, Eva and Charlie are here now?" Jeff asked, looking at Carl curiously. "That's mighty kind of you, boss."

Carl wasn't fishing for compliments, he was trying to get answers, so he cut right to the point, not acknowledging Jeff's compliments. They felt strange to him somehow, as if Jeff didn't fully mean it. "I was wondering if you knew anything about them. I'm always curious about those that come to the ranch, even if it's just temporary, you know. Any idea what their story is?"

Jeff thought for a moment, running a hand over his stubbled chin. He let out a low whistle. "Well, I reckon Eva's a pretty quiet little thing. She never put up a fuss about anything. And Charlie is a sweet kid too. Not likely to get any trouble out of either of them."

Carl nodded. "I thought as much."

"Yeah, Jim could get a little bit rowdy, but she always welcomed him home with a smile on her face, even if he had us sorry lot in tow." Jeff chuckled fondly. "We could put a lot of drinks down and he'd always want to bring us back to his place and play that damned fiddle of his. I reckon it kept the baby up, but Eva kept him out of our hair and never let on if it bothered her."

Carl nodded. "Yes, I've heard he was a fan of the bottle. It was pretty obvious with the way he acted during the last few months he worked here, too."

Jeff nodded. "Yeah, it was getting pretty bad. We tried to get him to slow down but you know how a man's pride can be, and we didn't wanna overstep either. Didn't seem right to tell a grown man how to conduct himself. Still, he could be right mean sometimes. I felt sorry for his wife, putting up with his temper the way she done. But I guess that all ended when he got killed."

Carl and Jeff were shoveling snow as they spoke, clearing the path to the cellar. Carl paused with his hand on his shovel, debating whether or not to ask another question. "I don't know much about how he was killed," Carl said. "Only that it happened. I don't want to say anything stupid, you know, that could upset Eva while she's staying here. It's hard though, not knowing the details."

Jeff nodded. "Yeah, it's certainly a little sensitive, that's for sure. But she's a strong woman, even if she's just a pretty little thing."

Carl didn't like the way his skin prickled whenever Jeff talked about Eva that way, but he tried to push it as far from his mind as possible. There was no reason for it. He was just feeling protective. Carl already knew that Jeff could drink heavy himself; it sounded like he and Jim may have had a lot in common. Eva was too good for any of them.

"So, what happened to Jim, anyway?" Carl finally asked outright, eager to get Eva out of his mind.

"Well, I can tell you some things, but Eva probably doesn't know about them, and probably shouldn't," Jeff said, lowering his voice. Carl's interest piqued and he stepped closer to Jeff, frowning.

"Things she doesn't know about?" he asked. "What doesn't she know?"

"Well, it's mostly rumors, but we tried not to talk about it in front of her, out of respect for the dead. She hasn't been around much these days, anyway."

*Because she's been homeless,* Carl thought to himself. But instead of showing any of his frustrations, he simply gave a quick nod. "You can tell me though," he said. "I would like to know."

Jeff nodded. "Well, a few of us boys were at the saloon the night it happened. Jim was pissed off at his brother, Clarence. The two of them got into it over something stupid. You know how it can be when boys are drinking. The smallest thing can seem huge, and both had a temper on them. Well, Clarence left the saloon for the night to get away from Jim; he was really ticked off too, but one of the boys saw Clarence was still there, waiting outside behind the saloon, when he left to go home. Eventually, Jim left too, but he didn't make it far before he got shot."

"So, you think Jim was killed by his own brother?" Carl asked, perplexed.

"Me and just about anyone who heard the two of them fighting," Jeff said with a quick nod. "It's not like they was just yelling, Clarence was threatening Jim and telling him he didn't deserve what he had, that he was a good for nothin' waste of a man. I can't imagine saying a thing like that to anyone, let alone my own kin. On top of that, Clarence skipped town before the funeral even happened."

"Clarence took off?" Carl asked. "Did anyone get a chance to ask him what happened?"

Carl thought about it for a moment, trying to see both sides of the story. The rumor mill in a small town could be pretty rough to anyone unfortunate enough to get on the wrong end of it.

If Jeff was right, Jim was shot in cold-blood and his brother was responsible. Then, he had run right out of town to avoid the repercussions. Still, there was no evidence that he had done it. A lot of people in this town could lose their temper and end up responsible for murder. Well, not anyone Carl associated with, he hoped, but he was just trying to keep an open mind. He would hate to be accused of killing his own kin if he hadn't done it. But the truth did seem remarkably clear in this case.

"I appreciate you telling me what you know 'bout the whole thing, Jeff," Carl said. Jeff nodded back, and they continued their shoveling in silence. The whole yard was thick with snow, but there was enough of a path made that Maggie would be able to safely make it to the house, and any of the other staff who needed to get anywhere.

Speaking of the sweet woman, she came barreling toward them as soon as she heard Carl's voice. Her deep brown hair was tied up in a loose bun that she was patting into place, when she emerged from the ranch quarters where she lived and offered Carl a bubbly smile. "Why Mr. Spencer! I think it's about time you come in and I make you some breakfast, don't you?"

Carl smiled. "Breakfast sounds good to me," he admitted.

Maggie shook her head at him, tut-tutting like an old mother hen, despite being only 37 years old. She was older than Carl, plump, optimistic, and maternal, and he had many fond memories of growing up on the ranch and Maggie always being there too. Maggie's own mother had been the Spencer's housekeeper before she had passed away, and it felt to Carl, and always had, that Maggie was a part of the family.

"You practically leapt out of bed to clear this path for us, didn't you? You didn't even grab an apple or anything! What have I told you about that, Carl?"

"Carl sighed, not particularly loving being scolded in front of Jeff, but knowing there was no stopping Maggie once she got on about his eating habits. "I know, I know. But everything is fine, and you've managed to get to the house without breaking your neck. I think that's worth my while."

"You're impossible," Maggie said, shaking her head good naturedly. "Is it true that there's a new housekeeper here? Jim's wife?"

Carl chuckled. Leave it to Maggie to be one of the first to know. "Yes, she's staying here with her boy, Charlie. You'll meet them inside if they're awake, but if they aren't, don't wake them. We can have an early lunch. The two of them need a bit of rest."

Maggie understood the implications in his tone, and she nodded seriously. "Of course, Carl, I'll make sure they are taken care of."

He smiled at her, knowing that she would be true to her word. She headed inside and Carl finished what he was doing and followed her in. As he suspected, Eva and Charlie weren't up yet and didn't appear until the early afternoon. By that time, lunch was already being made and Carl saw them emerge timidly from the bedroom together.

"Good afternoon," he said, offering them a bright smile. "How did you two sleep?"

Eva beamed at him, and his smile broadened. She looked like a whole new person. "We slept like our bed was sent straight from heaven itself, Mr. Spencer. Thank you."

"Carl, remember?"

"Carl, of course. I swear, it feels like we've been blessed by God." Eva ruffled her son's hair and Carl couldn't help but notice the pretty blush that was creeping across her face. It reminded him an awful lot of the one she displayed at the table the evening prior. He had laid awake far longer than he cared to admit, thinking about the look on her face when their hands had touched. Would her lips feel as soft as those hands?

He had to force himself to stop thinking about her. That was how a man got himself into trouble, and as far as he was concerned, he wasn't the kind of man who could do right by a woman, anyhow. He liked things done his own way and he wasn't about to try and change himself for nobody. He had never been a pushover and he wasn't about to start now. There was little compromise in Carl Spencer's world.

Carl had given up on the idea of true love long ago. He had devoted his life to the ranch and had thrown himself into it wholeheartedly. He often told people he was married to his work, and he had never allowed himself to slow down and develop a real relationship. He'd been eager to please his father and prove himself worthy of inheriting the ranch, which hadn't left him a lot of time for women. Most women would never have understood the way he was, anyway. Being soft and approachable didn't come natural to him, and he had learned to keep his distance. He didn't really think there would ever be a woman out there who could put up with him, and he wouldn't start thinking that way now about Eva. No sir. She might have thought he was a saint, but that was the furthest from the truth. It made him anxious just thinking about it.

"I'm just trying to do right by you, Eva," Carl said. "Your husband left you two in a tough spot, and now I realize that part of that is my own fault for letting him go. So, you and the boy have a place here until you get back on your feet. There's nothing more to it than that."

She seemed confused by his straightforward reaction, and her perfect brow creased. Still, even though he could see the concern in her eyes, she didn't let her smile falter. Charlie wandered away from his mother and began exploring the house.

"Well, I'm eternally grateful for what you are doing for me and Charlie. I forgot what it felt like to sleep in a proper bed. I didn't realize we slept so late!"

Carl was about to reply when Maggie came into the hallway, her face rosy and joyful, just as always. "There you two are! How are the clothes? Do they fit you both?"

Carl was surprised by this turn of conversation, and he looked to Eva. Yes, her clothing had changed since the night before. How had he missed that?

"They're perfect, Maggie. Thank you so much. And Charlie just loves those little suspenders! He feels very dapper in them, I think. He was looking at himself in the mirror for the longest time. I think they remind him of his pa."

Eva spoke with such a dazzling lightness that Carl couldn't help but stare. She truly was a breath of fresh air. How could any man raise a hand to this woman in anger? She'd implied that Jim had been a mean drunk and it made Carl seethe with a fierce, protective instinct he hadn't even known he had.

Maggie squealed in delight. "I'm so glad they fit! I just wanted to let y'all know that lunch will be ready in a tick, so why don't you get your hands all cleaned up and come to the table once you're done."

Carl smiled wryly at Maggie, always giving the most sound, motherly advice, even to fully grown adults no longer in need of it. Still, he secretly enjoyed all her fussing. She was a comfort to him, truly.

"There!" Charlie's little voice said, startling Carl out of his thoughts. His little voice was surprisingly close, and Carl looked down at the floor, where Charlie was lying beside him, playing with his boot laces. He had untied one side and was busy untying the other.

"Hey!" he shouted, pulling his leg up so the boy couldn't touch the boot any longer. "Don't do that!" Carl barked. Charlie shrank back in fear.

Carl was startled by his own reaction, though it had simply been reflexive. He had never liked anyone messing with his things, particularly if he was wearing them at the time. It made him feel real uneasy. Carl liked to be in control of everything around him and the boy was a sudden variable that he hadn't prepared for.

Carl headed toward the kitchen and sat down at the table, just as Charlie began to wail. He tried to ignore it and took a bite of the food that Maggie had laid out for them. The boy needed to learn respect for other people's things, although he had to admit, he had overreacted. It had been a harmless act just a little boy playing games, but what was done was done and there was no reason to worry over it now.

But, there was because suddenly Eva was there, standing in front of Carl, stern faced and with the wailing child on her hip, and he sighed. So much for a nice meal together. He continued eating, trying to ignore the glaring mother on the opposite end of the table.

"You don't need to yell at him like that, you know," Eva said. "If he's doing something wrong or that you don't like, you can just ask him to stop it. He knows what no means."

"I told him no," Carl said firmly, taking another bite of his food as if to prove a point. He wasn't enjoying this conversation at all, and he wished with all his might that it was over.

"No, you shouted at him! You can say it in a normal voice, he'll listen. I've been raising him to do right by other people." Eva stared him down with such conviction that Carl wondered how any man ever spoke against her, but he supposed she hadn't with Jim, if the stories were to be believed.

"If you are trying to teach him to do right by other people, then teach him not to mess with another man's things." Carl spoke evenly, despite Eva's clear anger. He was already feeling terrible but couldn't figure out how to fix things.

"He's learning, and he will know better. But it's not like he broke anything. I don't see why you had to yell at him like that. It even scared me. It was so sudden. And so loud."

Eva shifted the little boy in her arms. He was still crying, and it grew more intense with every word his mother spoke. It was giving Carl a headache. He hated himself for the way he had scared the little boy, which was making him agitated and irritable. The more the situation escalated, the more on edge Carl became.

"Does he always carry on like that?" Carl asked. "You're going to have to get a handle on that, you know."

"Yes, well, he's three years old, and you're a grown man, Carl. There's no reason to lose your temper. That's what children do." Eva looked just as surprised by her courage as Carl was, and he glanced up at her for a moment, letting out a sigh.

Hearing her call him by his first name felt good. Although, he was starting to feel angry, too. Who did she think she was, telling him how to conduct himself in his own house? He had done a lot to make sure she and the boy were comfortable, and she was still attacking him. It was starting to tick him off. All he wanted to do was have his lunch in peace and get back to work, but she wasn't going to let that happen.

"You don't get to come into my house and disrespect me like this," he said, standing up. His appetite was long gone, and he was getting tired of pretending to entertain this conversation any longer. "If the boy touches my boots, I'm not going to like it. Same as if he touches any of my other things without asking first. You do that before doing anything around here."

Eva shook her head in disgust and Carl felt a mixture of shame and anger surge through him. He was about done with this situation. "Forget it. I'm leaving. I have a feeling if I don't, that boy will never stop crying."

Carl stood up from the table and headed out the door, wondering just where in the hell things had gone so wrong and wishing that he could begin the entire day over again.

# Chapter Eight

Eva watched in shock as Carl stormed out of the house, holding Charlie close to her chest. What on earth had gotten into that man? She regretted being so grateful for him. That hadn't lasted long at all.

"Maybe this was all a mistake," she murmured to herself.

"No, honey," came a soft voice from the hallway. It was no mistake. It's the Lord's work," Maggie said. She had been watching the whole thing from the doorway, waiting for Carl to calm down or leave, whichever came first. Usually, he left and then would return a calmer man, but every so often he liked to see a fight through to the end.

"I'm just not sure about any of this," Eva said. "It's a nice offer and everything, but I can't stay here if he's going to be cruel to my son," she sighed, her chest tightening. She felt on the verge of tears herself. Everything had seemed so optimistic just moments ago. Her son was warm and well fed, wearing clean clothes in a beautiful home. She finally felt like a real woman again too, with a bedroom for herself, even with its own vanity. She had done everything in her power to make a good impression on Carl, but no matter how hard she tried, she couldn't always be watching her four-year-old son any better than any other mother could.

"Sweetheart," Maggie whispered to Charlie. "Carl didn't mean to be cruel. And he definitely didn't mean to frighten you so." Eva looked at the sweet woman and sighed. Maggie was a kind person, with big, sparkling blue eyes and soft, chestnut hair. She looked middle-aged to Eva, and she seemed confident in what she was talking about. "He's just not used to children. It can be hard on a man who thinks he should be able to control every little thing around him."

Maggie chuckled and approached the two, holding out a gentle hand to the little boy. "Is it all right if I hold him for you, Eva?"

Charlie's tears had calmed a bit, now that she and Carl weren't fighting anymore, and she nodded, allowing the small boy's form to shift from her and onto Maggie. Maggie sat down at the table and held Charlie on her lap, looking at him with a bright smile.

"Guess what happened while you were getting dressed, Charlie?"

Charlie sniffled and clung onto Maggie as if she were his own mother. It was heartwarming and Eva allowed herself to regain her composure as she watched the two. "What happened?" Charlie croaked.

His sulky voice made Eva smile, but she hid it in case he might think she was laughing at him. He had always been so sensitive.

"I remembered what you told me and started making that chocolate cake you wanted," Maggie said in a conspiratorial whisper. "It's in the oven right now, and by the time we finish eating our lunch and playing outside, it's going to be all done and ready to ice!"

Charlie sat upright and looked Maggie in the eyes with a small, adorable gasp. "Really? You really are making a chocolate cake?"

"I really am, sweetheart," Maggie said, squeezing Charlie into a cozy hug. "And if you like, you can even help me mix the icing!"

"I don't know how to do that," Charlie said with a slight pout. "Would you help me?"

"Of course, I'll help you," Maggie said. "As long as it's okay with your ma that you're my kitchen helper, and I'm yours."

"I bet it will be!" Charlie exclaimed.

"Well then, you had better ask her, hadn't you?" Maggie said in another conspiratorial whisper. "And if she says yes, you can eat your lunch and then make some frosting for that cake with me."

Charlie's excited golden eyes found Eva's, red-rimmed, but no longer full of tears. "Ma, can I help Maggie? Please? I want to help make frosting for her cake!"

"Not my cake," Maggie corrected, shaking her head firmly. "Our cake. But especially for you, Charlie."

Charlie grinned proudly and looked back to Eva, looking much happier now that he might get the chance to be Maggie's little helper.

"Of course, you can help make some frosting, Charlie," Eva said with a soft laugh. "I think that's a great idea. And I'm sure the cake will taste heavenly. I can already smell it."

"Yay! Ma said I can help!" Charlie exclaimed, looking up at Maggie with a bright smile. "It's going to taste so good!"

"Yes, it is, sweetheart," Maggie said, nodding in agreement. "But we don't get any yet because it's still baking, and you still have some lunch to eat. Do you think you could do that while I check on everything? I want to make sure we have all the ingredients we need for this frosting of ours."

"Yeah!" Charlie shouted, slipping off Maggie's lap and running to his seat at the table, where his lunch was waiting for him. Maggie stood and walked over to Eva, and they both watched him eat silently together for a while. Then, Maggie turned to Eva, speaking in soft tones.

"I know that Carl can be a little bit intimidating, but he would never harm a hair on that little boy's head."

Eva froze, prickling a little at the comment. She was so protective of her son that she hadn't really considered how she might come across to other people. "It's just a little bit hard to trust people with him," she admitted. "I don't like it when he's scared, and angry men just make me so anxious after everything with my husband."

Maggie nodded. "I remember him, alright."

Eva felt a lump forming in the back of her throat. She shook her head, angrily trying to will her tears away.

"I've been the cook in this home for many years now," Maggie said. "I grew up on this ranch and I'm some ten years older than Carl. I've seen that boy turn into a man and I can tell you for certain, he would never harm that little boy, or anyone else for that matter. That's the honest truth."

Eva was quiet, letting the words sink in. She was starting to feel bad for the way she had reacted. "Do you think I was too hard on him?" she asked Maggie, looking to her with apparent concern.

Maggie laughed light-heartedly. "No, dear. That's just what Carl does," she replied, still chuckling to herself. "He has a bit of a hot temper, but it cools off quick. It's better that he walked away because when he stays, then he says things he regrets, and I have to hear all about it."

Eva couldn't help but smile at the thought of Carl confiding in Maggie, turning to her for advice like a son might to his mother. "Well... Do you think he will want us to leave now because of all this?"

Maggie shook her head. "No, I don't think that's what he will want. I think he'll think about what he did; he likely regretted it immediately but couldn't figure out how to say so. Trust me, he will come round. He just takes time to adjust to new things. He's like an old dog, set in his ways. But he has a good heart."

Eva could only hope that Maggie was right. She nodded, her gaze following Charlie and Maggie as they disappeared into the kitchen before she headed back to the bedroom to compose herself better after everything that had happened. When she emerged, Maggie and Charlie had just finished with their icing, and Charlie was looking tired. She smiled and picked him up, carrying him to the bedroom to lay him down for his afternoon nap.

Eva sat with Charlie until he was asleep, and then left the room, looking for Maggie. "I'm feeling a bit restless," she admitted, and Maggie smiled.

"Well, you're here now," she stated. I know Carl mentioned having you start next week, but if you're up to it, I can show you around, and you can look around for something that needs doing. How does that sound?"

Eva nodded gratefully. "Yes, please. I'm afraid I'm going to go crazy without something to do. And I'm anxious after what happened. It would be nice to feel like I'm helping out. The sooner the better."

Maggie nodded sympathetically. "Of course, dear. Right this way!"

She led Eva to a cleaning closet where dusters and rags were kept and buckets she would need for mopping. A duster and broom were leaning in the corner. Eva looked to Maggie with a grateful smile. "Thank you so much. Where do you think I should begin?"

"I'd recommend the study," Maggie said. "It's been out of order for a while now. Anna's a sweet girl but she isn't great at taking initiative with organizing certain things. Carl would never admit it, but he does need that sort of help sometimes. He has so much to keep track of, and it would do him a great deal of good to get some kind of system set up in there."

"Okay, I can do that," Eva nodded eagerly. She had always had a hand for keeping things organized and it was a relief to feel like that might be useful in her new job.

"Wonderful! I will be in the kitchen if you need anything, dear."

"Thanks, Maggie."

Eva headed to the study and looked around thoughtfully. If organizing needed done, she would happily do it. The most cluttered space appeared to be Carl's desk, so she set to work. She tried not to snoop, purposefully avoiding any close inspection of the papers scattered about. Jim had been so controlling of their finances that he'd get furious if he caught her near his things, and she decided to clean out the drawers. They betrayed a bit of a frazzled mind, despite the meticulous records that he clearly kept. She tidied everything in them as best she could, taking everything out to dust and clean before putting things back inside in a more organized fashion.

The last drawer she opened surprised her, however. Inside sat a framed portrait of a handsome, young man.

"How did you get in there?" Eva asked. "You're far too handsome to be stuck away in here." She sat the portrait on the cleared off desk and gave it a proper dusting, then attended to Charlie who had woken from his nap.

She was dreading seeing Carl again after the conflict earlier in the day but was hoping he would be pleased with her work. And so, she waited with hidden anticipation for him to come home from his labors, but when he did, he was quiet and avoided her, so she kept out of sight, figuring the afternoon's outburst had ruffled his feathers. She wanted to stay out of his way and avoid any conflict. It already felt like she and Charlie were walking on eggshells, and she spent the next hour in discomfort.

Before supper, Eva was helping Maggie set the table and Charlie was playing quietly in the bedroom. It seemed he, too, was reluctant to be near Carl and chose to play with his little soldiers under the bed instead. That was fine with Eva. She would check on him in a bit. She only hoped he wouldn't be too timid to come out and eat his supper.

"You were in my study."

Eva nearly jumped out of her skin. She hadn't noticed Carl enter the room, and he was standing behind her, his voice full of barely contained anger. "Yes, I was cleaning it up a bit. Maggie suggested that I-"

"Stay out of there!" he exclaimed. Eva turned to face him, flinching as he held up the portrait she had placed on top of the desk. "You have no right to rifle through my drawers and put things where they don't belong!"

He looked furious, and Eva's heart raced as she backed away from him. She felt just like she had when Jim was about to strike, and it took everything in her power not to cower in fear. "I'm sorry, I was just trying to help."

"Well, it was no help, and you violated my space and my privacy. Never move a thing in this house, is that understood? Your job is to clean, not to change my office around to your liking."

"Y-yes," Eva stammered. "I understand. I'm sorry."

With that, Carl stormed off, leaving Eva behind, trembling like a leaf. Maggie was standing silently behind Eva and placed a hand on her shoulder. Eva shrugged it away and felt a surge of adrenalin push her forward. She couldn't stand it; this was all too much.

There was no way they could stay here. Not a moment longer. Charlie was frightened enough already, and now Carl was upset again. She couldn't stand being near a man with a temper like her late husband's. It wasn't good for her, and it wasn't good for her son. She would make her own way, just as she had done before. They could get by without Carl Spencer's help.

Eva headed to the bedroom to pack. As nice as it was to be in a real home, it never would be one for them. They would be leaving first thing in the morning. And that was that.

# Chapter Nine

Carl threw the portrait of his father back into the bottom drawer of his desk, hard enough to shatter the glass. Fortunately, his temper had been just restrained enough to prevent that, but he was furious. The last thing he needed to see that day, especially after treating Charlie so harshly, was a reminder of everything he was trying not to be.

His father had been cold and cruel towards him, and he had vowed to be a better man. But was he proving to be? How would he ever be able to say he was when he couldn't even stop himself from barking at a little boy? He felt horrible about everything, and now he had gone and berated Eva too. But how was she to know he had put it away for a reason. He couldn't stand those glaring eyes in the frame reminding him that he would never be good enough. It sent Carl into a spiral of self-doubt and emotional unease. His father had never loved him, and he would never be loveable to anyone else, either. The way he had been acting was proof enough of that. Why couldn't everyone just leave him in peace?

"Tea, Mr. Spencer," Maggie said, entering the study quietly. Carl flinched at her reference to his father. That meant that she was unhappy with him.

"Thanks."

"You know I told that poor girl to come in here and give you a little help with the organizing. It's not really your strong suit and we both know it."

"She put the portrait of my father right on my desk, Maggie," Carl said, glowering at the teacup. "I don't want to see that."

"You're not your father, Carl, but you're certainly doing a bad job of showing it to that poor girl and her little boy. What's going on with you?"

Carl looked away, still fuming but feeling guiltier than ever. "I don't know if I am better, Maggie. This has been really hard. I don't know what I'm doing."

"What you're doing is messing things up for yourself," Maggie said with a firm nod. "She wanted to help you out, to pay you back as she put it, even after you treated her son the way you did. She's a kind woman, Carl, and you're hurting her because you're scared. Because we don't usually keep soft things around here and she and the little one are."

"Soft, yeah," Carl said with a low sigh. "Soft and a pain in my neck."

"You're going to scare them right off if you keep it up. I haven't seen her since you yelled at her and I'm worried she might be planning to leave. Are you really going to drive her back out into the cold because she thought it would be a nice gesture to help you out? She doesn't know anything about your father. All she saw was a picture of a handsome man most people would be proud to display."

Carl glared down at his hands, then looked up at Maggie, finally meeting her sharp, blue eyes. "So, how do I fix it then, huh? How do I be less like him?"

"What you needed from him was the kind of softness you see in her. Maybe that's what's got you so on edge."

Carl furrowed his brows as he considered Maggie's words. He had needed more softness from his father? Well, he supposed it would have been better than getting the rod all the time. "So, how do I fix things?"

"Go and talk to her. Let her know she's wanted here. Not just wanted, but even needed. She's not a stupid woman, Carl, and she's been mistreated enough. She's learned enough by now not to let it happen again, so you'd better not let it."

Carl nodded, looking away in shame this time, rather than in anger. "Yeah... all right. I'll talk to her. Thank you, Maggie."

"Take your tea first and calm your nerves. Everything's going to be fine, just be honest with her."

Carl sighed as Maggie left the room. He drank the warm tea she had left for him and sat in the study quietly for a few more moments before standing up and making his way to Eva's door. He knocked gently, more conscious than ever of his own gruffness.

"Yes?"

Eva's voice came to him muffled through the wood. Carl sighed. "Would you mind coming out to speak with me for a moment?" he said, trying not to sound demanding but not knowing what he would do if she said no. "In private?"

"All right, but Charlie is playing and I'd rather not leave him for too long." When she opened the door, Carl's stomach dropped to see the suitcase she'd brought sitting open on her bed. She was packing.

"What's all that?" he asked, frowning.

"My things, or what's left of them," Eva said, avoiding his eye as she spoke. When she finally looked up, he saw a fire in hers that made him pause. She was a strong woman, there was no doubting that. He only wished he had known how to manage things better. "I'm leaving with Charlie in the morning. And I apologize for any inconvenience we may have caused you."

"Eva, no... I don't want you to leave. I'm sorry for the way I behaved. Truly. I really just don't know how to act around children and I will really try to do better with him." Carl found himself stammering as he searched for the right words, feeling overwhelmed and anxious.

"You didn't just yell at Charlie, you know," Eva said, looking at Carl hard in the eyes. "I thought I was doing a nice thing and it turned into... well..." She looked away for a moment before looking up at him bravely again. "I thought you were going to hit me."

Carl was stunned. "Hit you?" he replied. "I would never. I would never harm a hair on your head, or your son's, Eva."

Carl let out a low exhale and pinched the bridge of his nose in thought. How could she believe that he would strike her? She crossed her arms over her chest and lifted a brow at him, waiting. He sighed again before continuing.

"I overreacted. You see, the picture you found was of my father. He was an unkind man. He was cruel to me as I grew up and I've always felt like I'm living in his shadow. Like... like I'm just here trying to prove to myself that I'm worth something, you know? After behaving the way I did with Charlie, I felt horrible. It reminded me of the way my father treated me. Then, I went to my study, the place I go to sit with my thoughts, and there he was again, staring straight at me. It was unexpected, and I just snapped. I truly am sorry. But please know I would never hurt you."

Eva listened quietly, then glanced over her shoulder before stepping out of the bedroom and closing the door. She didn't want Charlie to overhear any more than he might have already. "I didn't mean to upset you with the portrait. I had no idea."

"Of course you didn't. It was terrible of me to have acted the way I did. I know you were just trying to help and I feel awful for ruining that. But if you stay, and you continue to work for me here, I promise I'll try harder. Do better. I want to prove to myself as much as to you that I'm better than that."

A tender smile curled Eva's beautiful lips and Carl found himself awestruck. He froze in place, waiting for whatever was coming. "Carl, no matter what, you're worth something. Don't let anyone tell you otherwise."

She reached up to touch his cheek in a natural, comforting gesture, and he found himself leaning into it for a moment before they were both suddenly aware of the intimacy. Eva withdrew her hand quickly and Carl stood up tall, pretending that he hadn't just melted into Eva's fingertips.

"I know that I don't deserve to have you here after what I've put the both of you through today, but I'd like to apologize sincerely and ask that you stay. Just until the time we've agreed to. It would really tear me up knowing that you and Charlie are out there on your own struggling through this winter."

Eva sighed. "Well…"

Carl looked away, already bracing himself for rejection. He didn't know if he could handle that and he looked up, interrupting her answer. "Before you decide, is it all right if I apologize to Charlie? I don't want him to be scared of me, even if you end up leaving tomorrow."

Eva looked surprised, then nodded. "Sure, if he'll let you. He's been glum this afternoon."

"I understand," Carl said, feeling another nagging sense of guilt tugging at his chest. "I'll just be a moment."

Eva nodded, then granted Carl entry into the room. He could see the top of the little boy's head under the bed. He was murmuring to himself, holding two little soldiers in his small, chubby hands. Carl knelt on the ground.

"Hey, Charlie," he said, his tone as gentle as he could manage to make it. "I'm sorry for getting mad earlier. I got startled and didn't know how to use my grown-up voice very well. I hope that you can forgive me."

Charlie looked up at him, his eyes wide and curious. "You scared me," he said. "Why'd you get so mad?"

"I think I was a little bit scared too," Carl admitted. "I've never had a little boy around the house before and I didn't know what to do."

"Oh," Charlie said, thinking this over for a moment before looking up at Carl with a big smile. "It's okay!"

"Well, thank you for forgiving me. Maybe sometime soon I can show you where I used to play when I was little. I'll see if Maggie can help me get it all set up for you."

"Are there toys?" Charlie asked, his eyes wider than ever.

"There are, but they were put away a while back. We can get them out for you, though, so you can have somewhere special to yourself while your ma works. Would you like that?"

"Yeah!" Charlie exclaimed, looking over to Eva with the biggest grin Carl had ever seen. "Can I, ma?"

Eva was watching the scene with an expression that Carl couldn't quite read. She didn't look angry, at least, he could tell that much. She looked conflicted with a mixture of happiness and concern. "Yes, Charlie. We'll stay here a little longer so you can see the toys."

She cast a meaningful glance at Carl as he stood from the spot where he had crouched on the floor. He nodded to her in understanding. "Thank you," he said gently, putting a hand on her shoulder. Again, the contact was so natural, but so intimate that when they were aware of it happening, they both turned away and he dropped his hand immediately.

"You're welcome," she murmured. "We'll give it a little longer, but if I feel like we're in your hair, we will find another way to deal with all of this."

Carl nodded. "All right," he said. He left the room feeling lighter than he had in months, then went to find Maggie so that she might help him set up the playroom for Charlie.

# Chapter Ten

Eva was feeling uneasy. She had promised to give Carl another chance, but she wasn't feeling overly optimistic about his ability to really change his behavior. She had been hoping for years that Jim would get back to his old self again and remember that he loved her enough not to take it out on her when things went wrong, but that never seemed to happen and she had been sorely disappointed waiting for nothing. She was learning that some things weren't likely to change at all, and a bad temper was one of them.

Still, she had to hope for the best. Charlie had become much happier after Carl had spoken with him, and that had made her feel a lot better about everything. She could only hope that it would last. If it didn't, well, she would just have to figure something out.

She was feeling a little on edge because Maggie wouldn't be working that weekend and that meant she was in charge of the meals. She wanted to make something special to smooth things over, so she settled on an old family recipe. It was one of Charlie's favorites, and she hoped that Carl would like it too. If not, she could fix him something else, but she hoped the casserole was good enough to work its way into any man's heart.

She scoured the kitchen in search of a dish before stepping into the dining room and realizing that it was all the way on top of the China cabinet. Eva wasn't a tall woman, but that was no matter. She pulled one of the chairs over and stood on it but found herself still straining to reach the silly thing.

Her fingertips finally brushed the handle of the dish as she pushed up on her tiptoes to try and maneuver it as carefully as she could into her hands. The last thing she needed was for Carl to come home to a broken dish, after everything else that had already happened.

Eva's heart surged with adrenaline as she felt the chair begin to wobble uncontrollably beneath her feet. She flailed in an effort to try and grab on to something, but her fingertips only brushed the smooth, polished wood of the cabinet before feeling nothing but air as she lost all sense of balance. She let out a soft cry as she fell.

"Eva!?"

She barely had the chance to process that Carl was making his way toward her before she realized she was already on the ground. She'd heard his voice just as she blinked her eyes open. A sharp pain in her wrist thundered through her body and she cried out, curling up in pain and cradling her hand to her chest in agony.

"Eva, are you all right?" Carl asked, breathless as he reached her. He had moved quickly from wherever he had been to get to her. She felt his strong arms lifting her up from the floor and cradling her close to his body. She had had the wind knocked out of her so it took a moment for her to speak or even process what was happening. She was fighting back tears as Carl took her hand gently in his and stroked her wrist with his other. "You're hurt."

For a moment though, the pain left her and she felt only the electrifying sensation of Carl's fingertips brushing against her skin. Her breath quickened as she realized her body's proximity to his, knowing that should have been the last thing on her mind. Carl had been more worried about her destroying the family heirlooms hiding in the cabinet. Still, it was impossible to ignore his closeness and she hid her flushed face as he examined her wrist closer. "I'm going to get some ice for that," he said, helping her gently to her feet before disappearing into the kitchen. He came back several moments later after fetching ice from the box and wrapping it in some cloth. "I can send for the doctor; he comes out this way."

Eva shook her head emphatically. "No, no need. I'm fine, really."

"You have a sprained wrist, Eva. That's hardly fine," Carl said. She felt touched by his concern and looked away before her blush deepened.

"It's nothing I haven't dealt with before," Eva murmured, feeling embarrassed by the fall. "I'm just glad I didn't break your casserole dish."

Carl chuckled. "It wouldn't matter if you broke it, Eva. What matters is that you're all right."

Eva looked away just as Charlie came running into the room. "I'm hungry!" he declared. Carl grinned.

"Me too, but your ma's had a bit of a spill, so how about I make us some lunch?" Eva was surprised by the offer, and even more surprised by the gentle tone he took. He appeared to hide a secret soft spot behind his rugged form.

"You don't have to do that, Carl," Eva said quickly. The last thing she wanted was to be any more trouble to him. What if he held it against her later? She didn't want to risk that. "I can just-"

Carl held up a hand to stop her from continuing and gestured to one of the dining room chairs. "I want you to sit down and relax, while I make us something to eat. You've done plenty today already. It won't take long, all right? I promise I can throw something together if I have to. It's not my first rodeo."

Eva sighed, still reluctant to sit. But Carl's eyes were unwavering upon her and she could feel herself submitting. Even though it made her uncomfortable, he wasn't allowing her to argue and she ended up finally taking a seat with a slight flush on her cheeks. Charlie was oblivious to the strange dynamics going on between his mother and Carl. He was simply satisfied knowing that something was being made to eat. Eva stroked his hair as he played on the floor beside her and Carl went to the kitchen. Twenty minutes later, Carl emerged with a plate of buttered bread, three bowls of beans, and some fried potatoes. It was a bit of an odd combination, but Charlie was happy, Eva was grateful, and it smelled divine.

"All right," Carl said, his voice lighthearted as he placed everything on the table in front of them. "Lunch is served."

Charlie stood up and held his little arms up in the air, waiting for Eva to pick him up to place him in his chair. "Up!" he exclaimed.

Eva started to stand but Carl rushed over to intercept him. "Ma hurt herself, remember little man? She needs to rest her arm right now. So, just let me pull the chair out for you and you can climb on up there yourself."

Charlie looked up at Carl with wide eyes, holding his pudgy little arms in the air with unmistakable intention. He was waiting for Carl to pick him up and get him situated. Carl had clearly never had a child approach him like this before, so he found himself looking to Eva with desperation in his eyes. Eva looked back with barely concealed amusement and lifted a brow toward him, nodding her head toward the child as if to say, "Go ahead." Carl hesitated a moment.

"You want me to pick you up?" Carl asked Charlie, whose arms were beginning to wave impatiently now.

"Yeah! Up!"

"Um…"

A laugh, poorly concealed as a cough escaped Eva's mouth. Carl shot her a look and Eva did her best to keep a straight face. Carl bent down and carefully lifted Charlie into his arms. He stood there awkwardly for a moment as Charlie gasped and let out a bright laugh. "Wow! I'm high! Let's go there!"

"Go where?" Carl asked, looking at the boy, whose bright eyes were fixed on the cabinet.

"There!" he exclaimed with a giggle. Carl hesitated before reluctantly following the child's instructions. Eva watched from her seat, a warmth spreading across her chest from the fumbling man's efforts to appease her son.

"Here?" he asked, shifting Charlie in his arms. His brow was furrowed and Eva guessed that he was worried he might be holding him wrong. But Charlie seemed perfectly content, and she had no reservations.

"Yeah! I need to see in there."

"Oh really? Why's that?" Carl asked.

"I never did before," was Charlie's simple reply. The smile Eva had been repressing spread tellingly across her face. It widened when she heard Carl's reply.

"Oh."

Carl stood there for several moments, feeling unsure of himself. He looked uncertain of what he was doing, and he glanced over to Eva, who let out a soft chuckle and spoke.

"Charlie, honey, come to the table now. It's time to eat and you don't want it getting cold. Mr. Spencer worked hard to make us this food and we won't be wasting it."

A look of relief spread across Carl's face and she caught his eye.

"Okay, ma. Let's eat!"

Carl took this as his cue to bring Charlie to the table, and he gently placed him in the chair nearest his ma before taking his own. He cleared his throat, still looking a bit embarrassed. He snuck a peek at Eva, and she knew she had been caught looking at him with an amused but gentle expression on her face. She looked down at her plate quickly, unable to hide the smile that was forming on her lips from witnessing the small moment he had shared with her son.

"This looks amazing, Carl. Thank you so much for fixing us lunch. I'll make it up to you," Eva said, her tone soft and sweet.

"You don't have anything to make up to me," Carl said. "You didn't mean to get hurt, and I just want you to focus on feeling better. Okay?"

She moved her food around on her plate with her fork. "Okay. Thank you."

"My pleasure."

They ate their lunch with light, casual conversation before Carl gathered the dishes and took them to the kitchen. He washed up before returning and looking over to Charlie. "Now, I've gotta get some work done outside, and your ma needs to rest some. Maggie's at work, so that means you're the man of the house right now, all right? If you or your ma need anything, you just get me from the barn outside and I'll come in and see to it that you two are taken care of. Got it?"

Charlie nodded enthusiastically. "Got it!" he cried.

"Good boy." Carl pressed a hand on top of Charlie's head and headed back outside. Eva watched him go, a confusing wave of emotions washing over her. Seeing her son being treated so kindly by a man was strange. Her husband had been okay with him at times, but he was an irritable drunk and hadn't always treated him gently. It was bittersweet, really, to see the way Carl was. Charlie surely missed his father in certain ways, but there were so many things that he hadn't been getting from him. A simple pat on the head, for example.

She sighed, looking down at her injured wrist, remembering Carl's promise to come inside and look after them if they needed anything, and wondered if there was more to the man than most people knew. Well, she doubted that he was going to open up to her willingly, and she wouldn't do anything to push it. She already felt like she was on thin ice with him as it was. Even so, she found herself thinking about Carl long after he'd left, waiting for the sound of the door to indicate that he'd come back home again.

# Chapter Eleven

Before Carl knew it, it was beginning to feel like the most natural thing in the world to have Eva and her boy there. Although he had most definitely felt a charge between them when he had tended to her; one that had kept him up all night thinking about it for several days in fact, he truly enjoyed just simply spending the afternoons having lunch with them. Even Charlie had begun to warm up to him more, and he was really enjoying the little boy's playfulness and bright energy. The first time the boy had asked Carl to pick him up had been an awkward moment. While it left him feeling exposed and embarrassed, it also made him feel a strange sensation of warmth. Carl had never experienced anything quite like it before.

But it had opened up a floodgate and the little boy had grown attached, especially since his ma was having a hard time with her wrist. Now, though, it was Monday and she was feeling significantly better, so Carl didn't feel quite as worried about spending extended periods of time outside again.

"Carl!"

Carl's lips pulled into an irresistible smile when Charlie ran to greet him at the door. "Hey, cowboy!" Carl said, chuckling when Charlie threw his arms up in the air expectantly. He lifted the boy and grinned as he squealed in excitement. "You been looking after your ma like I told you?"

"Yeah!" Charlie exclaimed, squealing as Carl flew the small boy through the air. "Ma's good. Horsie?"

"Honey, Mr. Spencer's just got done working, we should let him rest."

Charlie's face fell as Eva appeared around the corner, watching them play with a soft look on her face.

"Nonsense! I'm no old man, I've got time for the little one," Carl said, setting Charlie down on the floor. Charlie bounced on the ground with a giggle. "Horsie?"

*"Horsie?"*

"I'm the cowboy and you're the horse!" Charlie stated matter of fact. Carl chuckled.

"Ah, I see. You wanna wrangle some sheep, do you?" He grinned. He was familiar with the game and found himself crouching on all fours. Charlie laughed excitedly and hopped onto Carl's back. Carl chuckled and began roaming the room, going every which way the little boy pointed him to. Eva laughed from the doorway where she stood watching them, her arms crossed over the apron against her chest. Charlie's bright amusement made it even more fun for Carl, and soon he was rearing and kicking, giving the little boy a bit of a challenge.

Of course, he was careful, keeping a supportive arm curled behind his little body in case Charlie slipped.

"Well, look what we have here!" Maggie chimed, her voice causing Carl to stop in his tracks. She had very rarely seen the playful side of him. In fact, his own father would have never dreamed of getting down on the ground for anyone. "Looks like we've got a regular buckaroo living with us now!"

"I'm a cowboy!" Charlie exclaimed. Carl nodded, sitting up on his knees while carefully removing the little boy from his back and setting him safely on the ground in front of him.

"That's right, he is," Carl said, ruffling Charlie's hair. "And someday you'll look just the part. You can come work with me on the ranch here and I'll teach you all about real horses."

Charlie gasped in excitement and ran over to Eva. "Ma, I can be a real cowboy! Mr. Spencer said he would teach me!"

"That's wonderful Charlie," Eva said softly to her son, patting his head.

Carl got himself up off the floor and looked over to Maggie, already able to guess what she was there to say. As if on cue, she spoke.

"All right, everyone. Time to wash your hands and get to the dining room. I'm about to serve up some supper."

"Okay, Maggie, thank you," Carl said, chuckling as he watched the little boy take off running to get himself cleaned up. He was a huge fan of mealtimes, just as Carl had always been. In fact, food had been one of the only comforts that Carl had during his upbringing. His father had so rarely shown him affection but when he was served a meal by a smiling Maggie, he had family that cared about him. Still, he had a real fondness for mealtimes and made sure not to miss a single one.

"I'm starved. Ready for some supper, Eva?" he asked, venturing a look at the beautiful woman. She seemed to be getting more and more by the day. His gaze ventured to her hand, and then to her stunning, golden eyes. "How's the wrist feeling today?"

"Much better, thank you," she said, demonstrating by moving it around and showing its range of motion. He watched skeptically, knowing she was the type who would downplay her injuries to not cause a fuss. "And I just want to thank you again for making sure Charlie and I were taken care of while it was healing. It really means the world to me. And to him, too."

Carl waved a dismissive hand. "Aw, Eva, that isn't anything worth thanking me over, but you're welcome, of course." Carl looked away from her golden gaze, his heart tremoring oddly in his chest. Whatever effect this woman was having on him, he wished it would give him a break.

"Well, unfortunately, not everyone is well versed in human decency. But you really astound me sometimes, Carl Spencer. And you have my everlasting gratitude." Eva's voice was as gentle as her gaze when he finally dared to meet it, and Carl found himself struggling for words. Fortunately, he didn't have to try for long because Charlie appeared, flying towards them like a hornet, and held his hands up for his ma to inspect.

"I'm ready for supper now!" he exclaimed. "Can we go to the table?"

"Go on ahead, sweetheart, I'll be there in a moment," Eva said. She smiled to Carl with a strangely knowing look on her face before she disappeared to get herself cleaned up as well. Carl shook his head before heading to his bedroom. He was still in his work clothes and preferred to have his supper dressed in clean clothing before he relaxed for the night, so he washed himself up and took his time doing it, too, not sure he could face Eva again quite so soon after the way her look had made him feel. She was quite a woman, he knew, and he wished that he could just get her out of his mind sometimes. Never in his life had he felt such a powerful desire to be close to a person, her skin, her touch, her warmth, and softness. But there was more to it than that. There was a way she touched him that wasn't physical; something he felt that he had no idea how to even analyze. She was something special and he felt like a special kind of man for the way he caught her looking at him some moments.

It was just because he was a generous man. He had opened up his home to her and her son, and the three of them were getting along better than he had anticipated. She was just looking at him the way anyone would at the person who offered them a way out of an exceedingly tricky situation, maybe because he had money, or because she respected him, or felt a sense of gratitude. Whatever it was, he was happy to see that look, and he only wished that it might be more than those things. Even though he wasn't quite certain what more would mean.

When he finally emerged, he was cleaned up and in clean, more comfortable clothes. He felt bad for keeping them waiting; it was rare for supper to be served before he made it to the table. But mother and son were sitting patiently at the table, chattering idly as Maggie bustled in and out the dining room setting out the dishes.

When Carl took his place, he felt the warm eyes of both Eva and Charlie upon him and again, his heart felt incredibly full. It was a world apart from when Carl sat down at this very same table with his father, who was quiet and stern and seemed to have no room for him in his thoughts, let alone his emotions. He was never greeted with a kind smile or an inquiry about his day. At most, his father grilled him about his chores and the ranch's inventory and then took his leave once he had filled himself up.

Even when he had grown into an adult, mealtimes had been the same; impersonal, quiet, awkward, and Carl found himself finding much more pleasure in the food before him than from his own father's company. It was kind of sad, now that he thought about it, but then, his father had been a very distant figure, incredibly aloof. In fact, most of the time Carl had felt like he was a bother to the old man, and even now, seeing his face had made Carl feel worthless. He was an adult now. He was running the ranch on his own. He was worth something.

But even more than that, he had earned these warm, genuine smiles from Eva and her boy, and somehow that felt better than anything else he had ever felt on the ranch. He wanted them both to know just how much he appreciated them, and he wished with everything in him that he wasn't so closed off. Even though he was starting to really love spending this time with them, he also knew he couldn't admit it aloud, and he had his father to thank for that.

The rest of the food was served, and they dished up their plates and began to eat. Carl was ravenous after spending all day out on the ranch, and he barely had the wherewithal for conversation or even small talk as he tucked into his dinner.

"Boss!"

Carl frowned in confusion when he heard Jeff's voice. He had let himself in, and he sounded panicked.

"What's the matter?"

"The fence broke! One of the steers kicked Earl into it and he went right through, now they're looking to escape from the hole there. We're trying to patch it up as quick as we can but we could use some extra hands."

Carl frowned, immediately getting to his feet, and heading to the door. "Is Earl all right?" he asked, following Jeff to where it had happened. He would have to finish his meal later.

"He's all right but his wife is already taking him up to see the doc. She wanted to make sure."

Carl nodded, glad that he had allowed the young man to bring his new wife with him to live at the ranch quarters until they were able to afford their own space. She had heard all the commotion herself before taking her husband up to town. Carl hoped the injuries weren't too serious and walked up with Jeff to examine the damage done to the fence. He let out a low whistle.

"This will take some work to fix but it shouldn't be too long," Carl said. Jeff nodded and soon the men were immersed in their work as they took turns keeping the steer at bay and away from the broken area of the fence.

Finally, the fence was fixed to Carl's satisfaction and he headed inside. They were beginning to lose daylight but evening hadn't quite fallen and he figured he could enjoy the rest of his supper now in peace.

But when he arrived inside the house, something was wrong. Eva and Maggie were running about frantically and Carl stopped Eva by the shoulder. She had hardly even noticed him come in. Before he could ask what was wrong, her voice came out fretful and scared. "Carl, have you seen Charlie? We can't find him."

"He's not in the house?" Carl asked, frowning and glancing about the place in concern. Maggie appeared then and shook her head, looking just as frazzled as the young mother.

"I don't know Carl, we're still looking."

All pangs of hunger that Carl had disappeared and he immediately turned back around and headed deeper into the house to begin his search; a sense of urgency pressing upon him quite unlike anything he had ever felt before. He had a little boy to find.

# Chapter Twelve

"I'll look in the kitchen again," Maggie said.

Eva was in a panic and she nodded quickly to Maggie in acknowledgement. "I think I'll check the bedroom again. Maybe he was hiding after I put him down, and I missed it."

Eva walked to the bedroom, shaking. Where had Charlie gone? He normally didn't get out of bed after she laid him down. He might call for her to get him something every now and again but to disappear was entirely out of character. And although they had been in Carl's home for a little while at that point, her son didn't really know his way around.

"Charlie?" she called, feeling overcome with anxiety. "Come on out, Mommy needs to talk to you!"

She felt a spike of panic after rechecking every nook and cranny of the bedroom and still not finding her son. She didn't hear a word from him and came back out into the hallway, where she met Maggie standing there, just as concerned and out of sorts as Eva.

"He wasn't anywhere in the kitchen, either," Maggie said, running a hand across her forehead and massaging her temples. "I just can't fathom it."

"Do you think he could have gone outside?" Eva asked, suddenly consumed by an entirely new wave of panic. "It's going to be dark soon!"

The night's events played out in Eva's mind. They had finished their supper and she had tucked the little boy into bed. She helped Maggie finish cleaning up the dishes and tried to get some tidying done, since she was finally beginning to feel better and able to move her wrist again. Of course, that meant she hadn't stayed in the bedroom to supervise her son, but he had been sleeping soundly through the night for a long time now. When she went to check on him, he was gone. She had never felt a fear like this in her life.

Why would he have gotten up? Had he been taken? Had he wanted to explore outside? Was he sleepwalking? She had never seen him do it before, but what if he had this time? Had he called her name and waited for her to come to him? Had he had a bad dream and gone looking for her? The guilt and the worry was too much to bear, and she began to search the living room again, wondering if he had crawled behind the sofa and fallen asleep. She had to find her son.

Maggie continued her search as well. Nothing was turning up, until suddenly, Eva heard Carl whistling from down the hall. She frowned and made her way over fast, only to find him carrying Charlie on his hip, as if it were the most natural thing in the world.

"Charlie!" Eva cried, running toward them. She threw her arms around Carl and her son, not even thinking twice. She didn't realize how awkward it was until she pulled away and heard Carl clear his throat gently. "Thank you so much, Carl," she said, trying to fight away her embarrassment while taking hold of her little boy. Charlie went easily into her arms and she held him tightly. "Where was he?"

"Oh, he was just fine. He decided to do a little exploring. I found him in my bedroom playing with my shoehorn."

Eva shook her head with a sigh before squeezing her son close to her again. "Charlie, apologize to Mr. Spencer for going into his bedroom without his permission."

"Sorry, Carl."

Carl's lips twitched in amusement. "Atta boy, you remembered to use my first name."

"Ma don't like it though," Charlie said. "Am I gonna get in trouble?"

"No sweetheart, not this time," Eva said. "But you are definitely going to be getting into bed and staying there. And from now on, you won't be leaving that room after bedtime, do you understand? Or you will be in big trouble."

Eva's words lacked any real conviction, although she did try to sound as stern as she could. The last thing she wanted was to ever worry about her son's whereabouts again. Right now, she was too relieved that he was okay to give him a proper scolding.

"I love you, Charlie, you know that?" she murmured, hugging him close again. Charlie giggled.

"Yeah, I know! I love you, ma."

When she looked up from embracing her son, she caught Carl looking at them with tenderness in his gaze. Then, he put his hands in his pockets and continued whistling, heading to the dining room to finish his supper without a word about any of it.

Eva sighed with relief, carried her son to their bedroom and laid him down in bed. She was going to have to talk to him about all of this. Once he was nice and cozy, tucked into bed, she sat beside him.

"Charlie, do you understand why mama was upset?"

"I got out of bed?" Charlie asked, his precious eyes fluttering closed after all the excitement.

"Yes, you got out of bed, but then you went into Mr. Spencer's bedroom and I didn't know where you were. I get scared when I can't find you."

Eva was doing her best to understate the dread she had felt when she couldn't find him. Every worst-case scenario had been playing out in her mind and she couldn't imagine what she would do if anything were to happen to him. But as much as she wanted him to understand, she didn't want to scare him either.

"I was just playing," Charlie said.

"Yes, honey, I know that, but you were missing from bed and Maggie and I couldn't find you. Did you not hear us calling for you?"

"No, ma, I was explorin'." Charlie looked at her with his big eyes full of wonder and awe. "Mr. Spencer has a big room with lots of stuff in it!"

"I understand that, sweetheart, but I didn't know if you had gotten hurt, or if you were lost somewhere and needed help. It made me real scared thinking you might need ma's help and she didn't know where you were."

She watched her son's expression soften in concern and he put his little hand on hers. "I didn't get hurt, mama, but I won't get out of bed like that no more."

"I appreciate that, sweetheart. It's okay to make mistakes, but please try not to scare ma like that ever again. I always need to know where you are. If you get up and want to play, just tell me, okay? We can do something else until you're ready for bed, but sometimes, bedtime means bedtime, remember."

"Okay, mama." Eva gently stroked her son's hair out of his face and she gazed upon him as he drifted off to sleep. She stayed at his bedside for a long time, not feeling up to leaving the room. She just wanted to stay by his side.

Eva felt a lump forming in her throat and she tried swallowing it. It felt like everything that had been going on was just becoming too much. She hadn't had a chance to slow down and process everything that had happened. She had lost her husband, lost her home, and she had almost lost her son.

She let the tears fall, crying softly and trying to do her best not to wake him from his sleep. She curled up on the big bed beside him and covered herself up, allowing herself a moment to really reflect. She had been homeless. She had even gone to the extreme of stealing to feed her son. And now, they were here, under this man's roof, feeling like some kind of family.

Eva forced herself to stop these thoughts. She couldn't let herself get attached to the idea of the three of them,. They were only here on a temporary basis, and there were conditions to that. She had to work for Carl and save up enough money to venture out on her own. She was so grateful, but she couldn't help but feel a sense of foreboding, considering the fact that all of this would one day end.

As crazy as it seemed, she was feeling a connection with Carl. He seemed to fill something in her life that she hadn't realized she was missing. He was a strong, capable man and she hated to admit it, but there were moments when she could feel herself drifting off thinking of his touch on her wrist. He was so concerned and so tender towards her, and she felt incredibly blessed and cared for. She wasn't used to that.

Jim had been the only man she had ever been with, and while things had seemed picture perfect at first, his desire to care for her had faded along with his care for himself. The more he relied on the alcohol, the less of a husband and father he was. She had forgotten how nice it was to have a capable man around. Not only was he sober, but Carl was considerate in ways he didn't even need to be. It went beyond being an employer, but that was just his nature. He treated Maggie like family, and he never even had second thoughts about the kindness he expressed towards Eva after her fall. Eva convinced herself that anything he was doing for them, he would have done for just about anybody. He was just that sort of man.

Still... she couldn't help but think back to the way he had been looking at her as he held Charlie after finding him playing in his bedroom. There had been something in his eyes, something pure and genuine. Something deep. Maybe he really did feel more. Maybe her feelings were mutual. It was something she wouldn't let herself linger on for too long it was hardly appropriate. She had found herself in this man's home and was working for him, she wasn't there to explore any sort of romance.

What she couldn't deny was that, in some of her quiet, private moments, she couldn't help but wonder what it might be like if he took her into his strong arms and treated her as a lover would. To touch his cheek and feel his beard underneath her fingertips. Were his lips soft the way she imagined, or would they be rough like the rest of him? She couldn't help herself wondering, especially after the way his touch had affected her.

She had been with her husband for several years, but there was something more charged about the way Carl's fingertips had felt against her skin. She was doing her best not to read into it, but the intrusive thoughts kept coming back to her. Eva hated to even give herself the temptation of finding love again. Would she even recognize it? She was getting ahead of herself, but the draw between them felt real and intense, and she wasn't one to laugh in the face of a fate.

Eva shifted in bed and sighed, glancing over to her small son. She had been worried before, about Carl and Charlie. She didn't want the man to be put out by having a little boy in the house, and the way he had reacted to him at first had been surprising and difficult for her to understand. She had been ready to pack her things right then and there, and had begun to do just that, but he had come to them and apologized. He had taken the time to talk to Charlie, something many adults wouldn't even think to do.

She had felt much more at ease with him since then. And ever since, the two boys had developed a close bond. The way he held her son on his hip seemed the most natural thing in the world, and Charlie loved it. He needed a strong man to look up to, someone who could call him a cowboy and promise to teach him things all young boys deserved to learn. But that came with responsibilities. Would Carl really live up to his promises, or would her son end up attached to a fleeting figure? A man with no follow through, just like his father.

It was all too much for Eva to process and she closed her eyes, feeling suddenly exhausted by everything that had transpired that night. Before she could even change into her nightclothes, she drifted off into a deep sleep, and found herself in a perfect world, where she and Carl were raising Charlie on the ranch and they would never have to leave.

# Chapter Thirteen

The night of Charlie's little mishap remained with Carl. He replayed the moment when Eva had thrown her arms around him in a warm embrace. He had wanted to take her into his arms and embrace her back, but he didn't want to give the wrong impression, and he felt he wasn't worthy of it anyhow. She would only end up rejecting him, no one would ever truly see his softer side. His father had shamed him for any of his sentimentality, and he had learnt to keep his feelings locked tightly away in a box, in an effort to avoid any further hurt.

And that was perfectly fine by him. It had to be. He could observe from a far and enjoy those fleeting moments of tenderness at a distance.. Once in a while, Charlie could provide Carl with a precious moment of laughter and sentiment without the rejection that came after.

A child was so different from an adult. If he had allowed himself to hug Eva, there was no telling what might become of him after that. It would have revealed the fact that she was on his mind so often, that he had feelings of a different kind for her. She didn't need to know that. She wouldn't feel that way anyway, and worse if she did, it wouldn't last. She could do much better. Carl was an irritable man set in his ways; he had already shown his short his temper. How could she want to be with someone like him? Someone so much like Carl's father.

So, he had refused to hug her back, despite it being what he had wanted to do the most.

When Carl woke up the next morning, he realized he had slept in. He squinted out his window, frustrated that he had let it happen, and knowing he needed to refocus on his work on the ranch. He walked outside before getting his breakfast and ran into Jeff, offering him a lopsided smile.

"Fence is holding up great, boss. None of the steers escaped during the night and Earl is doing better too. His wife came back with him late last night and all he needs is a couple days bedrest to make sure his head's right."

"That's good to hear," Carl said, genuinely relieved that Earl was going to be all right, and that they hadn't lost any of their cattle. The last thing he needed was to deal with a hit to his business.

"Well, we have it all under control. I'm gonna go tend to them now, I just wanted to give you an update."

Carl smiled at Jeff. "I appreciate it."

"Sure thing, boss!"

Carl and Jeff parted ways and Carl went to the barn to check the feed boxes before double-checking the stores and refilling wherever was necessary. Then, he groomed Smokey before deciding that the barn could do with some cleaning. He started on that and did his best to make sure everything was up to standard. The ranch hands were good for a lot of things, but none of them had Carl's particular eye.

He climbed up to the loft to double check everything was in its place up there and paused. There, he spotted the old tire swing he had used as a boy. It had fallen from its tree when a branch snapped during a storm and his father had never bothered to put it back up for him, even though it was Carl's favorite. He picked it up to inspect its condition, seeing if it was still in working order. He was pleased to find that it was and it gave him an idea. There was another little boy on the ranch now, and if he could set the tire swing up for him, he may love to play on it just as much as Carl did when he was growing up.

It would feel good to do something for the boy; something his father had never done for Carl. It was still cold out, but it never hurt a child to play outside, even when there was still snow on the ground. Besides, his mother would be there to supervise him, and Carl could when he had the time.

He carefully lugged the tire swing down from the loft, unsheathing his knife to cut the old rope off. He paid attention to the way the knots were formed, as he had never hung a tire swing before, and when he was satisfied that he knew what he would need to do, he rolled it over to was it with water and some lye soap, just in case there were any critters who had made it home. It had been up in the barn's loft for so many years..

When Carl was satisfied that the tire was in good shape, he headed out the barn in search of some decent rope and caught Jeff again as he was heading into the ranch quarters for lunch. "Hey, do we still have that rope that we got last summer or did we use all of it already?"

Jeff thought for a moment and shook his head. "No, boss, we don't have any like that right now. I'd have to run to town for more. Do you want me to do that?"

Carl shook his head. "Nah, it's okay. I can do it, it's no problem."

"You got it, boss!"

Jeff set off again back to the ranch quarters. Carl's stomach was rumbling, but he was eager to get going with his new project. He could grab a bite in town if he really needed to. Maggie would scold him for not giving her warning about his trip, but he could deal with her later. All he could think about was getting that tire swing so that Charlie could have something to play on.

"Carl! Long time, no see! Good to see you around these parts," Carter, the owner of the general goods store greeted Carl with a pleasant grin. Carl smiled.

"Good to see you too, Carter. I've got a question for you."

"Oh, yeah? What's that?"

Carter set down the glass jar he was polishing and set his gaze on Carl instead. Carl approached, looking around briefly at the shelves to his right, and spotting the rope he was after in the back. He felt so satisfied that he would be able to leave with exactly what he needed and approached the counter and smiled again at Carter. "Ever put up a swing?"

Carter chuckled and adjusted his glasses. Carl had always liked the man. He was small and wiry, with round, wire-rimmed spectacles that made him wise and unthreatening. "I have, yes. What you need it for, Carl?"

"There's a project I'm working on for the ranch and I want to make sure I do everything right. I wouldn't want any kids getting hurt because I used the wrong thing."

Carter nodded. "Kids you say? Well, why don't you grab that rope over there and I'll show you the best way to secure it. I didn't know you had kids on the ranch."

Carl glanced over his shoulder as he walked across the shop and grabbed the rope. He brought it over to the counter and sat it down. "My housekeeper has a young boy. Not Anna, but someone who'll be staying 'til spring. It got me thinking he might like to get some fresh air and I remember really loving that swing when I was a little boy."

Carter nodded with a smile. "That's a mighty nice idea, Carl. Well, here, this is how it's done. What kind of swing have you got?"

Carl watched Carter work as he answered. "Tire swing. I know how to secure the rope to the tire, but I'm wanting to make sure that it's all set up proper on the tree."

Carter nodded. "That's wise," he said with a chuckle. "Well, just watch me and then try it yourself. Then, you should be all set."

Carl grinned. "Thank you, Carter."

Carter smiled brightly. "My pleasure, Carl."

They worked at the rope for a while, then Carl paid for it, along with some jerky and a few apples. He was getting mighty hungry but he was focused on getting this finished before the day ended.

"Thanks again for your help, Carter, I think he's going to enjoy this." Carl really hoped that would be the case. It would feel real good knowing he had done something nice for the child, especially after everything he had gone through.

"Happy to help, Carl. Let me know if you hit any snags. I'll be off work around five, I can ride over and help truss it up if you need."

Carl smiled at the offer. "That's mighty kind. See you around, Carter, I appreciate this a lot."

He rode back to the ranch, chewing on some jerky and thinking about the knots that he would need to tie to properly secure the tire to the tree. Once he was back at the ranch, he finished his last apple and headed back to the barn, grabbed the tire and carried it outside, looking for the perfect tree. He needed something strong that would withstand the weather, something he could trust to stay secure, no matter what winds it had to contend with.

After a few minutes of searching, he found the perfect one. It was set back a bit from the barn and the stables; a big, sturdy redwood that had withstood the test of time since Carl was a boy. He considered it something of a good luck charm, as it often blocked the house when the winds were howling and protected those within by collecting the snow. He smiled to himself as he carried the tire over before unslinging the rope from over his shoulders. He would need to climb up high to secure it to the thickest branch, but he was happy to do so. It wouldn't be the first time he had climbed this giant.

He scaled the distance quickly, then worked at the rope until it was secured on one of the sturdiest branches. When he was done with that, he hung on and slowly slid down the rope, making sure it would hold his weight as well as the weight of a tire with a child on it. It held firm, and he made it to the ground very satisfied.

"Carl, there you are! What on earth are you doing out here?"

Carl was startled at Eva's voice and he turned around to greet her confused gaze.

"Afternoon Eva. I was just…"

Carl suddenly felt embarrassed by what he was doing, though he couldn't for the life of him figure out why. It wasn't like he was doing anything wrong, but he felt exposed doing something nice for the boy; something that he wished had been done for him fifteen years ago.

"I was testing this rope," he replied. re. Eva looked over at the tree, and then to the ground where the tire lay. She smiled at Carl as she put the pieces together, followed quickly by a frown. Carl was confused.

"You climbed down the tree before you knew that rope was even safe? Carl, you could have broken your neck!"

Carl opened his mouth to protest, feeling warmth from her concern and shame from being scolded. "It was fine! I wouldn't have done it if I didn't think it would hold me. I just wanted to make sure."

"Well, good thing you didn't get hurt," Eva said, letting out a sigh that made Carl shoot her a teasing grin.

"I'm fine, Eva, nothing happened. And the rope is safe enough that Charlie will be able to use the swing without any accidents happenin'."

Eva looked to him, her expression full of surprise and warmth. It caught Carl off guard and he couldn't help but stare. "What made you think to do this?" she asked.

Carl froze. Should he share his childhood memory of his own father and the swing that sat on the ground unattended after that storm? How his father had grown sick and tired of looking at it and ordered Carl to move it up to the loft. No, she didn't want to hear anything about that. Instead, he just shrugged. "I thought it would be a fun thing for the boy. It's always been something I wanted to put back up, anyway. It was knocked off during a storm some time ago."

He could settle with half the truth. That would be enough. Eva smiled.

"Charlie has never been on a swing before. He's going to be so excited when he finds out that you did all of this for him."

"Well..." Carl looked away, feeling flustered and inarticulate. But Eva would understand. She didn't seem to think any less of him for his awkward silence. "I'm just hoping he can get some fresh air on the nicer days. I know what it's like to be cooped up inside. No growing boy can handle that for too long a time."

Eva nodded. "You're sure right about that. He has been getting restless. That may be why he disappeared the way he did the other night."

"It may just be," Carl agreed with a nod. He was so lost in their easy conversation that he almost didn't stop to wonder what she was doing out there. He frowned. "Is something wrong that you came out to find me."

Now it was Eva's turn to shy away. "Well.. I noticed that you didn't come in for lunch, so I was getting worried about you and I wanted to see if you would be comin' in for dinner. It's getting late, you know, and you can't tell me honestly that you had a proper meal in all this time."

Warmth filled Carl's chest and he shifted his weight, looking from Eva to the ground. "Well, I had a bit of jerky and some apples on my ride, if it makes you feel any better."

"It doesn't," Eva replied, causing a broad smile to break out on Carl's face.

"Well, I beg your pardon, ma'am. I'll come in and eat, don't you fret. Just as soon as I'm done out here."

"See that you do, Carl. Otherwise, I'll tell Maggie not to save you anything and you'll go to bed hungry for being stubborn as a mule."

"You wouldn't dare, Miss Hall." Now, they were both grinning and Eva shrugged a coy shoulder.

"I just might. Stubbornness never did a man any good. Especially when he ain't eating proper meals."

Carl sighed. "Yes, ma'am. I'll be in soon. I just want to finish with this first."

"All right. I'm glad to hear that. And I'm also glad that I can report to Maggie and let her know that you're still alive. She was about ready to have a fit when you weren't inside for lunch."

Eva laughed and Carl found himself entranced by the sound. It was a physical force, somehow. "Well, Maggie is prone to fretting for no reason," he said. "Don't worry about her. Just let her know I got caught up on a project. She knows how I can get."

Eva nodded. "I'm starting to see that myself," she said with a wink. She turned away and headed inside before Carl even had a chance to think of something to say in return.

Carl was left in a daze from the exchange, his heart fuller than he could remember it ever feeling before. But he couldn't let himself get too distracted, he wanted to finish setting up the swing for the boy before the sun set. He wouldn't be able to use it 'til morning, but it was going to be a very nice surprise.

Carl worked until there was almost no light left in the sky and when the tire was finally secure, he smiled at the result of his efforts. He held the rope in his hand, debating whether or not to try it out for himself. After a few moments of hesitation, he did. It was just the thing he needed to say goodbye to the old memories of his disappointing childhood, an act of defiance. He placed one foot in the middle of the tire and launched himself forward, pulling it up into a swinging motion as it swayed back and forth, a gentle groaning of the branch holding its weight. It was as solid as could be, and, finally satisfied that his work was complete and safe for little Charlie, Carl headed inside a happier man.

# Chapter Fourteen

The next morning, Carl was up to unveil the swing to Charlie. Everyone in the household was excited and there was a big hullabaloo as they layered him up in his winter clothes, ready to venture outside and enjoy the winter weather for the first time that year. Eva was excited to see Charlie finally get to go outside and play. He had loved being outdoors with her when they had their own home, but she had always felt cautious about taking him outside on the ranch. It wasn't familiar to them, and she didn't want to get in the way. She knew Charlie would want to see all the animals and she didn't want to interrupt anyone's work. Especially Carl's. She felt underfoot enough already, so she had gotten in the habit of telling Charlie that it was too cold to play outside.

"All right, buckaroo, you ready for this?" Carl asked once they had all gathered around the redwood tree.

"I'm ready, Carl!" the little boy exclaimed, the jubilance in his voice reaching all of the adults and making them chuckle.

"Great, get on over here and I'll put you in it."

"Swing time!" Charlie exclaimed, running through the snow into Carl's awaiting arms. He lifted the boy easily into place and Eva felt a tug of warmth at seeing the way the two interacted. It was heartwarming to see the bond between them growing, even if it caused her concerns. She knew that her son would be devastated when spring came if they were to leave the ranch.

"Mama, I'm on the swing!" Charlie called, pulling her away from her thoughts. Eva smiled at her son.

"I see that, honey! What do you think?"

"I like it a lot," Charlie confirmed. "Push me, Carl!"

Carl chuckled and pulled the swing back before letting it go, allowing it to coast gently in the push.

"Faster, faster! Push me harder!" Charlie cried, wiggling his little feet in excitement that had them all laughing.

"You sure about that, partner?" Carl asked, lifting a brow to Eva. She gave him a nod to signal that it was okay and Carl grinned as Charlie cried out happily. "Yes! Higher, higher!"

"You got it, cowboy, but you need to tell me if I should slow it all down."

"I won't, Carl! I want to go high!"

Carl chuckled. "All right then, here we go!"

Carl pulled it back as far as he could before letting it go with a push. Charlie squealed in excitement, but quickly it turned into a fearful scream. Carl looked to Eva, alarmed, before reaching for the swing to still it. But midair, Charlie began to flail and let go of the rope, tumbling from the swing just as Carl caught hold of it. Charlie fell to the snow and let out a piercing wail. Eva knew that he wasn't hurt; she could tell when he was just scared or startled, and she ran to the little boy to scoop him up from the ground.

"It's all right, sweetheart. You're okay," she quietly spoke, rocking him soothingly as she could. Charlie was in hysterics and Carl stood frozen behind the swing, with a look of sheer guilt plastered on his face. He was beet red, and he abruptly turned around and hurried off as Eva and Maggie consoled Charlie the best they could. Soon, Charlie stopped crying and they took him inside.

"I hate that swing!" Charlie announced once they got inside.

"Hush now, darling, you don't mean that. It's a lot of fun, you just got a little scared your first time is all. It's okay to be. Now, you know not to go so high, so you won't ask again, right?"

Charlie nodded and Eva smiled, wiping the drying tears from his cheeks. She sat him on the table to examine him for any scrapes or bruises, but found none . He had mostly been startled to hit the ground the way he had, but there had been enough snow to cushion his fall that it had barely hit him. Still, he had been afraid and she couldn't blame her tiny son for that.

"Can you do me a favor?" she asked, whispering conspiratorially as she smoothed the boy's hair away from his face. Charlie looked at her with a dubious expression, but he didn't answer or deny the favor either, so she went on. "I don't want you to tell Mr. Spencer that you hate that swing out there, all right? I know it wasn't fun to fall off it on your first time but it wasn't the swing's fault either, now, was it? Mr. Spencer worked really hard to set that up for you because he thought it would be something fun for you, something you would like, and he didn't have to do that at all, now did he?"

Charlie sighed and shook his head. "No, mama."

"That's right. It was nice of him to do that, wasn't it?"

Charlie nodded.

"We were all excited this morning and thought it was very nice of him, now didn't we?"

"Yes, mama."

"Do you want Mr. Spencer to feel bad by making him think you don't like his present?" Eva felt a strong, protective urge over Carl's feelings in the matter. She had seen just how much he had put into setting the swing up, and the last thing she wanted was for him to feel responsible for the minor accident.

"I didn't like falling off," Charlie said with a sulky pout. "It was scary."

"I know it was scary, sweetheart, but you aren't going to fall out of it every single time, you know?"

"But what if I get swung really high every time?"

"I don't think anyone will ever swing you that high again," Eva said with a tremendous effort to repress a giggle. "I think we all thought you would like it, but then you got scared and there was a little accident, that's all."

Charlie thought this over for several moments before nodding resignedly. "A little accident, that's all."

"That's right, sweetheart. But it's all fine now, hey, and you didn't even get any bumps or bruises. It might have just knocked the wind out of you a little. I'm sure it was all very scary, but before that happened, it was really fun, wasn't it?"

"It's fun if I don't go too high," Charlie said.

"That's right. Now are you going to tell Mr. Spencer you don't like the swing?"

"No, mama. The swing is fun if you don't fall off." Charlie screwed up his brow and looked around. "Where did Carl go?"

Eva had been wondering the same thing herself. She felt a knot in the pit of her stomach when she thought about how mortified he had looked. She couldn't stand thinking he was beating himself up over this, and she patted Charlie's head.

"I think I'm going to go look for him and see, how does that sound? You and Maggie can play for a few minutes while I do that."

Charlie nodded, and Eva went to the kitchen where Maggie was getting some hot chocolate ready for the little boy after his exciting time on the swing. "Maggie, do you mind keeping an eye on Charlie for a few minutes? He's still a bit shaken up, but I want to check on Carl. I think he is, too."

Maggie looked over at Eva with a gleam of something in her eyes that made Eva feel a little bit embarrassed. It was like she knew something she wasn't saying, and Eva looked away, trying not to betray the unsettling feeling. "Of course, honey. I'll bring this out to the little soldier now and we can have a nice chat while you find Carl."

"Thank you so much, Maggie, you're a blessing. Truly."

Eva hurried outside, grabbing her shawl, and slinging it over her shoulders. She had seen Carl head off toward the barn and she made her way there, following the big boot prints he had left in the snow as he walked away from the source of his shame.

Eva stepped into the barn and looked around, concerned when she couldn't see him there. Finally though, she looked up and spotted him sitting in the loft, pinching the bridge of his nose and hunched over on a hay bale.

"Carl?" she called gently, making her way over to the ladder. She began to climb, not waiting for him to answer. When he saw her, he let out a sigh. "I'm so sorry, Eva. I should never have set up that stupid swing."

Eva made it up to the loft and sat on a hay bale opposite Carl. "Charlie is just fine, Carl. You didn't do anything wrong. He was having a great time until he panicked and let go."

Carl shook his head. "No, it's my fault it happened. I pushed him too high. He's just a little thing. I should have known better. What in the world is wrong with me?"

Carl went back to pinching his nose and looked away in frustration. "All to prove my old man wrong. I put that boy in danger. I can't believe it."

"What do you mean?" Eva asked gently. Carl sighed. "It's nothing," he muttered.

"It doesn't sound like nothing," Eva said, applying gentle pressure on Carl to open up. Of course, she would accept it if he didn't want to, but she hoped that he would. "Go ahead, you can tell me if you want to."

Carl sighed heavily and leaned back, finally removing his hand from his face. "That swing used to be mine, you know. It fell down and my old man didn't want to put it back up for me. I had a pretty complicated relationship with him. He nearly let it rot, then had me store it away. I guess I just thought I could kind of show him, or myself, by putting it back up, by letting a kid really just be a kid, you know? I thought it could be a symbol, in a way. It sounds ridiculous."

"It doesn't, Carl," Eva said with a shake of her head. She kept her tone low and gentle. "It was a beautiful gesture and it was an empowering one, too. Accidents happen, you know. Kids get into all sorts of mischief. It doesn't mean you did anything wrong."

"I'm the one who pushed him like that," Carl insisted, shaking his head. He couldn't seem to get over it and Eva found it incredibly endearing. It showed just how much he truly cared about Charlie and she felt comforted to see that. Jim would have told their son to walk it off, even if it had been his fault entirely. But Carl didn't have to blame himself the way that he was and Eva couldn't stand seeing him beating himself up.

"You pushed him because he asked you to, Carl. And you checked with me first. I don't think any of us expected him to react to it the way he did. It can't be helped sometimes. These things happen and he's perfectly fine. He's having some hot cocoa with Maggie right now."

Carl sighed. "I'm glad he's okay. But I still feel terrible."

"Carl, I really wish that you wouldn't. You didn't do anything wrong and, in fact, it was the sweetest thing anyone has ever done for him. He was having fun. The only part he doesn't like is going too high or falling out. And now we all know better, right?"

Carl sighed and was quiet for several long moments before offering Eva a nod. "I suppose that's true. You're sure he didn't hurt himself?"

"I think his four-year-old pride was hurt more than anything else," Eva said with a smile. "But he's entirely fine. And we're going to go back outside tomorrow and try the swing again. He really did enjoy it, and if he didn't, he wouldn't have asked to go even higher, right?"

Carl nodded and Eva smiled again. "Please don't beat yourself up over it anymore. Charlie was worried about you, so I told him I'd come and find you. Why don't you come in with us and see for yourself that he's all right?"

"I'm not quite ready yet, Eva. I just need some time to think about everything." Carl avoided her eyes and Eva felt a pang of sadness gripping her insides.

She stood to leave, but faced Carl first, putting a delicate hand on his broad shoulder. It was just the most natural thing for her to do and she didn't even think twice about it. "Kids get hurt all the time, Carl. It's not going to do either of you any good to hold on to it like this."

Carl grunted and Eva pulled her hand away, feeling uneasy for the contact.. She could tell he didn't want to talk about it anymore, so she climbed down the ladder, left the barn, and went back into the house, leaving him alone to fight his demons.

# Chapter Fifteen

Carl eventually made his way down from the loft, unable to block out the horrible voice of his father playing in his mind. He hated that the man was still right there with him.

*That little boy could have broken his neck because of you. What kind of a man are you? You're worthless!"*

Carl tried to drown the voice out by throwing himself into his work, but all day long, whenever there was a quiet moment, he found himself hearing it again and it was driving him mad. Nothing he had ever done was good enough by his father's standards, and now he had proven him right. Of course Carl was worthless with his hands. Of course he had built a death trap for the little boy to play on. Of course he had pushed the little boy too hard and jerked the swing, causing him to tumble off into the snow. He couldn't get the sound of that scream out of his head. It was as loud as his father's.

Carl tended to every single animal that day, examining them all closely to make sure they were as healthy as could be. He brushed the ones that needed it and did everything that he could to avoid going back to the house, including taking that swing down. He didn't think he would be able to face Charlie, and he had no intention of going in until he was tucked safely into bed for the night.

But of course, there were some things he was sorely missing. He helped himself to something to eat from the ranch quarters kitchen, knowing that, once again, he was exposing himself to Maggie's scolding but not worrying about it anyhow. Not with the way he was feeling.

His father would have told him he didn't deserve a nice meal anyway, not after what he had done. He had made a tremendous mistake and he should pay the price for that. He knew it and so did Charlie. The child was probably furious with him. Even worse than that, he was feeling unsafe, which made Carl feel even more terrible. He had only wanted to do a nice thing. Charlie would never want to play on the swing again.

Carl decided he would take the swing down. It had already become the source of a horrible memory. The last thing he wanted was to leave it up as a reminder of his mistakes. No, he would take it all down in the morning, but right now, he was still feeling too sore to go anywhere near it.

Eventually, Maggie came out, knowing that it was not his intention to eat at home that night. She wasn't going to let that happen.

"Carl Spencer, you get inside this instant. I'm not going to let you miss another meal, not while I'm here to stop it. Do you understand me?"

Carl sighed and nodded, allowing Maggie to lead him inside. He did his best not to make any eye contact with Eva or Charlie and sat down in his seat silently, brooding. Maggie sighed at him as she disappeared into the kitchen to serve the food, and he could feel Eva's eyes upon him. He had hardly eaten over the past two days and now that there was food in front of him, he focused on it, making no conversation. Everyone was okay with that and respected his silence, and they ate quietly, not bothering Carl with small talk.

"Remember when I fell off the swing, ma?" Charlie asked, making a hot wave of guilt wash over Carl. Eva shot a look at her son and raised a brow before Charlie added. "It was fun before that. I wanna swing tomorrow too."

Carl wasn't convinced and he simply continued eating.

"We are going to swing again tomorrow, honey," she said. "Maybe Mr. Spencer will come along."

Again, he felt shame redden his cheeks and said nothing, only looked at his plate and continued to eat. He knew his body needed the food, but he didn't feel hungry in the least. Everything felt heavy in his mouth and didn't settle well in his stomach either. Instead of feeling satiated by the meal, he felt nauseated by it, so he soon stopped eating and pushed his chair back, waiting for a good moment to exit. But it was rude to leave before everyone was finished with their meals, and he sat at the table waiting.

Finally, Charlie hopped off his chair after asking Eva if he could be excused, but of course, she was still picking at her food, and Carl didn't feel quite free to leave yet. Charlie ran over to Carl and climbed into his lap. He looked down at the little boy in surprise. Didn't Charlie hate him for what had happened? Carl certainly hated himself. He didn't really understand what was going on, but he felt a confusing mixture of emotions from the boy's simple act.

"Carl, will you tell me a story?" he asked, looking up at Carl with those adorable golden eyes.

"You want me to tell you a story?" Carl asked in surprise. "What kind of a story?"

"Any story! You tell good stories!"

Carl was quiet for several moments as he considered his options. He wanted to tell the boy a good one, of course, and he began the tale of Goldilocks and the Three Bears, one he remembered from when he was young.

Charlie giggled hysterically when he made a big show of acting out the different voices for the mama, papa, and baby bears, and soon they were both laughing out loud.

When they came to the end, Charlie tugged on his shirt sleeve. "Can you tell me another one, Carl?"

"Another one?" Carl replied, his voice surprised and theatrical in a way that made the little boy laugh again.

"Yeah, another one!"

"I don't know if I remember any other ones," Carl said.

"Make one up!" Charlie exclaimed. "Please?"

Carl thought about this for a few minutes before nodding agreeably. "All right, buckaroo. Let's see..."

Soon, they were immersed in a wild tale of cowboys roaming the prairies, looking for a bear that had taken one of their friends. The bear was misunderstood, of course, and simply wanted someone to babysit his baby bear, while he went out to look for some honey. The entire time he spoke, the little boy sat in his lap, hanging on to his every word. Finally Carl could feel Charlie surrendering to the sleepiness in his eyes and he slumped against Carl, still looking up at him. "Will you tuck me in tonight?" he asked, his voice almost impossible to understand as he spoke through a yawn.

"Sure, if it's all right with your ma."

Carl looked up, startled to find that Eva hadn't moved from her spot at the table and was watching the two of them with a tender smile. "It's all right with me, Carl. You know where his bed is."

Carl nodded and picked the little boy up with him as he stood. He carried Charlie over to the bedroom before laying him down gently. He had already been changed into his pajamas before supper, so he didn't have to worry about any of that, thankfully.

"Carl?"

"Yes, Charlie?"

"Thanks for being my friend."

Carl was speechless. If there was one thing he hadn't expected to hear that night, it was this. He found himself choking up and unable to respond, but fortunately, he collected himself before the boy could notice.

"It's no problem, little cowboy. I'm happy to be your friend. Thanks for being mine, too, and I'm sorry you took a spill earlier today."

Charlie laughed. "It was just a small accident, it's okay. Will you cover me up, Carl?"

Carl did as the little boy requested, then stood awkwardly for a few moments, not sure what else needed doing.

"Do you and your ma pray at bedtime?" Carl asked, trying to remember what he had done before bed when he was a young boy.

Charlie nodded. "Mm hmm, we thank God for you every single night and for always having food to eat."

"Well, that's mighty nice of you Charlie. I pray for you too." Carl felt his voice wobble as he spoke the words.

Charlie smiled and nodded as if he had expected nothing less, and Carl chuckled. "All right. Let's say a bedtime prayer now. Will you say it with me?"

Charlie nodded. "Is it the one with the sleep?"

Carl smiled. "We can do the one with the sleep," he replied, knowing which one the little boy meant.

"Now I lay me down to sleep, I pray the Lord my soul to keep. And if I die before I wake, I pray the Lord my soul to take," Carl said softly. He smiled as the little boy recited the prayer with him in a whisper. He was about to leave when Charlie stopped him.

"Wait, we didn't do the asking part yet."

"The asking part?"

"Yeah, the asking part! Like this!" Charlie held his hands together again and squeezed his little eyes closed. "Please bless Carl and Maggie and everyone who has a heart fulla love. And thank you for this place to live and the nice food and for Carl, too. He's a really good friend and made a swing I can play on, so I hope you can do something nice for him too Lord. Amen."

Carl was speechless but uttered a soft "Amen" in response to the little boy's prayer. He placed a hand on Charlie's head and smiled down at him. "Good night, Charlie."

"Good night, Carl."

Carl smiled and left the room, turning out the light and closing the door slightly, just enough that they could hear the little boy if he called, just as he had seen Eva do before.

When he emerged, Eva was clearing the table and she stopped to smile at Carl.

"You see? They bounce back. And he really likes you, Carl. There's nothing to beat yourself up about, all right? Just let it go. Every day starts anew."

Carl nodded and Eva smiled. "You know," she said, "I knocked his head against the doorframe when he was a tiny baby. He screamed so loud that I thought I had killed him. But sometimes, things seem a lot worse than they really are.

Try and remember that. He's a loud little boy, but when he's actually hurt, he's quiet as a mouse."

"Stoic," Carl said with a chuckle.

"That's right," Eva said, returning the smile. "And he's forgotten all about his fall. You should too."

Carl smiled, realizing Eva was right. Even if the boy did remember, he didn't harbor any resentment at all. Carl had been in turmoil all day over it, but to the little boy, it had just been another thing that happened and nothing more. "Yeah," Carl said. "I suppose you're right."

"I would like to think so," Eva said with a little teasing smile that made Carl's heart pound in his chest. "I'm just going to do these dishes now, Carl. Have a good night."

Carl nodded. "You too, Eva. And thank you."

They exchanged a meaningful look that brought that unfamiliar warmth to Carl's chest. He gave Eva a slight nod, then retired to his bedroom, feeling as if he were walking on air.

# Chapter Sixteen

"Morning, Eva," Carl greeted with a slight nod. If he had been affected by their conversation the night before, he didn't appear to show it. Eva smiled back, trying not to reveal her disappointment.

"Good morning, Carl. How did you sleep?"

They were standing in the hallway together; they had both been heading to the dining room for their breakfast.

"I slept okay, thanks. I think I'll move the swing to a better spot this morning. I took it down last night after Charlie's fall and I reckon it would be better in the barn. It's warmer in there anyway, without the wind, and he might not be so tempted to go too high if it's indoors. I know how boys can be."

Carl spoke quickly, as if he were embarrassed by his thoughts Or maybe he was more concerned about the fact that he had taken it down in the first place. Eva hadn't quite been able to figure out why Carl had taken it all so hard when Charlie had gotten hurt. Sure, it was hard to see a child in pain, but obviously there was much more to it than he had been letting on. He had mentioned his father when he was young... Perhaps that had a lot more to do with his reaction.

"I think that sounds like a wonderful idea, Carl. That would be a nice spot for Charlie to play." Eva smiled at Carl and he gave her a quick, handsome grin before heading to the dining room to grab a hard-boiled egg from the table. He headed out the door with it, peeling it on his way to the barn. Eva watched him go just as Maggie emerged from the kitchen. She saw Carl leave too and tut-tutted, shaking her head with a bemused smile on her lips.

"He's something, isn't he?" Eva asked, looking to Maggie. Maggie chuckled and nodded. "He sure is."

"Did you know he took that swing down yesterday?" Eva asked.

Maggie nodded. "Yes, I saw it outside on the ground in a heap. He felt really bad about your boy falling how he did."

"Yes, I know. We talked a little bit about that last night. He said that he had a complicated relationship with his father. What do you suppose that has to do with Charlie and the swing?"

Maggie sighed. "Carl's father could be incredibly cruel, but I'm worried he would be upset to know I told you that. I don't normally talk about people's personal business, but I would just hate for you to give up on him and leave us so soon. When Carl was young, I'd hear his father berating the poor boy left and right and it didn't stop when he grew up, either. It went on and on until the day that man died of a bitter heart. Carl always did his best to please him, but it just never seemed good enough. He could make Carl feel like he was well near worthless, and it felt like he did it on purpose, too. I always felt real bad for Carl."

Eva's heart broke hearing this, and it made more sense of what Carl had mentioned in the loft, and why he couldn't let it go. He felt like he had failed Charlie, and he was feeling worthless like his father made him feel. "That's terrible," she said softly, her eyes wandering to the window. She could see Carl outside, dragging the swing with him, the rope slung over his strong shoulders as he headed back to the barn. "No child should ever be made to feel that way, especially by their parents. Charlie's dad could be hard on him too, thankfully, Charlie was still so young, he could still see his pa in a positive light, and I did my best to protect him from a lot of what went on. If Carl's dad acted like that until he was grown... Well..."

Maggie nodded. "Carl wants to be his own man, to make his way in the world without being reminded of the way his dad made him feel, but sometimes, when things don't go according to plan, he feels like a failure. That's why he took it so hard yesterday. He works every day to be a better man than his father was, and made him out to be, and he doubts himself when things go wrong. He is really hard on himself."

"Why do you think his father treated him that way?" Eva wondered aloud. Maggie sighed.

"Well, he wasn't so bad at first. But Carl's mother got depressed after she had Carl. She wouldn't do anything during the day except sit on the sofa and stare out the window. Eventually, she reached her breaking point, and one morning everyone woke up and she was gone. She left a note saying she had left and not to look for her. Carl was just a baby, but his father blamed him for it and resented him for the rest of his life. The poor boy could do nothing right by him because his father felt like having a child was what lost him the love of his life."

"She just left in the middle of the night?" Eva asked, shocked. Maggie nodded.

"That's right. And, of course, he looked for her, but she was never seen or heard from again, at least not by anyone here. Rumor has it, she went out east to live with her relatives. But no one really knows for sure. And from that point on, nothing could make Carl's father get over it. He felt like his son cost him everything and there was nothing the boy could do to earn his father's love. He tried his whole childhood and always fell short. I don't think the poor thing even fully understood. It was truly heartbreaking to see Carl's father go that way; from a bright, happy man excited to have the family he had always wanted, to a sullen, bitter old man with a heart hardened by how his life had become. And it was so frustrating the way that he blamed poor Carl for it all. People tried to speak to him about it on occasion, my own mother had words with him, but he was an angry man at that point and she couldn't afford to lose her job, so it was difficult for her to step out of place." Maggie sighed, clearly troubled by all of the memories. "I still don't see the sense in taking it out on the boy. It was evil, if I'm entirely honest. It was like his father just surrendered to the darkness in his heart."

Eva was quiet as Maggie spoke, overwhelmed with the sadness of Carl's upbringing. "So many things happened at the ranch before I came to be here," Maggie continued. "Carl didn't do anything wrong, and he didn't ask to be born into the family he was in, but I supposed love doesn't always make sense. I had heard about it happening to some women, that, they get awful sad after they have their babies. They don't know up from down anymore, and I think that's what happened with Carl's ma. It is tragic, really. It's something that has affected Carl his whole life, in ways I'm sure he doesn't even realize. I feel mighty sorry for that man, sometimes."

Eva listened to Maggie quietly. It made sense that Carl would feel that way if his father had been so cruel to him. He might not even realize the good in him that other people see and that his father couldn't. No wonder he tried his hardest to keep things under control. He must have felt like he had to do it to prove something, if not to his father then to himself. "Thank you for telling me, Maggie. I can't believe how hard it must have been for him."

"It wasn't easy, that's for sure. But it made him a lot stronger in ways that many people aren't. He has grit and determination, even if there are other things that bother him or hold him back in many ways."

Eva nodded. "I feel terrible. He took it so hard when Charlie fell. But these things happen all the time."

Maggie chuckled. "Children are accident prone, but Carl tries to prevent the possibility of any accidents, ever. He likes to keep everything running perfectly smoothly. But I think it's been really good for him to have the two of you here. He's been relaxing so much more, even though you may not see the difference in him yet. I know I've certainly loved having you two around." Maggie offered Eva a broad smile and Eva returned it, feeling warmed from head to toe that Maggie felt that way.

"I think you're one of a kind, Maggie, and I'm so lucky that we're here and we were able to meet you. It's been... confusing... to say the least, but it's also been the biggest blessing I may have ever gotten in my life, other than Charlie, of course."

Maggie chuckled. "Well, good. Why don't you get that little troublemaker in her and have some breakfast? I've got the porridge almost done, and the eggs are all set out already."

Eva smiled. "I saw that, thanks Maggie. Carl took one on his way out."

Maggie tsked. "I got into the habit of making them in case he wants to get outside early without sitting down for a proper meal. I swear, that man wouldn't eat at all if he were left to his own devices."

Eva laughed. "Well then, he's very lucky he has you." She and Maggie exchanged grins and Eva went to retrieve Charlie and get him ready for the day. Once he was all washed up and dressed, they sat down to eat together.

"Where's Carl?" Charlie asked almost immediately. Eva chuckled. Charlie sure had latched onto the man.

"He's moving the swing into the barn for you."

Charlie's eyes widened comically, excitement shining in his face. "The barn?" He wiggled in his seat. "I wanna see the barn!"

Eva laughed. "I know you do. You've been asking for a while now to go outside and take a look."

"Yeah! I can swing in the barn. Are there animals in there?"

Eva smiled. "It's mostly for supplies, but there are pens for the goats. They're very friendly, I think they would like you a lot since you're such a nice little boy."

Charlie beamed. "Can we go outside and play on the swing when I'm done with breakfast?"

"I don't know if it will be ready by then. Let's wait until Carl - er - Mr. Spencer - tells us it's ready to go. We don't want to put any pressure on him to get it finished if he has other work to do first."

Charlie nodded. "He runs this whole place, ma, did you know that?"

Eva smiled at her son. "I did know that. It's very impressive, isn't it?"

Charlie nodded and began eating, his mind far away as he imagined all of the untold wonders that were waiting for him in the barn.

Eva continued with her breakfast, her mind wandering in a different direction. She couldn't stop thinking about Carl's family. How hard must it have been for him as a young boy to be betrayed by the one person who was meant to love him unconditionally? Well... in a way, they had that in common. Her husband had sworn to love and protect her, and instead, he had become the one she needed protection from. It was one of the hardest things in the world for her to process, that sort of betrayal. He had been her salvation after losing her parents, but eventually all of that disappeared completely and he created a special sort of torture for her to, one that had an impact on their young son as well.

She missed Jim, of course, but she certainly didn't miss the fear of not knowing what sort of a mood he was in that day. She didn't miss hiding herself away from the world to nurse a black eye or covering bruises on her arms with long sleeves on a scorching hot day. And she didn't miss the yelling towards her and their son. Charlie was safer now, no longer exposed to the violent whims of his unstable father, and she grieved Jim. Of course she did. But she had been grieving him since he had taken to the bottle and left behind whatever promises he had made to her. She missed the good and decent husband and father he had once been. It was tragic what happened to him, and tragic that it had led to their homelessness, but she was beginning to feel a sense of freedom that she hadn't realized she never had. She could be herself now without walking on eggshells. She felt safe to be who she was around Carl. She had even stood her ground with him, and he had respected her, and her son, as well.

How she had gotten to comparing her husband to Carl was shocking. It brought a blush to her cheeks. The embarrassing truth of the matter was that she had thoughts about him that were improper, living in his home, and being a recent widow. But she had hardly been able to help herself. She supposed it was only natural after all, but it wasn't proper or intelligent. Everything in her life seemed so unstable in so many ways, and if she made another wrong move, she'd be risking everything. A good home for Charlie. A good relationship with Carl. The peace and comfort she had found at the ranch. What if she was wrong about it all?

"All done, ma! May I be excused?"

Eva smiled at her son, grateful for the distraction from her anxiety-inducing thoughts. She nodded. "Remember, we won't be bothering Mr. Spencer about the swing and the barn until he's done, all right?"

Charlie was already scrambling out of his seat and running to look out the window, his eyes fixing upon the barn with excitement. "Yes, ma."

"Good boy."

Eva smiled privately to herself and stood, clearing the breakfast dishes, and taking them to the kitchen, trying not to let her mind wander back to thoughts of Carl and what could be if the circumstances between them were somehow different.

# Chapter Seventeen

Carl dusted off his hands and looked over to Jeff, who finished tossing the last hay bale into place. Jeff nodded to Carl, acknowledging the successful end of that task and Carl grinned. "That should do it, then," he said. "We have to do the feed bags now."

Jeff nodded. "You got it, boss."

They headed outside to where the feed bags were stacked and began to haul them into their spot in the barn. Jeff glanced across to Carl. "I saw the darndest thing yesterday. Thought you might wanna know about it, seeing's you've got his kin staying here and all."

Carl perked up at the words and his eyes found Jeff's. "Oh? What's that, Jeff?" He heaved up a bag of feed and sat it on his shoulder, moving behind Jeff towards the barn doors.

"I saw Jim's brother Clarence back in town. You know, the one most people are saying shot him? He's been making his rounds again, drinking like a fish over at the saloon."

Carl frowned. "Clarence is back in town? What does he want?"

"He didn't really say, though he was asking about Eva and the boy. I didn't tell him nothing though, figured it ain't my business and to leave well enough alone. Especially if he's capable of doing what he did to his own brother, if you know what I mean."

Carl's stomach sank but he did his best not to let it show. "Yeah, I think I do." He was quiet for several moments as he processed the news, then spoke up again. "Do you think he will be coming around here?"

Jeff shrugged. "It seems like a good bet, you know. Charlie is his nephew and all, and it ain't like he was convicted. I don't trust him as far as I could throw him, so that's why I knew I needed to say something. He may come skulking about, looking for a way to get to the lady and her boy. But I don't like him, boss. He ain't nice people. Ornery and an alcoholic to boot."

"You think he'd want to hurt them?" Carl asked, now unable to hide the concern in his voice. He had been trying to stay calm and appear impartial. If he showed too much investment, someone might suspect his feelings for Eva, and he wasn't prepared to confront those yet. It was private, for one thing, and for another, he wasn't even entirely sure what those feelings were. "I want to keep them safe here, you know."

Jeff nodded. "Yeah, I know, boss. I don't really know what he would do to be perfectly honest with you. I just know he's bad news and I think he ought to be locked up for what he done to Jim."

Carl nodded. "I might be inclined to agree with that," he said, not only out of his keen sense of justice and morality. He didn't like the sound of it one bit.

It didn't take them long to finish with the feed bags and when they were done, Carl thanked Jeff for his help and headed back inside. Nature called and he was hoping to get cleaned up for supper before it got too late. Sometimes, he had to wait until Charlie was done getting bathed and by then, he was likely to be late for dinner.

Carl walked toward the bathroom, lost in thought. What was he going to do if Clarence came to the house looking for Eva and Charlie? Could he refuse to let him in? Would Eva even want him to do that? They were family after all. She was his sister-in-law, and he was Charlie's uncle. And besides that, she might have no idea how dangerous he was, as nobody had seemed to have the heart to tell their suspicions.

Carl sighed and opened the bathroom door, then froze. Eva's body was before him, stepping carefully out of the tub and as naked as the day she was born. He wanted to look away, out of respect for her, but he was mesmerized by what he saw. She was like an angel emerging from the depths of sacred waters, and he stared at her in shock until his eyes saw the scars lining her back. He knew what they were. He'd seen those kind of marks before and knew a whiplash when he saw one. She'd been beaten repeatedly, and he felt a sudden fury that overcame him. His anger turned to sadness and before he could stop himself, he stepped forward and reached for her, his brow knitted with overwhelming sorrow. Nobody should ever treat a woman that way, but especially not this one. Carl was beside himself.

"Carl!" Eva gasped, turning to face him. He had startled the life out of her and he stood there awkwardly for a moment as he processed what he was doing. How could he have been so careless?

He ventured a look at her face, expecting to be met with fire, but she didn't look angry. Her face was flushed, her eyes flickering, but it wasn't the passion of anger he saw in them.

Eva backed away a step, throwing her arms around herself to try and cover whatever she could.

"I-" His mouth was so dry he could hardly speak. "I'm so sorry, Eva. I didn't think to knock." He grabbed a towel and handed it to her, keeping his eyes fixed on the ground to try and save her from any further embarrassment.

Eva took the towel and wrapped it around herself, while Carl took his cue to leave. He willed his legs to work and turned around. "I'm so sorry, Eva," he mumbled. "I don't know what I was thinking."

"It's okay, Carl," she said softly. The sound of her gentle voice in his ears vibrated through his whole body and Carl retreated from the room without another word, shutting the door firmly behind himself.

He was shaken all through and went to his bedroom immediately, frustrated with himself for the mistake he had made. How could he have approached her like that? She was probably mortified, even enough that she would want to leave.

Still, he couldn't help thinking about the look on her face. It hadn't been anger. It hadn't even been surprised. If he didn't know any better, he might even have thought that she didn't seem violated at all, but rather affected in another way. A way he couldn't dare let himself believe. Not after what he had seen.

She had been perfect in every conceivable way. The image of her body was burned into his retinas and there was no way for him to forget it. Even with the scars crisscrossing her back, she was the image of perfection. If anything, those scars made her seem more angelic. A woman who had survived terrible strife and still ended up the most immaculate and gentle creature he had ever seen. He was still furious that any man thought he had the right to hurt her like that, but he would never let that happen again. And he would tell her that. It was hard for him to pity Jim's death after seeing the scars he had left on his poor wife. And when it came to Jim's brother, Clarence,, the apple didn't fall far from the tree. And for a brief moment, he thought that Clarence had done the world a favor.

His life now with Eva and Charlie was the last thing he had ever expected, but it was happening and he had to hold onto it. He couldn't just ignore that kind of a gift, but he also didn't feel entirely worthy of it. He would do whatever he could to protect Charlie and Eva while he had them. Nothing would stop him, no matter what it took.

## Chapter Sixteen

Eva dressed slowly, her body still tingling from Carl's look. It had been so long since anyone had looked at her that way. It had electrified her and she was longing for more. She almost wished she hadn't been so startled. If she had been still, would he have come closer still? What might have happened?

Eva walked to her bedroom; quite certain she wouldn't be able to face Carl again while she was feeling this way. Her whole body was on fire, and her mind was consumed by the memory of his eyes on her. It felt magical, making her lose sight of everything else. She wasn't sure she would have had the self-control to resist him if she hadn't stopped things when she had. Imagining what might have happened if she hadn't been so startled left her mind reeling with the possibilities. What if he approached her again later, during a moment where she was less exposed, less shocked? She genuinely didn't know if she would be able to stop herself from allowing it.

Of course she would have to try, though. It wasn't proper. He wasn't her husband, for one thing. How could she let herself get entangled with a man when she had her small son to take care of? She had feelings for Carl, increasingly strong ones, but she felt a responsibility to be cautious before letting herself give in to them. That was assuming Carl even wanted the same thing she did, but one look at his face had told her he did. She wasn't alone in this torturous desire. But she couldn't get emotionally involved with a man who wasn't willing to take on the responsibility of fatherhood. Carl and her son had bonded, sure, but that wasn't the same thing as being a dad to him. And she definitely felt like she was getting ahead of herself.

Her desire for Carl was complicated by her situation, and she would have to tread carefully. As much as she was attracted to him and the life they could have together, she wouldn't do anything that could hurt her son.

Then, she heard Charlie's little footfalls as he ran towards the bedroom. He had been spending time in the kitchen with Maggie while Eva bathed, but he knew she was done now and he knocked rapidly on the door before letting himself in.

"Mama, supper is ready and Maggie had to go home so she told me to find you."

Eva smiled at her son, who beamed back at her. He was really thriving. She wouldn't have recognized him from the starving little boy he had been only a few weeks ago. She would never be able to express her gratitude toward Carl enough for the turn in their fortune.

"Good boy for coming to get me, sweetheart! Have you washed your hands already?" Eva took a glance at herself in the mirror, knowing that she would be encountering Carl at the dinner table after their awkward moment together. She hadn't taken much consideration to her appearance since Jim had lost himself to the bottle. She still took care of hygiene, but she had other things besides being pretty to worry about. But for some reason, now she had an urge to groom her hair into place and try to look as presentable as she could. Not that it could take away the fact that the man had just seen her naked.

"Yeah, Maggie helped me get washed up for supper after we set the table!" Charlie was bouncing with excitement and Eva couldn't help giggle. Her son was quite possibly the most adorable thing she had ever seen and she was so grateful to have him. He really was the light of her life.

"You helped set the table? What a big, strong boy you're becoming!" Eva exclaimed, taking her son by the hand. They walked together to the dining room, Charlie walking straight upright with pride. She lifted him into his seat before taking her own place at the table. Carl wasn't there yet, which she felt a fleeting moment of gratitude for, but it also made her feel a little silly for the way she had been primping just moments before. He was going to skip the meal, considering what had happened earlier. He didn't seem too shy about avoiding situations that made him uncomfortable and she was sure that this was one of them.

To her surprise, Carl emerged just a few moments later and took his seat, clearing his throat and situating his napkin as if nothing had ever happened.

"Evening, Charlie. Eva."

"Carl!" Charlie exclaimed. "Did you do good at work today?"

Charlie's innocent question made Carl chuckle, and Eva felt some of the tension disappear. He was trying to play it cool and act as if nothing had happened between them. She was grateful for it, and for her son's positive and oblivious energy. It was a good distraction, probably for the both of them.

"I did, friend. And guess what?"

"What?"

"I got the swing all finished. It's in the barn for you now so you can swing inside. And if you fall down, there's lots of straw on the ground so you don't get yourself all banged up."

Carl grinned broadly as Charlie bounced in excitement. "I can't wait to swing tomorrow! Can I, mama?"

Charlie looked intently at Eva, and Carl fixed his eyes upon her, too, making the heat rise in her cheeks. "Yeah, can he, Eva?"

Eva laughed and shook her head, resisting the urge to hide away from Carl's gaze. "Of course you can, sweetheart, just as soon as ma's done with all her work."

"It's the weekend! You don't gotta work the weekends," Carl reminded her. "Just have some fun with your boy. I think it would be good for you both."

Charlie nodded enthusiastically. "Will you come too, Carl?"

Eva turned her eyes to Carl curiously. Had he been too worked up by the incident with the swing to be present for another try? She didn't expect him to agree and she was surprised when an easy smile creased Carl's face.

Carl chuckled. "I think I could manage that."

"Yay!" Charlie cheered and Eva allowed him to express his excitement before gently shushing him.

"We're inside, sweetheart. We have to be polite at the table, remember?"

Charlie nodded, but it didn't wipe the big grin from his face as he scooped up his fork. "Yes, ma."

The meal went on without any incident Even though Eva avoided Carl's eyes, knowing what had happened between them, she felt relaxed to see that he wasn't acting strange. He was composed and considerate, even though it was clear that he was avoiding her eyes too. The whole thing had been embarrassing, but there had been a lot more to it than just that, and they both knew it.

Once they were finished eating, Eva sent Charlie to play in his room and she collected up all of the dishes. "Here, let me help you with those," Carl said, standing from his seat and reaching out his hands. "Maggie had to leave early today to see to some family who just came into town for the weekend, and I wouldn't feel right having you stuck with doing all these dishes on your own."

"All right," Eva said quietly. "Thank you."

Carl nodded and they went into the kitchen together. Eva took one side of the double sink to wash in, and Carl took the other to rinse and dry everything before putting it all away. They worked in silence for a few minutes before Carl spoke. "I just wanted to apologize again for what happened earlier. I never meant to do anything to make you feel uncomfortable," he said, glancing at her before looking back down at the sink, his forehead creased in shame. "I'm sorry. I'll make sure to knock next time."

Eva shook her head. "You didn't do anything wrong, Carl. It's okay."

Carl was quiet for a moment. "Those scars on your back, Eva... They're..."

Eva nodded, "Yes, it was Jim."

Carl's hands clutched the dish towel tightly, his knuckles turning white. He let out a low breath and dropped the towel on the edge of the sink. "No man should ever treat a woman that way, you know that. I'll never let someone treat you that way, Eva. I promise, that will never happen again."

Eva was surprised by the conviction in Carl's voice, and she nodded. "I don't plan on ever letting that happen to me again, either, don't worry. I have to be really careful now, you know, with my decisions. Who I end up with, I mean. I've got a son, you know... It's... particularly important for me to make sure I don't make any more mistakes."

"I understand that, Eva. Definitely. I just want you to know I'm here, no matter what happens, all right? No one will ever hurt you again."

Eva was touched by Carl's words and looked down into the sink, unsure of what to say in response. "Thank you," she finally whispered. "What about you, huh?" she spoke up. "I can't be the only one with a scar or two. I know you've had a rough go of things... with your parents..."

Carl smiled sadly. "My scars aren't visible ones. But you're right. They're there. We may just have a lot in common, you and I" he said, shifting his weight from one foot to the other.

Eva nodded and without thinking, she took Carl's hand and gave it a gentle squeeze. They stood this way for a few moments before she thought about taking her hand back, feeling suddenly self-conscious about what she was doing. Carl cleared his throat but offered her a quick smile, squeezing her hand back.

Eva was overwhelmed by a powerful desire to feel Carl's lips against her own and she wondered if he was thinking the same thing. When she dared to look into his eyes, they were fixed intently upon hers, dark and smoldering. Her pulse began to race and she instinctively leaned in towards him. He was doing the same and she was sure that something was about to happen.

Before their lips made contact, though, a shriek from the other room made Eva's pulse spike. She dropped Carl's hand and ran toward the sound of her son's voice. "Charlie?"

Carl was right on her heels and she soon found her son crumpled on the ground with his arm clutched to his chest.

There was blood. "What happened, Charlie?" Carl asked, looking around.

"The kitty got me!" Charlie wailed. Eva picked up her son and cradled him to her chest. "It's all right, sweetheart, it's just a scratch. Were you playing rough with her?"

Charlie shook his head no, his little lip quivering. "I didn't hurt her, she hurt me first. I just wanted to pick her up and..." Charlie trailed off then looked to Carl, who raised his brow at Charlie. Eva was confused for a moment until Carl filled her in on what she was missing.

"We talked about that, didn't we, buddy? The kitty doesn't like it when people pick her up, hey? She gets mad and thinks she's going to get hurt, so she tries to get away and her little claws are sharp. Do you remember me talking to you about that? It wasn't long after you got here, so maybe you forgot." Carl paused and waited for Charlie to answer as Eva began to clean the cut. She was pleasantly surprised to find that Carl speaking to Charlie proved the perfect distraction she needed to clean his wound without any more needless crying. She managed to get him all bandaged as Charlie sniffled and took deep shuddering breaths.

"I thought she might like it this time because we've been playing, and I thought we were friends now."

"Friends can still scare each other, though, buddy. Remember how you got scared of being pushed too high up in the air on the swing? That's how the kitty feels. She doesn't like being up too high and she sometimes gets scared and wants to get down. She didn't even know she was hurting you, she just wanted to feel safe." Carl ruffled Charlie's hair. "Does that make sense, little man?"

Charlie sniffled and nodded. "Sorry, Carl. I won't do it again."

Carl smiled. "That's all right, buddy."

"I'm okay," Charlie said, looking down at his bandaged arm. "Mama fixed me."

"That she did," Carl said with a private grin to Eva. "She did a real good job, too."

"Yeah, ma's real good at stuff like that. You should get her if you ever get hurt, Carl."

Carl winked over Charlie's head at Eva and it made her whole body warm. "I just might do that. Come on, let's have some dessert, what do you think? Maggie made us a pie for the weekend, but I don't think she'd mind if we had a piece a little early."

"Pie!" Charlie exclaimed, hopping up and running to the dining room. Eva began to follow and stopped to press a hand against Carl's firm arm, appreciatively. "Thank you," she murmured.

"My pleasure," Carl said, his body stiffening a little at her touch. But his face was gentle and he smiled at her as she passed him to follow Charlie. Eva did her best not to think too much into what just happened because, for the first time in a long time, she was starting to feel like something was finally going right.

# Chapter Eighteen

The next morning, Carl's head was flooded with thoughts and feelings unlike any he had ever experienced before. He felt cloudy, full of a strange optimism laced with a bitter knot in his stomach. He couldn't get the night before out of his mind. He had nearly kissed Eva. Kissed her! How could that have happened? More than that, why did he regret so much that he hadn't?

He had been out of his mind with desire for Eva, and part of him had been distraught the moment that the possibility of a kiss had been interrupted. He found himself wishing that he had never let the cat inside that night. If he hadn't, he would have finally felt the softness of Eva's lips against his own.

Of course, they wouldn't have been able to foresee what had happened. And it had been for the best. Eva wouldn't want to be with a man like Carl. Carl was strict and stubborn. He had never known love for a day in his life and that was for a reason, he figured. Why would he drag her down with him? No, he couldn't allow that to happen.

Still, everything in him had wanted that kiss. Nothing had ever felt more natural before. She was everything he never knew he wanted, and she was right there at his side. But he couldn't have her. He wouldn't put her through the hell of being with a man like him. There was no way it would be fair on her or Charlie. She would just end up disappointed, and he would end up with a broken heart.

Still... it was shameful just how many times thoughts of her body had run through his mind. She was so beautiful in every conceivable way. He hadn't ever intended on seeing her unclothed, but he would be a liar if he said he regretted it. As much as it may have been inappropriate, it had been wonderful. Just as almost kissing her had felt. But that only served to make him feel worse. He had never been shown love, how would he know how to show it to this woman? It was a lost cause and Eva deserved so much better than that. She truly did. He wasn't going to let her throw her life away on him.

And yet, he had a feeling that the next time one of those moments happened between them, he wasn't going to have the self-control to stop it.

Carl forced these thoughts away, electing instead to focus on the tasks ahead of him. He dressed and headed out the door, not even bothering to say good morning to anyone on his way out. He would head to town and that would be that. He didn't even know if he could look Eva in the eye after all that had happened, and he had to vow to keep his hands and eyes to himself because he didn't think he would be able to manage wherever it may lead.

Carl mounted Smokey and they rode into town to pick up the mail and place a few more feed orders.

"Morning, Carl! How's the swing going?" Carter said with a bright smile when he entered the general goods shop. Carl smiled back.

"It's great, Charlie loves it."

"I'm happy to hear that! Hold up good on the branch out there?"

Carl nodded. "It did, yes, but I moved it into the barn. Seemed safer and a little warmer for the little guy. It gets really chilly up there some days."

"Ain't that the truth," Carter said with a chuckle. Carl gave Carter a nod and began to browse the shop. He paused when he saw a beautiful piece of lace on display. He touched it gently, noting how delicate and soft it was. It was pure white and it made him think of Eva immediately. He pictured how she might wear it in her hair, or maybe sew it to a garment. He loved the thought of the way it would look against her skin or wrapped up in her pretty hair. She deserved to be adorned with things like this. Pretty, feminine things. Could having her husband be so cruel make Eva feel like less of a woman? Well, he wanted her to feel whole, and feel just as beautiful as she was.

Without a second thought, he picked it up, and took it to the counter. He made small talk with Carter as he paid, vaguely registering the sound of the bell as another customer entered.

As he headed to the door, he couldn't help but overhear the conversation being had behind him.

"Morning," Carter greeted someone as Carl continued browsing.

"Morning. I figured you might be the man to ask. You have any idea where Eva Hall and her boy are staying?" Carl froze in front of the door when he heard mention of Eva's name. A sinking feeling fell to the pit of his stomach and he glanced at the man speaking. He was young and handsome, thin with black hair slicked back. He looked so much like Jim that there was no mistaking him. This was Clarence. "I'm their kin and they got forced out of my brother's home. I'd like to check in on them, make sure they're well taken care of."

Carter shot a look towards Carl, who gave a slight shake of the head before opening the door and stepping outside, suddenly desperate for fresh air. He heard Carter's reply, "Afraid I can't say that I know," before the conversation was cut off by the door shutting behind him.

Clarence was actively looking for Eva and Charlie. Carl didn't want them to have anything to do with the man. He could be dangerous. He would have to be vigilant. On the plus side, he did know what the man looked like now, even though it made him feel sick to his stomach.

Carl began walking away when he heard the door to the shop open again. He strode toward Smokey, eager to get as far away from Clarence as possible, and quick. But he cringed when he heard the man's voice calling to him.

"You! Hey, you're that big ranch man. You seen Eva and Charlie around?"

Carl pretended he didn't hear him and hurried up the street, eager to put as much distance between himself and this man as possible. But he wasn't having it. Clarence sped up to a jog and intercepted Carl, pulling at his coat and staring at him dead in the eyes from below. "Hey. You know Eva Hall? I'm looking for her. My brother's Jim, her husband. You oughta know of them. Oak Bend ain't that big, and Eva's one of the best-looking ladies around. Come on, help me out here, I've been looking for days."

Carl stopped and sized the man up. He was lankier than Carl, but just as tall, with a smug-looking smile plastered on his face. He was clearly entitled enough not to care for boundaries and dead set on finding Eva, enough that he was willing to stop a stranger dead in his tracks. He'd also called Eva one of the prettiest women in town, which Carl personally didn't care for comin' out of his mouth, and it made him agitated and prickly. He instantly despised this man.

"Afraid I can't help you with that," Carl said, putting his arms behind his back to hide his fists, balled up in anger. "I heard they moved out of town once Jim was killed."

Clarence didn't flinch when Carl mentioned the way his brother died.

"I'm not sure where they would have gotten off to, she don't have a family besides me. I come to see they're taken care of."

"Well, I'm just telling you what I heard. Good luck, mister."

Carl departed quickly, deciding not to take a second glance behind to see if the man was still following him. The last thing he wanted was to look suspicious. He didn't like that he was there asking about Eva and Charlie, and he especially didn't like that he had had to talk to a man who murdered his own kin. Not only that, but Clarence clearly coveted Eva from the sound of things, and Carl was eager to keep him at more than arm's length. He feel not one iota of guilt about lying to him and he intended to make sure he never found them.

Once he had passed the town limits, Carl tried relaxing his tense shoulders as he made his way back toward the ranch, his mind swirling. He hated that Clarence was back in town. It gave him the feeling something bad was about to happen, and he couldn't stand the thought. He headed inside, eager to distract himself from the unsettling experience.

"Carl!"

Charlie's little voice reached Carl all the way from the dining room table, where Charlie was sitting, drawing with pencil chalks. Carl grinned at the little boy, but inside his chest had tightened with a protective surge of energy. He wanted to make sure they were both okay, and the idea of Clarence coming anywhere near them made Carl sick, whether he was Charlie's uncle or not. Kin didn't necessarily mean that the boy would be safe, and he was grateful no one in town had told Clarence where he might find Eva and

Charlie yet. Maybe the townsfolk had protective instincts of their own, especially if the rumor had made its way around.

Carl's thoughts were interrupted by Charlie getting up from his seat and running over to him, abandoning his drawing to see his friend. Carl's heart warmed when Charlie took his large hand in his own small one. The little boy tugged at it gently, leading him toward the table. "I made a draw-ring for you! Look!"

Carl gazed down at the paper and smiled at the rough figures on the page.

"Did you, now? I didn't know you were an artist. And who do we have here?"

Charlie's picture showed three figures, a large man, a woman, and a little boy. A portrait of a happy family.

"It's us, Carl," Charlie said with a bright smile. "This is ma," Charlie said, gesturing to the figure with long hair. He pointed to the one beside her and then looked up at Carl with round eyes. "And this is you! And I'm here." Charlie gestured to the smallest little figure and then looked to Carl proudly, waiting for his reaction.

Charlie smiled brightly at the man, entirely unaware of just how heavy an implication the innocent drawing could have on the adults in question.

"That's us?" Carl asked, studying the image with emotion pulling on his chest. He just didn't think he was the kind of man that such things could happen to.

"That's a good piece of art, buckaroo," Carl said, placing an approving hand on Charlie's head, but he had to turn away.

"Thanks, Carl. Do you want to draw one with me?"

Carl was still feeling shaken from seeing Clarence, and this little boy needed a pa. More than that, he wanted one. But Carl could never be one. How could he when his own father had never set any kind of example?

"Hm? Draw with you?" Carl asked, distracted by his thoughts.

"Yeah! It's fun. Maggie got me all this stuff so we can make pictures."

Carl didn't feel like drawing pictures with Charlie. In fact, he was starting to feel like the walls were closing in on him. He needed to get the hell out of there and get some fresh air. He was feeling panicked and overwhelmed all of a sudden.

"I've got some more work to do, but why don't you work on a new picture for your ma, huh? Some of the animals, okay?" Carl said, his throat closing up around the words as he spoke.

Eva emerged from the kitchen but he turned and walked out the front door before she had a chance to see the expression on his face. He wondered if she had seen Charlie's drawing, but he couldn't stick around to find out, it was all just too much.

He walked down the porch steps, running his hands through his hair, and not even bothering to put his jacket back on. The burst of freezing air was refreshing and he took in a deep breath, walking through the snow to a spot overlooking the vast field where the steers were allowed to roam. They weren't out at the moment, but he eyed the scenic view, trying desperately to calm the aching feeling in his chest. Eva and Charlie were convinced he was a better man than he was. The both of them seemed to give him far more credit than was due and it was tearing him up inside. As much as he wanted to be the man they thought he was, he knew it was impossible. He would just disappoint them both.

Carl knew that he didn't know how to be a father. His own father hadn't done anything to help him become a better man. He made him doubt himself at every turn in fact, and he would never let himself be in a position to do to another little boy what had been done to him. He had always had a belief in the way that people grow up as a result of the way their parents raised them and they were often little replicas of the values they were taught. There was a phrase about that, wasn't there? The apple doesn't fall far from the tree. Well, Carl believed that, and he didn't want to be the rotten apple that rolled away from his father only to impact the little apple that was Charlie. Sure, Charlie's pa hadn't been much better. He had been a much crueler man than Carl was, that was for sure, but it didn't mean that Carl was perfect or better suited to being a father.

Another freezing gust of wind blew and Carl found himself shivering in it. He wrapped his arms around himself but he wasn't ready to go inside yet. He wasn't sure that he could face Eva and Charlie again right now. Instead, his eyes wandered around the beautiful scene before him. The ranch had always been the pride and joy of himself and of his father. Everything he was as a man was in this ranch.

The weather was still cold, and there were still a few months before his favorite time of the year would begin. The ranch was lively in the springtime. He was excited for the bustle of activity that the fresh weather would bring. New life everywhere. Baby animals would be born, the grass would be green and crisp, and everything would begin to feel alive again. Right now, the winter left things feeling a bit oppressed.

Carl had always been a gentler boy than his father might have liked. He had always tended to the animals with a patience and reverence that his father lacked. He was different but was he different enough to really be able to raise his own family? His desire to be the kind of man Eva and Charlie thought he could be was confusing, because he had always felt that he just didn't have it in him. But they seemed to think otherwise. Even though he had yelled at the boy when he first got there. Even though the swing had at first been disastrous. Even though he had lost his temper at Eva when she had uncovered his father's portrait and placed it upon his desk.

He felt like a terrible man for all of those things, and what was worse was that he was fond of the fact that they didn't think he was. He was leaning into it most days, forgetting his own low opinion of himself, but he couldn't let himself get lost entirely in the delusion that he had of this little family being his own in any way. It wasn't possible, he would just be as big a disappointment to them as Jim had been.

In fact, it would be worse because they had experienced a terrible thing with Jim and Carl would offer them some kind of hope. A nice house, a nice life, some kind of emotional security that he couldn't actually maintain. He hadn't been built to be a family man. Not as a husband and certainly not as a father. His own father had done nothing to guide him in showing love to other people, and he hadn't received an ounce of it himself. Whatever they were hoping for, he was empty of it, and the sooner they all realized it, the better.

Carl shivered, suddenly aware of just how cold he was. If he stayed outside like this much longer he could be prone to getting frostbite, which would mean he couldn't work out on the ranch. And that was all he really knew how to do. That was what he was good for. He was good at running the ranch and keeping things in order. He wasn't good with feelings. His own father had been a monster to him. What if he ended up hurting Charlie even worse than he already had? He couldn't let it happen. He wouldn't.

He turned away from the pasture and headed inside, bypassing the dining room entirely and heading into the bathroom to warm himself up in a hot bath.

What would it be like to be a father? His gut twisted at the thought. He imagined himself as his own father, sitting at the table and scowling down at Charlie, who might come home from school and tell him about some little accomplishment and hoping to please him. What if Carl wouldn't be pleased? What if he was just as cruel and stern as his own father had been? The hope in the little boy's eyes burned brightly, bright enough to make Carl feel protective of it. But that didn't mean it was going to stay that way. He was still his father's son, and his own father had been cold and merciless. He wouldn't let himself get swept up in Charlie's fantasies of being his son, and he had to put a stop to it somehow. Carl's father had ruined him as a man emotionally, and built him more to be a soldier, a worker, and a rancher. He would never be anything more than that, and it was time for them all to accept it.

# Chapter Nineteen

Eva had been watching from the doorway when Charlie took Carl's hand to show him the picture he had drawn. He had shown it to her first, of course, as she'd been with him while he drew it, and she was surprised to find that she had felt a strange reaction to it. The little boy cared a lot about Carl and of course in his mind it seemed perfectly natural for the man to fill the empty "pa" role in his life, but he didn't really understand what that implied between the adults. She had been curious to see Carl's reaction to it, to see how he felt, and secretly hoped that it might touch him because it showed just how much Charlie cared about him.

But Carl's reaction hadn't been positive at all. He seemed upset, actually, and had gone outside without so much as a coat on. When he returned he'd gone straight to the bath, then out to the porch even though it was supper time.

"Can you do your ma a favor and go play in the bedroom for me, sweetheart?" she asked Charlie, ruffling his hair. He smiled at her and her heart warmed. He was the highlight of her life, truly.

"Yeah, ma. Then can we have supper?"

"Of course we can. Now go play and stay there until I fetch you, understand?"

"Yes, ma!"

Charlie ran off toward the bedroom and she waited until she heard the door close behind him before she headed outside to the porch. She found Carl sitting outside on the porch swing, his hands stuffed into the pockets of his jacket and a knit cap settled on his head to protect his wet hair from the chilly weather.

"May I sit with you for a moment, Carl?" she asked him with a gentle smile. Carl nodded but said nothing, so Eva made her way to the swing and sat down beside him. "Are you all right?"

Carl lifted his arm in a partial shrug, still not speaking to her. Eva sighed and looked out at the barn, gathering her thoughts. Finally, she looked to Carl. "What's wrong?"

"What do you mean?" Carl asked, stubbornly avoiding the subject. Eva rolled her eyes inwardly; it was just like a man or a petulant child to deny the obvious emotional distress he was in. The whole thing was reminding her of Jim, and it was making her feel sorry for Carl, but annoyed with the way that some men just couldn't manage to express themselves properly.

"Charlie's picture bothered you a lot, didn't it?" she asked softly. "You could barely look at him after you saw it and you've been avoiding us. Don't think I don't notice, Carl."

Eva raised her brow at the man, who glanced in her direction and sighed. He pulled the cap off his head and clutched it, shaking his head. "I can't do it, Eva. I can't let Charlie think about me being his father. I can't be any use to a little boy, or even to you for that matter. I know you and I have... well. There have been moments where we are feeling really good together, but this isn't right. I'm useless to the both of you in the ways you need me."

"Carl, what on earth makes you think you're useless that way? That's so silly." Eva reached out to touch Carl's arm and he pulled it away quickly.

"No, Eva. What's silly is pretending I'm a normal man. A man who could be a husband or father. The boy thinks of me as someone who could be his pa, and that isn't right, you know. I'm not that kind of man. I wasn't raised to be soft and kind and to give love to little boys who need it. I was raised to be tough and to just get by." Carl ran his hand over his face and avoided looking at Eva. Her stomach sank when she heard his words and she swallowed before she answered him.

"You weren't raised to be that way, but it hasn't stopped you from showing a whole lot of love and compassion to the little boy in there. You're taking the picture too seriously, anyway. Kids draw things, they simplify things. You don't need to overthink it all, you know? He's not expecting us to run off and get married. He just likes the idea of you as a pa and he put us together in a picture. He's a little boy. He doesn't understand."

Eva tried desperately to reason with Carl but he didn't seem receptive to it at all and she felt terrible for just how awful he seemed to feel over the innocent little picture. She felt even worse because in a way, she had been hoping he would be flattered by the idea. Even like it. She would be lying if she hadn't thought about what their lives could be like together if things were a bit simpler. She didn't want him to know she had thought that though, especially since it seemed like he was spiraling into a really painful feeling. Not just for him, but for her. It meant that he didn't want to be with her, didn't want to be a parent to Charlie, just as she had been afraid of. Even though she had tried to make peace with the reality that they likely wouldn't be together, and it wouldn't be fair to Charlie for her to get her hopes up by being attracted to Carl, the reality was bitter and painful. But she couldn't let that show. No matter how much it was hurting her.

"It doesn't matter, Eva; he thinks of me as a man who could be his family. I don't care if he doesn't understand or not, in fact knowing he wouldn't only make it feel even worse. You have to understand that on some level. I'd just disappoint him. I don't know how to do any of this."

"Carl, you don't have to do anything you aren't comfortable with. We don't expect anything of you. It was just a drawing," Eva said, trying to keep her voice from cracking. Carl was really unhappy and she couldn't help but feel partially responsible for that. Had their almost kiss caused him enough pressure that he was having similar thoughts as Eva had been having? Imagining their lives together? Although she had tried to steel herself against the idea for Charlie's sake, it still stung that Carl was so dead set against it.

"I don't have to do anything I'm not comfortable with, huh?" Carl said, turning to look at Eva with a deeply pained expression in his eyes. "I've made a mistake in thinking this would be a good idea, Eva. I shouldn't have let you come here with Charlie, and I'm sorry for that. But we can make it right. I'll help you figure out a new place to go and try to fix my mistake now."

"Carl, what are you saying?" Eva asked, panic spiking in her chest. "I don't understand."

"I'm saying that this has all just been a mistake and I'm thinking twice about letting you two live here. I don't think it's a good idea any longer." Carl looked away, gripping his hands tightly in his lap. He shook his head as he battled with his thoughts. "I can't have you all here when it's going to mess with everyone emotionally. The boy can't think of me as his pa or your husband."

"You don't have to be any of those things, Carl," Eva said, attempting to plead with him. "Please just take a deep breath and calm down a little. It doesn't have to be so serious."

Carl glowered. "Yeah, well it is serious!"

"I really think you're overreacting, Carl," Eva said with a sigh.

This seemed to spark Carl's temper and he clenched his fists.

"I'm serious, Eva. I can't do this anymore and you can't expect me to keep trying to do something that ain't right. I won't leave you two out in the cold. I'll try and help you find a different job somewhere else. But you can't stay here anymore. I mean it." Carl's expression was dark and his knuckles were white as he clenched his hands.

"I don't know what to say," Eva said, looking around to try to keep the tears in her eyes from forming and falling down her cheeks. "I hate to leave like this. I'm sorry for what we've done to offend you, Carl."

Carl didn't answer for a long moment. "You will be fine, Eva. You and Charlie need to be somewhere better than this for the both of you."

"We love it here, Carl, I don't understand." Eva tried to grasp what had caused Carl to react so strongly. She thought they had been becoming close, and it felt good. Really good. And now she was being pushed away, right out of the house.

"All you need to understand is that it's time for the two of you to move on. It's what's best, and you can trust me on that."

Eva felt incredibly numb as the reality of her new situation hit her like a freight train. She had lost her place on the ranch, a place that had been starting to feel so much like a real home for herself and for her son. But it wasn't meant to be. Carl didn't want them there, and on some level she just couldn't understand why. She couldn't help but blame herself in a way. She hadn't pulled away from the moment they had shared together in the kitchen. She had wanted him to touch her, wanted him to kiss her. All of it had been her own desire and now she was paying the price for it.

"Okay. I'm sorry for everything and for being a burden on you, Carl. I'll start getting packed up now." Eva got to her feet and stood still for a moment. Her legs were shaking and she was afraid to lose her balance in front of him. After a moment she walked into the house and finally let the sob that she had been holding back erupt from her diaphragm. She was grateful Charlie was still playing in the bedroom as she had asked him to do, because she didn't want to alarm him by being emotional in front of him. Children could be frightened to see their parents showing emotions like that, although once in a while she did show Charlie that it was okay to be sad and would explain to him what was bothering her. But this felt far too personal to share with a three-year-old, and she wasn't ready to explain to him that they would be leaving the ranch. He loved it there so much and had come to really cherish Carl. He was going to be so heartbroken. As heartbroken as Eva felt.

She went into the bathroom to splash cool water on her face and compose herself before she had to face her son with the horrible news. A part of her was still hoping that Carl would come to his senses and she wondered if she should wait to talk to Charlie until she knew for sure that they were moving forward with the move. He did say he was going to help her find a new job so maybe there was some time left yet to talk to him. She was feeling far too upset to approach it with the little boy right now, and he was going to be having supper soon anyway. She no longer felt hungry, of course, but as soon as supper was served she retrieved her son and sat at the table with him, trying to pretend that everything was still okay. Still, she couldn't unlearn that the world as she knew it was beginning to crumble at her feet and the uncertainty and fear that was resting in her chest was enough to make her sick.

Carl didn't come inside for supper, and she didn't go after him this time. He had made it clear what he wanted, and trying to talk him out of it was pointless. They were going to be leaving the ranch, and that was that.

# Chapter Twenty

As much as it pained Carl to send Eva and Charlie away, he knew it had to be done. It was for the best. He couldn't be responsible for giving them any more false hopes or letting them think that he was something he wasn't, and Carl himself would be better off alone. He knew what he was, even if those two didn't, and he was doing all of them the biggest favor he could.

That night, Eva wouldn't look at or speak to him and he didn't push it. He didn't know what to say even if she did. They only passed each other after she tucked Charlie into bed and sat in the living room to read a book. Carl went to bathe and then took to his room, where he spent the night trying to figure out the best place for Eva and Charlie.

As he thought while, he remembered that Carter who owned the general goods store had children and when they weren't at school, he kept them there with him, as their mother had passed the year beforehand. If he could get Eva a job at the shop, Charlie would be able to stay there with the other children while she worked, and she would be able to pay rent for a room someplace, even with Carter. Clarence would figure out where she was working, which bothered him, but he could still protect her from afar. He knew Carter was aware of what a creep Clarence was and Carl wagered that the two of them combined could keep him at bay.

With his mind made up, Carl fell into a fitful sleep. When he woke up he felt like hell, but he was adamant about his decision. He dressed quickly and combed his hair, then headed out without even stopping to eat. He hadn't had much of an appetite since his conversation with Eva and it was more important than ever now for him to make sure she and Charlie were taken care of. Another benefit of having them there was that Carter was aware of his feelings about Clarence contacting them, so he might be able to intervene if the man came in asking after them.

He rode off into town after tending briefly to Smokey and headed straight for the general goods shop. Carter was just opening up when Carl arrived and seemed surprised to see him there so early.

"Urgent business, Carl?" he asked, looking Carl up and down. It seemed obvious that he thought Carl looked disheveled, and he was. He had dressed quickly and hadn't slept well after all, so it was likely that he embodied the hell he felt.

"Something like that. Is it all right if I speak to you privately for a moment?" Carl asked, shifting his weight.

"Of course," Carter said. "Tend to your horse and I'll meet you inside."

Carl nodded and dismounted, then tied Smokey to the post outside. When he was all set, he went inside and found Carter at the counter, stocking the candy jars. "All right, Carl, what's this all about?"

Carl sighed. "You know I've been keeping Eva Hall and her boy at the ranch. She's been working for me but I can't have a little one like Charlie underfoot so I really need to find a better situation for the both of them. I thought you could use a hand at the shop, you know? I know the kids are here with you a lot of the time and she's a good worker, no trouble at all. I just worry about the boy not having any other kids to play with. He's got to learn to socialize, and or else he'll be getting underfoot at the ranch. It's dangerous out there for a boy his size, and if he isn't kept occupied who knows what kinds of trouble he might get into or what it could cost my business."

Carl had been rehearsing what he would say to Carter the whole time he was riding toward town and now that it was out, he felt like he had lied outright. It was partly true, of course. He didn't want Charlie to get hurt. He didn't want Eva to get hurt either. But it wasn't the ranch animals he was afraid of causing them pain. It was himself.

"Well, that's a mighty big ask of you, Carl. Must be urgent if you're out here this early. Did something happen?"

"Well..." Carl paused in thought. "Sort of. The boy got scratched by the cat and I've just been thinking a lot about everything. They need to be somewhere safer and more suitable for a woman and a little boy, if that makes sense. Right?"

Carter was quiet for a few minutes and then nodded. "Sure, sure, it makes sense. Yes. All right, well I suppose I can keep an eye on Charlie with the other little ones for a little fee out of her wages. It would be nice to have another hand around here, we could maybe extend store hours. We get a lot of folks traveling through here at odd hours and sometimes we miss a bit of business for it."

"That's great, Carter. Thank you so much." Carl felt himself breathe a sigh of relief. That was one problem down.

"Where's she staying, then? Her and the boy?" Carter asked. "They won't be living at the ranch with you anymore, right?"

"Right... well, accommodations haven't been made. I suppose I could set something up at the inn." Carl frowned. He supposed she couldn't very well live in the store. But he hadn't thought that far ahead yet.

"Nonsense. I've got a little apartment upstairs they could stay in. It's too small for me and the kids but I used to live there when I first moved here and opened the place up. When I married Martha and she got pregnant with our oldest, I bought a proper house. Eva and her son can live up there for now, until they have the savings to live somewhere else."

"I appreciate that a lot, Carter. Thank you. I'm just going to head on home and tell Eva the good news. When do you reckon she can start?"

Carter thought for a moment. "As soon as you like, have her come by when she's ready."

"Will do, Carter. I appreciate it."

Carl nodded appreciatively to the man before leaving the store. He gave Smokey an affectionate pat on the muzzle. "Looks like things are working out, Smoke. We'll have the ranch back to ourselves in no time."

Even though he said the words, they left him feeling hollow. He mounted the horse before heading back to the ranch, trying his best not to let himself be affected by the miserable feeling that was curdling in his stomach. He hated the entire situation for so many varied reasons, but at least he was doing what had to be done. Any man in Carl's position would do the same, he was sure of it.

He found Eva in the living room dusting with a faraway look on her face. Carl entered the room and cleared his throat. "Good news, Eva. I've got a new job set up for you at the general goods store. You can work there and Charlie can play with the other kids. Carter's even got an apartment above the store he said you could stay in."

Eva whipped around to look at him, fire in her eyes that was so fierce it actually made Carl take a step back.

"You what?"

"I told you this isn't working out, Eva, so I talked to Carter and helped to find you a new job. Something you can do with Charlie around. I thought you'd be pleased." Carl was genuinely confused. He had put a lot of thought into the best way for her to stay on her feet and keep her son comfortable, and there wasn't much better out there of which he was aware.

"Why would I be pleased?" Eva asked, putting her hands on her hips. "You're throwing us away!"

"Throwing you away? Eva..." Carl was dumbfounded by the accusation and stood there feeling a lot like a child who was being scolded. His chest was tight as he tried to find the right words to respond with but before he could, Eva started in on him again.

"You are! You're throwing us away. I can't believe I was stupid enough to trust you!"

Eva's eyes were angry but brimming with tears. Of course she was too proud to shed them in front of him, and instead stormed off, leaving Carl standing in the room speechless.

Throwing them away? Carl didn't think he was really throwing them away. He was just trying to solve a big problem. Why couldn't she just see it from his perspective.

"Is it really true, Carl?"

Carl froze at the sound of Maggie's voice and let out a heavy sigh. "I got her a job with Carter at the General Goods store. He's a nice man, Maggie, and Charlie will have other kids to play with. He needs that."

Maggie came into view and stood in front of him, crossing her arms over her chest and looking at Carl with a brow slightly raised. "What have they done, Carl? Why are you doing this?"

"I don't owe anyone an explanation," Carl said, suddenly feeling a surge of agitation. The whole thing was immensely emotional. And private, for crying out loud. He didn't need everyone in his business all the time. He felt bad enough about it as it was. "This is my house and if things aren't working out they just aren't working out. It's going to be better for them both in the long run, just trust me on that. No one else seems to."

"I won't question you on this Carl, I was just curious what happened." Maggie shook her head and left the room. "Lunch will be ready soon."

The thought of food made Carl's stomach churn but he nodded in acknowledgement. Everyone would deal with this and they would see that he was right. It didn't make a difference whether they were upset in the moment or not, because the bigger picture was more important. He couldn't let them get any more attached to him than they already were, and now they would be closer to being independent and having a place of their own.

"We ain't staying at that shop, by the way," Eva said, suddenly in the doorway and fuming at him. "I don't need Carter's charity. We'll go to the boarding house."

Carl was numb as he processed what she was saying. "Eva, it wouldn't be any problem to stay in the apartment."

"It's not happening, Carl. I'll use what savings I've got from working for you and we'll stay at the boarding house. That's final."

Carl sighed, knowing that there was no use in reasoning with the woman. She was furious with him and her pride was bristling. He knew better than to test it.

"Fine, then we will get you all to the boarding house at the end of the week, all right? Once you're on your feet and can rent someplace proper, then you'll feel much better."

Eva scoffed. "I'd feel a lot better if you hadn't turned on us like a rabid dog, actually," Eva said coolly before walking away again. Carl sighed heavily, pangs of guilt painful in his chest. He wanted nothing more than to call her back and stop this from happening, but he already knew that it wasn't the right thing to do. He had made up his mind and he had done it for a reason. It was time for them to go.

"Lunch is ready," Maggie called. Carl sighed and ran his hand through his hair before heading to the dining room. He would eat just for Maggie's sake, but he wouldn't stay long. Thankfully, Eva and Charlie didn't appear for several minutes and he ate by himself quickly before disappearing outside where he threw himself into his work, not willing to let himself dwell on the situation for one moment longer.

He had done what had needed to be done and he had done it to protect them. Eva may feel like he was throwing them away, but Carl knew that he was saving them. And that was worth it.

# Chapter Twenty-One

"Charlie, calm down sweetheart. We will go on the swing later."

"I want to *now!*" Charlie exclaimed, his lip quivering in grumpiness. Eva sighed. The end of the week couldn't come fast enough. Everything felt awkward and painful now, and Charlie had picked up on the adult's energy and had been moody and agitated right along with them. She had hinted to him that their time at the ranch might be ending soon but hadn't outright explained the situation to him yet. She just didn't have the heart to do so. Even just the implication had been enough to shake her sensitive boy though, on top of the horrible energy that was in the house now between herself and Carl.

What a fool she had been to trust him! She had been beginning to think that he was special in a way. Far unlike any other man she had ever known. But he wasn't. She had been deceived. Everything she had heard about what a cruel and rigid man Carl was had been true, and she had let herself be duped by her own foolish hopes. And worse than that, she'd let her son fall for it as well, and now he was on a path of heartbreak. It was a good thing she hadn't let him kiss her. She couldn't imagine how much worse things would have been if they had begun any sort of real relationship. The idea that Charlie had of Carl as a pa was a fanciful notion in his head, but if they had any sort of relationship, then it would have been devastating to him because in his mind, it would be confirmed that Carl could be that type of man in his life. She had really avoided a terrible disaster, as disappointing as the whole thing was.

"Swing!" Charlie demanded. Eva sighed.

"All right, all right. I'll do the wash and you can swing if we keep the barn open so I can see you."

Eva wasn't in the mood to argue with her son right now, especially knowing that Carl could be coming out any moment now. The last thing she wanted was to be around him while she was already in a mood, and with Charlie acting up it would just be extra stressful. Neither of them needed that.

"Come on, sweetheart. We're going outside now," Eva said once she had gathered up the washing. "Get your coat on."

"Yay!"

Charlie ran to get his coat and Eva walked with him outside. He ran around her a while until she was done with the washing, building things in the snow that was still lightly peppering the ground. Most of it had melted at that point but it was okay. Charlie still managed to have fun playing in it.

Eva smiled at her son and opened the barn up so he could go play on the swing while she hung the clothes to dry. She could keep an eye on him from there, and he hooted and hollered in joy as he played while she began stringing the clothing up on the line.

"Beg your pardon, ma'am, but you're Eva Hall, ain't ya?"

Eva was startled by a crisp man's voice that sounded eerily like her late husband's. She turned to face a man who resembled him, though he was trimmer and a little bit taller, with slicked back hair and a cocky smile quirked upon his face. She felt her stomach drop, unsettled by the resemblance to Jim. "Yes..."

She didn't quite know what to say and clung to the shirt that she was holding, unable to form anything further than an answer to the man's question.

"Pardon me for the intrusion, but I'm Clarence Glass. Jim's brother. I thought I recognized you from the road, Jim sent the family a few photos over the years."

"Oh! A pleasure to meet you," Eva said with a clumsy curtsy. Clarence bowed slightly in response and then stood straight up again.

"The pleasure is mine, I assure you," he said with a chuckle. "Although I do hate to come calling under such tragic circumstances. My brother's passing has been hard for all of us, I'm sure."

"Yes, it has," Eva said carefully, glancing to the barn where Charlie had stopped swinging to look at the adults.

"This your boy?" Clarence asked, nodding in Charlie's direction. A protective instinct caused Eva to step in Clarence's eyesight to block his view from Charlie, though she couldn't explain why she had done it.

"Yes, my son Charlie. He favors Jim in many ways."

Clarence was taller than Eva so her effort to block his sight didn't have any effect. He simply nodded as he watched Charlie begin swinging again. "Yes, he does. He's a good-looking little boy, isn't he?"

"Yes," Eva said. "So what brings you here, Clarence?" She was eager to get the conversation off of her son.

"I wanted to check in on you two. After Jim passed I got to wondering about you and I just feel so guilty about it all. He was a good man but we never really saw eye to eye, and I never really knew you two because of it. But I also know that he had his troubles and that you two weren't left very well off. Our family was never really there for you, which is a shame, but I would like to make up for that now."

Clarence looked down at Eva with his bright blue eyes and Eva furrowed her brow as she tried to wrap her head around what Clarence meant by what he was saying. Jim's family had certainly been absent, and in fact lived out in Oklahoma. Jim had left home at an early age and managed to get himself to Great Bend, then put himself into school. He had loathed his family that much. He had said they were awful people. She'd heard of Jim's brother coming to town once in a while to visit him but Jim wouldn't let him near his home, they always met out at the saloon and she hadn't even spoken to the man before now.

"I'm sorry, but you're going to have to be clearer. I don't really understand what you're wanting from me right now," Eva said, playing with the shirt in her hands nervously.

"Well, Eva, I want to marry you." Clarence looked at Eva expectantly and she felt her stomach drop.

"You want to what?"

Eva was stunned and wondered if she had heard the man wrong. But he grinned and chuckled. "I said I want to marry you, Eva. I've got a job. I've got a little house all to myself. I would be able to take you and Charlie in and take good care of you. Better care of you than my brother ever did, considering his affliction. We would have plenty of space there, a bedroom for Charlie of all his own... it would leave you wanting for nothing, Eva. It's the least I can do for you and the boy. I would hate to see family stuck out on the streets, working for enough change to make it by just because my brother was a good for nothin'."

Eva took in Clarence's words, feeling a little bit lightheaded. He wanted to offer her security, a place to live for herself and for Charlie. A real home.

She looked past Clarence to the ranch house and felt her stomach tighten in a knot. This was what had begun to feel like home to them, but in just a matter of days that would be changing drastically. She and her son would be living in a boarding house, and she would be working for Carter at the General Goods store. She was perfectly happy to do anything she needed to do to provide for her son, but the thought of simply being able to be a mother, to have a real home for her boy... it was tempting.

"That's a very generous offer, Clarence," Eva said. "Are you sure you mean it though? Charlie's a small boy and he gets underfoot, and you and I don't even know one another. What if we don't get along?"

"Oh, I would see to it that we get along," Clarence said with a dismissive laugh. "Besides, someone as pretty as you ought to be easy to spend time with."

Eva blushed despite herself. She was flattered by the attention, and if she was being honest with herself, Clarence was incredibly handsome himself. He had similar features to Jim, but he was a more dignified sort and seemed to take immense pride in his appearance. It felt a little strange though, to just marry her husband's brother like that. Even though it could be the solution to all of her problems.

"That's a lot to think about," Eva said with a smile. "But if you give me a little bit of time to think it over, I will get back to you with whatever I decide. How does that sound?"

Clarence chuckled. "I think it's a fair answer. I really want to do right by you, Eva. Jim died and left you two homeless. It would be doing me a favor for my conscience if you accept my proposal, you know? I feel just awful about all of this. You both deserve better, and I would like to be the one to give it to you."

Eva nodded. "Well... thank you, Clarence."

"My pleasure, Eva. Now, I will be moving on but please do think about what I said to you. My home is open to the both of you, and I would love to be able to help you raise the boy. He takes after my family, and there's nothing more important than family."

Eva smiled. "I appreciate you saying that, Clarence."

"It's the truth. I would like to honor my brother's memory by marrying you, Eva. It would be as much for me as it is for you, and for Charlie. It's for Jim, too, you see? Here, take this," Clarence said, pulling out an envelope. He handed it to Eva. "Inside is my address so you can write to me if we don't see each other before you make your mind up. I want to be available to you no matter what you decide, all right?"

"All right," Eva said, taking the envelope. She noticed it was thicker than just an envelope with a piece of paper in it and she tucked it into her apron thoughtfully. "Thank you."

"My pleasure. It was really nice to meet you, Eva." Clarence gave her another bow and Eva attempted a less clumsy curtsy this time. "It was nice to meet you too, Clarence. Have a safe trip."

"Always!" Clarence said, turning away and heading back to the road. Eva watched him go, and when he was out of sight she went into the barn with her son.

"Who was that, ma?" Charlie asked, his eyes wide.

"That was your uncle Clarence," Eva said, biting her tongue before revealing anything more.

"I didn't know I had an uncle!" Charlie exclaimed. "He looks like pa."

"You're right," Eva said, feeling a small pang of grief at the mention. "He sure does. And so do you! It's a good family resemblance. You're all very handsome men."

Charlie puffed up with pride and continued swinging, content with the end of the conversation. Eva peeked into the envelope and her brows shot skyward. Inside was Clarence's address scrawled on a fancy piece of stationery, just as he had promised, and a wad of money. It wasn't an outrageous sum by any means, but it would help her out with the things she would need to buy for Charlie once they were living at the boarding house.

"I'm hungry," Charlie complained. Eva nodded.

"All right let's get inside. It's chilly out here anyhow."

"Yeah!" Charlie exclaimed. Eva took her son by the hand and walked him to the door, her head spinning with the strange encounter that she'd just had with the mysterious man from her husband's past.

## Chapter Twenty-Two

Carl had been passing by the window and had happened to see Eva talking to Clarence outside. It filled him with a hot surge of protective anger, and he rushed downstairs to the front door. But by the time he stepped out onto the porch, Clarence was already leaving, which unfortunately meant that he wasn't going to be able to chase the man off himself.

Carl was agitated by the sudden appearance and when he saw Eva and Charlie approaching the porch, he wasn't able to contain himself. Of course he knew who Clarence was and what he had done, but did Eva? What was going on?

"Who was that?" Carl asked, full well knowing exactly who it was. "What was that all about?"

Eva raised a brow at Carl, the woman's way of discreetly telling him to watch himself because her business wasn't any of his, but she gave him a quick smile and answered anyway. It certainly was Carl's business to know who was on his property, and he wouldn't think twice about throwing his weight around to say so if Eva wanted to be snarky about it. Of course she was too sweet for that and answered him, which made a little bit of his agitation melt away.

"That was Clarence Glass, Jim's brother."

"What did he want?" Carl asked. Eva shot him another look, one that Carl read unmistakably as saying it was none of his damn business what he wanted. Still, she pursed her lips and looked down to her little boy. "Charlie, why don't you run along inside and get your coat off for me like a good boy? See if you can find Maggie for some hot cocoa."

"Yes, ma!" Charlie exclaimed, releasing her hand, and running to the door.

Eva waited until her son was out of earshot to turn her piercing eyes upon him. Carl's heart betrayed him and thudded heavily in his chest. It wasn't any fair for a woman to be so pretty.

"Well, he wants me to marry him, actually," Eva said, sounding as if she couldn't even believe it herself.

"He wants to marry you?" Carl repeated, feeling a spike of adrenaline surge through his body. The nerve of that man. Killing Jim and stealing his family? It was downright dirty.

"Yes, and I have half a mind to do it," Eva said, fixing a glare upon Carl. "Seems the rest of the world just sees me and Charlie as rubbish, you know. Fit for tossing. But Clarence has a nice house, and money, and he wants to take care of us."

"You sure he just doesn't want to take advantage of you?" Carl asked. "You're a pretty woman, Eva, and he might not have the good intentions you think he does."

"Oh, like you do?" Eva asked with a snort.

"I never asked to marry you, now did I? You're comparing two entirely different things and I would appreciate it if you stay on topic."

"Well either way it doesn't matter what you think about it because it isn't your choice," Eva stated with the infuriating stubbornness that never seemed to fail to rile him up lately.

"You can't marry him," Carl insisted. "I heard that he's the one who killed Jim. It would be a huge mistake."

"You don't get to make any decisions for me, Carl. It's none of your business what I do or who I marry. And you can't just throw a rumor at me as a reason I should do what you say!

There's no proof of that and this town is full of gossip. You'd be foolish to listen to any of it!"

"Eva, I'm telling you, you can't trust that man! He's no good. I can't let you do this."

Carl was beginning to panic and feel incredibly desperate. The last thing he wanted was to see something bad happen to Eva and Charlie. He had already seen the way Jim had treated her. How much worse might it be with a man who would go as far as to kill his own brother in cold blood? He wouldn't let it happen. He couldn't.

"And just what are you going to do to stop me?" Eva demanded. "Assuming I even decide to marry him in the first place. What you are forgetting here is that it's entirely my choice what I do with my future, and if I want to be able to raise my son in a stable loving home where he isn't going to want for anything, then that's my business!"

"It really isn't a good idea Eva and you know it!" Carl insisted. "You'd be making a huge mistake. Think of your son!"

Eva's temper flared full force and she turned a hard gaze upon him, the fire in her eyes so potent that he felt scorched just looking at her. "My son is all I think about."

With that she pushed past him and entered the house, leaving Carl alone on the porch fuming. Why couldn't she just listen to him? He knew she was angry about everything that had happened between them, she felt like Carl had abandoned them, but that didn't mean he didn't care. Why couldn't she see that?

When Carl went into the house, Eva ignored him just as she did the rest of the night. Carl got sick of being cut off every time he tried to bring the topic up again, he just couldn't rest thinking that she and the boy would be in Clarence's grasp, but she wouldn't listen to a word he said. He retired early for the night, and when he woke up, he dressed quickly, determined to try again.

He emerged from his bedroom with a frown, looking around the house anxiously. Maggie emerged from the kitchen with a grim look on her face and Carl intercepted her. "Have you seen Eva? I need to talk to her."

"She left, Carl. She and Charlie left. Clarence, Jim's brother, got them this morning."

"You let her go with him?" Carl exclaimed, unable to help himself.

"Carl, do you really think I could have stopped her? She's a grown woman and she can make her own choices." Still, Maggie looked distressed and the painful reality suddenly hit him.

Carl's stomach dropped to the floor and he turned away feeling faint. He staggered into the study and sat down heavily on his desk chair, unwilling to believe it but having no choice. They were gone.

# Chapter Twenty-Three

"We could leave now, if you like, Eva. Right to my home. You don't have to do this," Clarence said, slowing his horse and buggy to a stop in front of the boarding house.

"I haven't made up my mind yet about marrying you, Clarence, but I really do appreciate you bringing us into town. I don't think I could stay in that house for another second."

It had been emotionally devastating to Eva to be around Carl that past week, and she was furious with him for planting the seed in her head about Clarence being dangerous. The thought of Clarence killing Jim boiled her blood and made her sick to her stomach, and she wished Carl had just stayed out of it. She could have gone the rest of her life without thinking that Jim had been murdered by his own brother. She had always known how much Jim hated Clarence, but with everything that was on the line now, Carl's words just put even more complications into everything.

"Well, there's time, yet. And you can stay with me now without us being married, though it would certainly appear improper."

"The plans have already been made, Clarence, but I appreciate the offer."

"Of course. Let me help you with your things."

Clarence helped Eva out of the carriage and she and Charlie took what was remaining and followed him inside. Once they were given the key to their room, Clarence set the bags down and looked as if he were about to make himself at home. Eva felt a twinge of unease.

"Charlie is starving. Let's have some breakfast."

"I want breakfast!" Charlie exclaimed. Eva smiled at her son and took him by the hand, heading out of the boarding room with Clarence behind them. She walked him down to the dining room, where a big table was all set and full of freshly cooked food. It was a feast, but Eva was too unsettled to partake in it. Her stomach was in knots and she simply sat down beside her son. Clarence sat across from them and helped himself to some food as Eva fixed Charlie's plate.

"I'd be a good husband, you know," Clarence said. "I don't ask for much. I know Jim was always demanding as a boy, so he was probably that way with you too. But not me. I just expect a few meals and a tidy home. I'm out of doors most of the time anyway so you would hardly ever see me. I'm an important and busy man."

Eva gave Clarence a polite smile, but she felt uneasy with his pushiness. She didn't want to marry him right at that moment, and the idea of it was making her feel sick. Her husband hadn't treated her well, so how could she trust this man to treat her any better? The stable home and promise of security was nice and all, but all she could think about was what Carl had said.

Had this man really killed her husband? His own flesh and blood? She tried to picture what he might look like drunk. When he was sober, Jim had cleaned up nicely, and he could have fooled anyone into believing he had a sweet and docile nature. Behind closed doors, however, he could be extremely cruel.

A blush rose to Eva's cheeks as she remembered the way that Carl's fingertips had brushed against her skin when he had seen her scars. He had been so upset at the thought of Jim hurting her, and he had told her to come to him if any man ever did it again. Did he mean that though? She couldn't trust anything anymore. Not after the way he had just thrown her out like she was a piece of stale bread. She had really thought she could trust him and that she and her son would have somewhere secure to stay through the winter. But winter wasn't over yet and he had tired of them all too quickly. Now, she would be starting all over again as a shopkeeper and living in the boarding house with several other people, most of whom were men who were just going through town. It wasn't the ideal environment to raise a son, but she would get on her feet in time. She simply didn't feel comfortable living in the apartment above the shop, either, because not only did it feel like charity, but it would put a lot of pressure on her at her job. What if she needed to move on and find something else? It all just felt too uncomfortable, and besides that, it stung that Carl had made all of those arrangements for her.

At least this way she would be doing it on her own with her own hard-earned money. She would find a way for her son to thrive, even if that meant marrying Clarence.

"Eva, I just want you to know that you're the most beautiful woman I've seen in a long time," Clarence was saying. She focused back on the conversation and looked at him.

"Thank you," she said quietly. The words didn't feel anywhere quite as flattering now as they had just the day prior before Carl had told her about what he might have done to Jim. She may have been desperate to find a good situation for her son, but there was no way she would marry a murderer.

"You're welcome," Clarence said. "So you're just not ready to settle down yet, huh? Can't say as I blame you. You could have any man in the county."

Eva smiled politely. "I'm not really thinking about that right now," she said. In truth, she had always sort of thought to herself that if she ever got out of her marriage with Jim, she wouldn't want to be with another man. It was risky and vulnerable, and she couldn't stand the idea of trusting someone to take care of her who would hurt her, or her son, the way Jim had. Besides that, she just never imagined there would be someone else who would appeal to her. She hadn't been around many other men during the past five years of her life, and the ones she had known held no appeal to her. Except, of course, for the one who had just thrown her out of his home. And now that she knew what a mistake that had been, she was reluctant to consider any other dating experiences either.

"Fair enough," Clarence said, taking a bite from his plate. He ate a lot, and he ate it quickly, with none of the table manners she had gotten so used to being around at Carl's house. "Lucky for me you're not or you might have gotten snatched up by now."

"I sincerely doubt that," Eva said, feeling a bit uncomfortable Clarence was referring to her as if she were just a steer being set up at auction.

"I don't have a doubt in my mind about it," Clarence said with a laugh before tearing into more food with his teeth. Eva looked away, trying to conceal how unappealing his table manners were to her. She felt like it was important to stay on his good side, especially if he was a dangerous man.

"Well, seeing's how you travel a lot and all, where is your house?" Eva asked, finding she had many questions for Clarence now that they were sitting together.

"It's just outside of Oak Bend, but not far. Stone's throw from town, really. I bought the place back in April and it's nice but it could use a woman's touch. I'm not great at tending to a home, myself."

Eva smiled. "That's understandable. I heard you've been gone from town for quite a while now. What kind of business were you tending to?"

Clarence dropped his fork on his plate. "Uh," he murmured, wiping his mouth with his napkin quickly. "Just... you know. Tending to some things. Family matters."

"Family matters?" Eva asked, noting how suspicious Clarence's behavior was. She felt uneasy and couldn't help but keep pressing him for details.

"Yeah, just some family stuff. It wouldn't interest you." Clarence set to work buttering a roll and Eva felt like he expected her to drop the topic.

"I see," she said quietly, choosing to pick at her own plate. His behavior was alarming but she didn't want to let on that she thought so. What if Carl was right and Clarence had fled town because he had murdered his brother? The fact that he could come to her so boldly and try and get her to marry him was sickening. That is, if the rumors were true, which wasn't proven. But the way he was acting now was really making Eva wonder.

"Right. Well, I best be getting off," Clarence said, standing up quickly after not even touching the roll he had just buttered for himself. "It was a pleasure to see you again. You have my address should you need anything. And I will come calling on you to see how things are going here. Let me know if you need anything."

"Thank you, Clarence," Eva said. She touched Charlie's shoulder. "Say goodbye to your uncle, sweetheart."

"Bye Uncle Clarence!" Charlie said brightly.

"Soon, he might be saying bye to his new pa," Clarence said with a wink that made Eva sick to her stomach. She forced herself to smile at Clarence before he left, then shook her head when she was sure he had gone.

"He's going to be my new pa?" Charlie asked, looking up at Eva in confusion. "I want Carl to be my new pa."

Eva sighed. "I don't think there's going to be any new pa any time soon, honey. Don't pay any mind to what he's saying. We're just talking about what might happen if we got married."

"You should marry Carl, not him," Charlie said. "I want to stay with Carl and go back to the ranch with Maggie. Uncle Clarence smiles funny."

Eva felt a twinge of annoyance at her son's statement. "I'm not going to marry Carl, Charlie, and you should just drop that kind of talk, all right?"

"Yes, ma," Charlie said, pouting down at his plate. Eva sighed and felt a twinge of guilt from making her son feel bad about it.

"Why do you think Uncle Clarence smiles funny?" Eva asked, ruffling Charlie's hair in an effort to soothe him.

"He smiles like something is funny but it doesn't match the rest of his face," Charlie said, pushing his food around on his plate. "He looks funny."

"I see," Eva said, wondering if her son was on to something. Clarence was being insincere. It wouldn't surprise her at all, considering everything else she knew now.

"Do we live here now?" Charlie asked, looking around at the dining room. A couple of men were filing in and sat at the opposite end of the table.

"We do for now," Eva replied. "But soon, your ma is going to find us the best place to live. And I'll make sure you're safe and taken care of no matter what. And when we're nice and settled in and I'm able to pay for everything we need, then we can think about things we want, too. I'll make sure you get a nice, comfortable bed and even some new toys to play with."

"That will be so fun!" Charlie said. "May I be excused, ma?"

"Yes, you may. Let's go upstairs and unpack now. I bet your toy soldiers are excited to get some air."

"Yeah!"

Eva smiled at her son and went with him up to her room. It was smaller than the one they had been sharing at the ranch, but it would do. She was startled when she heard raucous laughter coming from downstairs, and Charlie looked to her with panicked eyes.

"What was that?" he asked.

"It's all right, honey. It's just the other people who live here. It isn't going to be as quiet as it was at the ranch, but it's still nice."

"I don't wanna live here," Charlie whined. "I want to go see Carl and play on my swing!"

Charlie began to cry and Eva scooped him up in her arms.

"I know, darling, but we can't. Ma's going to work something out though, you'll see. Right now, we just need to be brave and strong and trust that God will put us where we need to be, okay?"

Charlie nodded, but it didn't stop his tears. She wanted to console him, to make him stop wanting the things that he couldn't have, but there was nothing she could say that would have that effect on the little boy. All she could do was to hold him and let him cry it all out and try to pretend that she didn't feel exactly the same way.

Still, a part of her realized that she couldn't keep her son in limbo any longer. He needed a home, and they both needed to get over the grief they felt over having to leave the ranch. If Clarence could give them that, then she would be able to do for her son what he needed done the most. He needed a home, and a father, and a family. Somewhere he could grow up and feel secure. And as far as she was concerned, there wasn't any proof that Clarence had done anything wrong by Jim, even if he was a bit overbearing.

Despite her desire to be with Carl and to have a home on the ranch, she knew she would never be able to have that. It broke her heart into a thousand pieces, and if Clarence wanted to pick those pieces up and give Eva and her son a chance to survive in this cruel world, she might as well let him.

## Chapter Twenty-Four

Nothing felt the same without Eva and Charlie in the house. Carl felt miserable and depressed. Maggie was just as miserable at first. She had really taken a liking to Eva and Charlie, and although she was frustrated with Carl, she was doing her best to try and be understanding with him. She was withdrawn at first, but when she saw how upset he was too, she tried making him his favorite foods to try and cheer him up, but they just sat on the table getting cold as they day dragged on. Everything seemed dark and dour without them there, and he knew it was his own fault for pushing them away, but he hadn't expected to take it this hard now that they were gone.

He had merely been trying to protect them, but he had driven them right into the arms of the enemy. How could he ever forgive himself? He needed to fix it. More than anything else in the world he needed to fix it.

"I can't believe she left with him, Maggie," Carl said, sighing to her and pushing his untouched food away. Maggie sat down at the table across from him and shook her head. "Well, if you're worried that she went straight home with him that isn't the case. I heard her bickering with him about it. She was insisting he take her to the boarding house. She needed time to think about his proposal."

"You know he probably killed Jim, don't you?" Carl asked, looking at Maggie with his stomach twisted into knots. "He killed Charlie's dad and now she's thinking about marrying him! It's not right."

"It wasn't proven, and unless it was I don't think she's going to take it all that seriously. The thing is, Eva's a fighter, a mother, but as a mother she needs to have somewhere stable for her little boy. If Clarence can give her that, there's a part of her that would have to be crazy to turn it down. She just needs somewhere to rest her head and raise her son. Somewhere proper, you know. And the sooner the better. So in her mind, I can see why she's doing what she's doing since she didn't feel like she had much choice in the matter. Still, I'm so worried about them. If he really is responsible for what happened to Jim, they can't be safe with a man like that, whether he gives them a home or not."

Carl listened numbly, but it sparked an idea. "If we could prove it, then she wouldn't marry him, right? He would go to jail."

"Well sure, but how do you plan on proving something like that?" Maggie asked. "If the sheriff hasn't managed it yet, what do you think we can do about it? It feels like a lost cause if you ask me, Carl."

"There's got to be a way," Carl said, springing up from his seat and grabbing his jacket. "I'm going into town, Maggie. I'll be back for supper."

"All right, Carl. Be careful!"

Carl didn't have to look at Maggie to see the look of concern she had on her face, but he couldn't help that. He ran to his horse and got him ready for the trip, then rode off to town like a bat out of hell. When he finally arrived, he made a beeline for the sheriff's office, then dismounted and tied Smokey up to the post outside.

"Sheriff White, may I speak with you for a moment?" Carl asked. The sheriff smiled and gave him a friendly nod.

"Sure thing. How's everything, Carl? Ranch business going well?" The sheriff stood to regard Carl and Carl nodded.

"Everything is great at the ranch. I just wanted to talk to you about the murder of one of my employees, Jim Glass. Do you remember him?"

The sheriff adjusted his hat and nodded. "Well sure I do. Poor man was gunned down outside the saloon one night."

"You know, rumor is that his brother Clarence is responsible, Sheriff. Did you know that? The man skipped town right after and only just came back. I think he's worth looking into."

Carl spoke quickly. He just had to do something about Clarence. He wouldn't be able to live with himself if he got with Eva and did something to hurt her. He had already seen the scars that Jim had left on her. The possibility of Clarence doing even worse made him feel sick to his stomach.

"Well, Carl, it certainly is peculiar, but unfortunately that isn't evidence enough of someone murdering his brother," the sheriff said, crossing his arms over his chest and leaning back on his desk.

"So, what evidence is there?" Carl asked. "I want to help with this. If Clarence is a dangerous man, I want to make sure that he's put where he belongs. Let me help."

The sheriff was quiet for several moments before tilting his head. "All right, well, we did get a couple of clues from the scene, but nothing that's strong enough to incriminate Clarence."

"I understand," Carl said, feeling a little bit defeated by the news. But he wasn't going to give up. There had to be a way to prove that Clarence had done it. Carl believed it in his gut and had ever since laying his eyes on the wormy man. He couldn't let Eva go through with it. If she married him, it would be the worst mistake of her life, and he would always blame himself.

"One last thing is that there was a pocket watch missing from Jim's body after the fact. Eva noticed it when we brought her in to take a look at the body."

Carl grimaced. The idea of the poor woman having to come in and witness something so horrifying really shook Carl to the core. The poor thing had gone through enough without having to identify her husband's dead body and try to remember whatever possessions he'd had on him that night. What an awful experience that must have been for her.

"A missing pocket watch?" Carl asked. "That's interesting."

"Yeah. Makes me wonder if it was personal. Eva didn't think that it was worth much of anything, though Jim had planned to give it to Charlie when he was older. That's all she really knew about it, so it seemed like it might be a sentimental thing."

"Something a brother might take, for example," Carl insisted. "A family heirloom, maybe."

"Maybe," the sheriff said with a nod. "But unfortunately, that just isn't enough evidence to bring Clarence in. If we can get our hands on him, we will ask him some questions, of course, but unless he confesses or we can get more evidence in the meantime, there's not too much we can do."

"Right," Carl said with a sigh. "I understand."

The sheriff nodded. "Well, sorry I couldn't be more help to you, Carl. I appreciate you taking an interest in the case. I can tell you really care about the people who work for you."

Carl nodded, his mind wandering to Eva for the thousandth time that day. "I do what I can for them," he said.

"Take care, Sheriff White. Thanks for taking the time to talk with me."

"Absolutely, Carl. I'll see you around."

Carl left the sheriff's office and walked directly to the boarding house. He didn't even bother to get Smokey; he was too riled up about everything that he had learned and he wanted to talk to Eva.

When he entered, he confronted a gaunt, elderly man. "Who may I ask are you calling for?" he asked him.

"Eva -"

"The new one," he said with a nod. "I'll get her for you. If you would be so kind as to wait here for me."

"Certainly."

Carl didn't like having to wait when he was so anxious to see Eva, but he was willing to do whatever he needed to. After what felt like a century had passed, Eva came down the stairs. He looked beside her, eager to see Charlie's face but disappointed to find that Charlie wasn't with her. He had really been looking forward to seeing him, he realized, and felt crushed that he wasn't coming. He could have used one of the boy's bright smiles or the way he exclaimed "Carl!" whenever he saw him.

"Eva, hi. How are you doing?" he asked, stepping toward her, repressing the urge to pull her into a hug.

Eva flinched back. "I'm fine, Carl. What are you doing here?"

Carl wasn't used to the coldness that was radiating from Eva and he felt uneasy in her presence, but he wasn't going to relent. "I just... wanted to see how you're doing. You left without saying goodbye. I was worried that..."

"Well you don't have to worry about us anymore, Carl. We're not your problem. And I've decided that I'm going to marry Clarence. I can't keep Charlie in the boardinghouse like this, he's terrified and a big fight just broke out a while ago. I've also been groped already by one man and it just isn't any place to raise a boy."

Carl felt his blood boil from the thought of anyone mistreating Eva and he started to reach out to her. "Eva, I'm sorry, I -"

"Don't worry about it, Carl. We're not your problem anymore. Clarence is coming to get us. I was just packing my things back up. We're not your responsibility anymore."

"Eva, please just listen," Carl said, finally allowing his instincts to take over and taking her hand. "The pocket watch that was missing from Jim's body, it wasn't worth anything. The sheriff thinks it's sentimental. Which means who else would take it but his kin if it were a family heirloom? Clarence has that watch, Eva, and if he does then it means that he's the one who killed your husband, or he knows the person who did. Either way I really believe he's responsible for it, you have to trust me. If he is responsible for this in any way, that means you won't be safe with him. Please listen."

Eva gazed at Carl; her eyes conflicted for a moment before she gently pulled her hand away from his.

"Goodbye, Carl."

"Eva -" Carl felt the air being pulled from his lungs as Eva turned away from him and headed back upstairs to her room. He cursed under his breath and then walked outside, wishing that he could meet Clarence right there and then and pummel him out of existence. But then Carl would go to jail and Eva would lose whatever hope of a home that she had. No, he had to try and be reasonable about this, as much as it killed him.

He walked slowly across town to where he had left Smokey tied up to his post and then mounted his horse, his mind full of the afternoon's events. How could he have let this happen? He had pushed Eva and Charlie out into an uncertain future, and the vulture had snatched them up right when they were the most vulnerable.

Carl ushered Smokey forward and he rode back toward the ranch, his chest so tight he was worried he might drop dead before he even made it back to the ranch. He supposed he might deserve it if he did. He had treated Eva and her son terribly, and now the consequences were greater than he could have ever foreseen. He wanted to protect them from himself, not hand them over to a cold- blooded killer. But he had done just that.

"Any luck?" Maggie asked when Carl trudged through the door.

He hadn't told her what he had planned to do, but simply shook his head. It was too difficult for him to talk about, so he simply slumped down at the table. Maggie brought him a hot tea and sat down with him.

"It's quiet here without them, isn't it?" she murmured. "I keep thinking I'm going to see Charlie rounding that corner asking for chocolate."

Carl offered her a pained smile. "It's quiet without them, yeah," he said. "But it won't stay quiet. I'm going to find a way to get them back here and fix my mistake. She can't marry Clarence, and she will see him for exactly what he is before anything bad happens. I'll make sure of it."

"I sure hope so, Carl," Maggie said, taking Carl's hand in hers and squeezing it gently. She stood from the table and retreated into the kitchen, and Carl realized that without Eva and Charlie there, they were both lost.

# Chapter Twenty-Five

For the rest of the evening, Eva couldn't get Carl out of her mind. She hated that he had come to her, hated that he had touched her again and sent another warm thrill through her body. She hated even more the fact that he was trying to protect her from Clarence, to keep her from him, when he hadn't been brave enough to keep her for himself.

Why couldn't she get that man out of her mind? She couldn't be with him, so no thoughts were wasted about him. What was worse, even though she didn't particularly want to marry Clarence, she didn't really know or trust him, it was sounding more and more like her only option, and a part of her wanted to marry him simply out of spite and hurt feelings over what Carl had done to her.

But it was far more than her anger at Carl that was driving her closer toward deciding to marry Clarence. Eva knew that she couldn't stay at the boarding house any longer than she absolutely had to. Which meant that marrying Clarence was the best choice she had right now. Sure, Carter had his little apartment above the shop, but it didn't feel right to take advantage of that kindness. She wouldn't be able to pay him for what it was worth, and besides that, it would be bad for business having a growing boy running around upstairs and having his tantrums, and staying there might cause the gossip mill to run wild. She wouldn't repay a kindness by becoming a burden on anyone else. She didn't want to be a burden to anyone ever again, especially after everything that had happened with Carl.

"Is Uncle Clarence coming?" Charlie asked, tugging on Eva's skirts. "I'm hungry."

"Yes, darling, he should be here any minute," Eva said. "How would you feel about maybe living at his house with me?"

Charlie was quiet for a few moments, and she knew that he was trying not to protest as he had earlier and say that what he really wanted was to go back to the ranch so they could be with Carl. Instead, he just offered her a little smile. "Sure, ma."

"All right, sweetheart. I will be going to talk to Uncle Clarence and if it goes well, we might go live at his house with him soon, okay?" Eva asked, just to make sure that her son was on the same page as she was. She didn't want him to go into hysterics because of something he didn't expect to happen happening.

"Okay, ma. You said I could have toys and a bed at his house."

"That's right."

"Okay."

Eva felt conflicting feelings from Charlie's easy acceptance of the news. She was happy that he was more comfortable with the idea now than he had been at first, but she had her own conflicts now. Was she really making the right choice for her son? Just as importantly, was she making the best choice for herself? The boarding house was a horrible environment for them to be living in. There were all sorts of ruffians and vagabonds running about the place, which made her feel unsafe. And they were loud. And crude. Clarence could offer her a way out or all of this, a way that had nothing to do with Carl. Security for her son was the most important thing, and she needed to feel like she didn't owe anyone anything. For once, someone felt like they owed her, even if it was Clarence, Jim's suspicious brother.

A gentle knock came at the door and Eva peeked out, relieved to find that it was Mr. Thornwhistle, the owner of the boarding house. He was a kindly, elderly man, but he let in all sorts and didn't seem to think twice about it. He couldn't afford not to, as he lost much of his fortune after the war had ended. All for a day's pay, she figured. "Evening Miss Hall. A Mr. Clarence Glass is here to see you. Said he was to join you for supper."

"Thank you, Mr. Thornwhistle. We will be right down." Eva smiled at the man, who nodded and closed the door behind her. Eva sucked in a long, deep breath before taking Charlie's hand. "Come on now, sweetheart. Let's talk with your uncle, all right?"

"You're going to tell him you want to marry him?" Charlie asked, looking up at Eva. Eva sighed, remembering what Carl had said to her about the pocket watch. She hadn't thought twice about it being missing when Jim died, of course, as she had been so distraught by the circumstances and barely remembered a thing about it, but now that it had been brought back to her attention again, she couldn't help but feel uneasy.

"I need you to be a good boy and not talk about any of us getting married, all right? Can you do that for me?"

"Sure, ma," Charlie said, an unmistakable note of relief in his voice. She had a feeling that he really didn't want her to marry Clarence, but he also wanted to be a good boy and support his ma, and to have a home and a bed and toys. She wasn't sure what the best option was, considering the circumstances, but she was going to figure it out. She had to. The pressure was on in more ways than one.

"Good boy. Come on now, let's not keep your uncle waiting any longer."

She walked Charlie downstairs to the dining room, where Clarence was seated at the table with a plate full of food already. He paused in his eating to smile at them, then stood and offered a bow to her. "Evening, my lady," he said, his mouth stuffed full of food. Eva tried not to show her disappointment before returning the greeting and sitting down at the table with her son.

"A pleasure to see you again, Clarence. How do you find your day so far?" Eva felt strange to speak to Clarence and was worried her words came out just as forced and rigid as she was feeling. Fortunately, he didn't seem to notice or care and simply smiled in response.

"I'm well, thank you! How are you and the boy?"

"Charlie and I are fine, thank you," Eva said, serving her son his supper before getting her own plate ready. She was feeling hungry after hardly touching her breakfast and practically running from the place during lunch, when the fight had broken out and she had been violated by one of the men there. Of course she had told the owner what had happened, and he promised to have a word with the man, but the man had already left town, so no justice was to be done for her honor. It didn't really matter, though. As much as she hated to admit it, she felt safer eating there with Clarence to protect her and her son.

"Well, good to hear. I've been getting things set up around the house today, you know, in case you choose to join me there. This doesn't seem the best space for a pretty young woman to be living," Clarence said, looking around at the other men distastefully as they filtered into the room and began to serve themselves supper. Eva shifted in her seat, wondering if she should just tell him now, outright, that she was ready to accept his proposal.

Still, there was something nagging at her and keeping her from doing so. It would be an easy solution to all of the problems she was having right now, but would it really be the best choice for herself and for Charlie? Especially if Carl was right?

They continued eating for a while, until finally Clarence stretched. "I'll be back in a moment," he said, nodding toward the bathroom. Eva smiled at him, her eyes drifting to where Clarence had draped his jacket over the dining room chair he was sitting in. If Carl was right and the pocket watch had been missing, that meant that whoever had it now was responsible for murdering Jim. He had been so proud of that pocket watch. It was the only family heirloom he had to his name and it would only be meaningful to someone in Jim's family. If Clarence had it, then Carl was right and Clarence was the one who murdered her husband.

She hesitated for a moment, realizing that she could search in Clarence's pockets and find out for sure one way or another if he was the one who had the pocket watch. If he did, there was no way she could marry him. If he didn't, then she wouldn't let any more rumors get in her head and keep her from doing what was best for herself and for her son. Charlie deserved the best, and she wasn't going to put him in danger any longer than she had to.

After a brief moment of debate, Eva stood and went to Clarence's seat. She glanced at Charlie, who was watching her curiously, before beginning to rummage quickly through Clarence's pockets. She didn't find anything in the two outside pockets, but when she went into the inside breast pocket, she felt the unmistakable metal. She pulled out the pocket watch and studied it for several moments, many memories flooding her mind. This was Jim's, certainly, and it had been in his family. And Clarence had taken it right off of his brother's dead body and kept it for himself.

The realization made her sick. There was no way she would ever be able to marry this man, and the fact that she had even considered it made her want to throw up. She dropped the watch back into his pocket and then returned to her seat, white as a sheet and shaken from head to toe.

"Are you okay, mama?" Charlie asked, putting his little hand on Eva's. She took a deep breath, realizing that the way she conducted herself right now might be the most important thing she could do, especially around Clarence, who was bound to return from the bathroom at any moment.

"Yes, sweetheart, I'm fine," Eva said, patting Charlie's hand with her free one.

"Why did you look in Uncle Clarence's coat, ma?" Charlie asked with a small frown.

"I had to know something, but can we keep that a secret between us, please?"

Eva's mind was whirling and she wasn't even sure how she was managing a conversation at the moment, but she was. Charlie nodded.

"It's a secret," he said with a reassuring little smile, and he patted her hand again. Eva took his little hand and squeezed it gently, proud to have such an understanding little boy.

"Thank you, darling."

Charlie offered her a sweet smile and then suddenly Clarence reappeared. Eva, still shaken, managed a smile to him.

"Welcome back," she said, pushing a dish toward him. "Would you like some more potatoes?"

"Don't mind if I do," Clarence said with a grin. A grin that certainly didn't reach his eyes or match the rest of his face as Charlie had pointed out. A grin that made her realize that she was sitting across the table from a stone-cold murderer.

# Chapter Twenty-Six

Carl pushed the rest of his breakfast away. He hadn't been able to eat since Eva and Charlie had left. In fact, he would say he was rather depressed about the whole thing. The house felt empty, but it didn't compare to the gaping emptiness that he felt inside himself. There had been something growing in there with the little boy's sweet smiles, and Eva's gentle nature. He was allowing it to grow and it had scared him. It had scared him so much that he had pushed them as far away as he could get them.

And now Eva was going to marry Clarence. A dangerous man who Carl was certain had murdered his brother. How could he have been so stupid? It seemed like no matter which way he moved he couldn't be happy, but he would have rather had Eva and Charlie home with him any day. He was haunted by his regrets and day by day, since they had left a couple of days ago, he felt worse and worse.

"Carl, you really need to start eating. I'm getting worried about you."

Carl noticed Maggie suddenly enter the room. She took his plate, but instead of going to the kitchen with it, she sat down at the table beside him. "You're really down lately, aren't you?"

"I really am," Carl said. "I feel just awful. I don't want Eva to marry Clarence. I can't stand the thought of it. I was so stupid…"

Maggie patted his hand, her brow knit in concern. "Dear, there's nothing to be done about it now, so don't fret so much. You thought you were doing the right thing, I'm sure… although I have to wonder what made you push them away the way you did. It seemed like things were going along just fine. Even better than fine, really."

Carl sighed, feeling the knot that had been in his stomach since Eva and Charlie left tighten painfully. He hated talking about all of this, but it was all he could think about so the words spilled from him freely. "I was scared, Maggie. It felt like they were prying open a piece of me that I didn't know very well. A part of me that wanted to love, and be loved back, but it didn't seem like I even knew how to do that. I was worried I would just hurt them both, the way my father had hurt me, or the way Jim had hurt Eva."

Maggie listened to him speak quietly, nodding her head when he finished. "So you thought it was for everyone's best interest if you got them away from you, is that it? Because you're so unlovable and worthless?"

Carl sighed, aware of how painful the words were even though Maggie didn't actually mean them and he knew she didn't. But it was just how he felt. "I suppose so."

"And that's because of what your father had been telling you, isn't it?" Maggie raised her brows at him expectantly as he digested her words.

"Well, yes. I guess that's part of it," Carl admitted. His father hadn't exactly adorned him with affection over the years. In fact, it had been quite the opposite, and he didn't know what it meant to be a good man.

"Since when did you listen to what your father said about you, Carl? Haven't I always tried to tell you that you're a better man than he was? He treated you awful, you know, you never deserved that and you don't deserve to alienate yourself from the things that make you happy, either. He may have ruined your childhood, but he doesn't have to ruin anything else. You're a man now. You have the power."

Maggie's words made Carl lift his eyes from the table in surprise. He had never really thought about it like that before. "Thanks, Maggie..." He paused in thought and then sighed. "The scariest part was how Charlie looked at me, you know? How he was just so full of love and acceptance. He didn't even seem to question whether I was a good man or not. He just believed that I was and he treated me that way. Eva at least gave me an earful if I messed up, but I think Charlie would have loved me no matter what and never questioned a thing. It's scary, you know. I don't want to do anything to damage something that... that pure."

"I'm sure you won't, Carl. In fact, you would only make it that much better. Charlie had a rough time with his own pa, and he looked at you like a hero. That's because you're a good man, and he had never seen a true, good man so consistently before. Now, don't get me wrong, children grow up. The day will come when they see your flaws and realize that you're human, believe me, but it isn't going to be a shock to him to see you as human because you're a good man. Anyone would be lucky to be part of your life."

Maggie smiled at Carl, who felt like the world's biggest fool all over again.

"If I was such a good man, then why did I kick them off the ranch? They were both happy here. I can't believe I did this. They'll never forgive me now." Carl ran his hands through his dark curly hair and shook his head. "I'd be lucky if they even speak to me."

"Give it some time, Carl. And one day you can talk to them yourself. Tell them what you were really feeling and apologize properly for it all. You'd be surprised how far you can get just by being honest with people. Emotions are powerful and sometimes even deadly, but they can mend and grow with time, and they ebb and flow like the tides. If you don't think you want to be without them, just be honest."

Maggie's words comforted Carl, and he nodded his head in thought. "You really think they could forgive me?"

"If they understand what you're saying, yes. If they can see what a good man you are deep down. And if they don't have hearts capable of forgiveness, is it really even worth anything at that point anyway? There's no sense in being all worked up over someone spiteful, now is there?"

Carl chuckled and shrugged. "I don't really know, Maggie. All I know is that I miss them a lot and I feel like a fool."

"Well, just because you did a foolish thing it doesn't make you a fool. I'd rather know you are being kind to yourself and forgiving yourself for your mistakes instead of holding on to them and hating yourself the way your father liked to see you do. You're better than that, Carl. And you deserve so much more than that." Maggie smiled gently at him and stood up. "Besides, you just wanted to protect them because you thought they would be safer on their own. You couldn't have known that Clarence wanted to marry Eva. If you had, things would have been different. And they still can be. She isn't married yet."

"Well, no, not yet..."

"Carl... let me tell you something. In this life, we accept the love that we think we deserve. You're lovable, and the sooner you accept that, the sooner you can have the happiness you deserve. I truly believe you could be happy with Eva and Charlie. You all have a special bond, and even though things got in the way, you can still have it. Nothing is impossible. All you have to do is believe you're worthy enough of something that special. And reach out to them honestly with everything you're feeling. Things will fall in place just as they're meant to."

Maggie winked at Carl and he smiled at her, feeling as if a big weight had been lifted from his shoulders. He usually kept all of his feelings to himself, but Maggie just had a way of making him feel safe. Plus, she gave the world's best advice.

Was it really true? Could he have the happiness he wanted with Eva and Charlie? He had been too afraid to believe what they were feeling about him. They could see him as a strong man, a man they loved, and there had been a part of him that truly wanted to see them both as his family. He had just been too afraid to admit it. He didn't want to mess anything up.

He had made a huge mistake. He didn't need to change anything about himself to stop being the kind of monster he felt like he was inside. What he had to do was stop believing that he was some kind of monster who didn't deserve their love in the first place.

The other thing he had to do was to stop lying to himself about something else that was really important. He was in love with Eva. Deeply, truly, passionately in love. And he had been terrified of that. The last thing he ever wanted to do was to hurt her, but there he was, going off and hurting her in the worst way possible. Driving her right into the arms of a murderer.

Well, he couldn't stand it. He was going to do everything in his power to get them back. He would grovel. He would apologize. He would get Clarence convicted of murder if he had to. Hell, he would even stand up in the church before God and object to their union and tell the entire world what he felt and why she should be with him instead. He would give it every effort he possibly could to be with Eva, and unless she told him outright that she had never returned his feelings, he wouldn't rest until she knew just how sorry he was and how much he wanted her to come back to the ranch.

Because there was something that he simply couldn't deny. He had loved her from the moment he had seen her stealing the food from his cellar. He had loved her deeply and truly with the first smiles they had exchanged. She had been on his mind from the moment they had spoken like a beautiful melody, and it was a melody he wanted nothing more than to hum along to his whole life if she would have him.

He wanted her back, and he was going to make sure that she knew it. Carl wasn't going to let anything stop him again. He loved her, and he had a feeling that she loved him right back. The way she looked at him had told him the whole story more than once, and he wanted to be Charlie's pa. Everything could work out between them. He knew it could. If only he could just convince Eva to believe that he meant what he said.

"Maggie?"

Maggie appeared soon after he called for her, and he offered her a sheepish smile. "I think I'm ready for some food now. Is it still out?"

Maggie beamed and went into the kitchen, exclaiming "Stay put and don't even think about getting it for yourself. I'm afraid the wind will blow you away. It's about time!"

After several minutes, she reappeared with a full plate of food and sat it down in front of him. Carl's stomach growled loudly and Maggie chuckled at him.

"You'd best eat that up right now before your stomach tries to escape so it can do it itself," she said with a laugh. Carl laughed too.

"Will do, Maggie. Thank you."

# Chapter Twenty-Seven

Once Clarence finished his supper, he wiped his face with a napkin and looked steadily at Eva. "Well, Eva, have you thought any more about my proposal?"

Charlie looked to his mother expectantly. He was prepared for her to say yes, for his mother to marry Uncle Clarence so he could have a bed and toys of his own, but she also knew that deep down, Charlie didn't want to live with Uncle Clarence. He would simply do whatever his mother told him was best, because that was the type of trust her son had in her.

"I'm just going to have to get back to you about this in the morning," Eva said with an uncomfortable look. "I'm afraid it has been quite a busy day and I haven't had enough time to think straight. Once I've slept on it I will let you know, all right?"

The truth was that there was no way she was ever going to marry Clarence now. He had murdered his own brother and was now trying to get his hands on his wife and child. There was something chilling about the way he smiled at her now, as if he were simply biding his time before getting what he wanted. There was a hint of impatience in his voice when he laughed this time, and once again she noticed how eerily accurate Charlie's observation was. His laughter didn't reach the rest of his face. He was a phony and a fraud and a killer, and she couldn't wait to get him out of her sight.

"That's perfectly fine, my dear. There's all the time in the world to decide. I will always have a room ready for little Charlie, and a loving home for his ma, if she decides to take it." Clarence stood and slipped his jacket on, and Eva found her focus on the breast pocket of the jacket where she knew her husband's watch was. If only she knew what to do. "I'll come back in the morning then. After a good night's rest, you'll be ready to be my wife!" He laughed and headed off, without even bothering with a formal goodbye this time. Eva watched him go and then took Charlie upstairs with her. She began to pack their things as calmly as she could manage while still going as quickly as possible.

"What are you doing, ma?" Charlie asked in confusion. "You're not going to marry Uncle Clarence?"

"No, sweetheart. And I don't want him to come back here and find us again. We're getting out of here tonight."

"Where are we going?" Charlie asked. "Back to Carl?"

Eva felt queasy at the mention of Carl. As much as she would have loved the security of the ranch house right now, things between herself and Carl were far too messy and strange. There was no way she would go crawling back to him. He had come to warn her about Clarence, sure, but he hadn't apologized for making them leave or even asked them to come back. That spoke volumes enough to Eva, and she felt like she had made a huge mistake in trusting him, even if he did care enough about her to try and protect her from Jim's brother.

"We're not going back to the ranch," Eva said firmly. "We have to go somewhere else. Maybe where we were before the ranch. Just for now."

Charlie frowned. "But it's cold there, ma!"

"I know, sweetheart, but it's only for now so that Uncle Clarence won't come find us, all right? I don't want you going anywhere with him, do you understand? It's important."

Charlie nodded, though he was clearly on the verge of crying. She sighed and gave his hair a gentle caress before packing the rest of their things hurriedly.

When she was finished, she didn't even tell anyone she was leaving. She just took Charlie in her arms along with her suitcases and began walking briskly down the road.

She knew the way to the hunting lodge by heart, fortunately, and managed to make it there before it was too dark. If nothing else, their situation would be less dire now. She had managed to save up some money from working for Carl, and they would be able to afford food, eventually. She considered taking the job and apartment with Carter, but now that Clarence was in the picture, she didn't want him knowing where she worked or lived with her son. She didn't trust him at all, and her instinct to protect Charlie was strongly driving her at that moment.

Her son and his safety would always be Eva's number one priority. When they arrived at the cabin, Charlie was tired and sniffling, but he resigned himself to the little bed in the corner that Eva made up for him. He fell asleep quickly, which she found merciful, but Eva couldn't relax herself and found herself pacing about the cabin the whole night through.

After several hours, a knock came at the door. Eva felt her heart race, and she cursed when she realized that she didn't have her rifle ready. In fact, she had left it in the closet at Carl's house. She had felt so secure with him that she had almost forgotten just how dangerous it could be out on her own as a single mother. How stupid could she have been?

But she couldn't ignore it. If Clarence had found them there, she would have had to confront him. She could lie her way out of it. Tell him she had decided to marry him but the people at the boarding house were just too noisy for her little boy to get a sound sleep.

She made her way to the door with her heart seized up in panic, but when she opened it, she blinked in confusion. "Carl?"

Carl was standing on the porch with his hands shoved deep into the pockets of his trousers. He looked awkward and concerned, and he took a step forward as soon as he saw Eva open the door. "Eva. Can we please talk?"

Eva nodded, dumbfounded, and stepped aside to let him into the cabin. "Yes, but Charlie is sleeping so let's try to keep quiet so as not to alarm him."

"Of course," Carl said, fixing a fond, tender gaze on her son. He was smiling sadly to himself and almost looked like he wanted to go over to the boy, but he stayed planted where he was.

"What are you doing here, Carl?" Eva asked quietly.

"Jeff saw you and Charlie pass by with all your things and told me about it. I had a guess where you had gone. Eva, did something else happen at the boarding house? Did Clarence hurt you? Did he hurt Charlie?"

Eva felt her throat tighten and she tried to will away the tears that had sprung into her eyes. "He didn't hurt me, or Charlie. But I couldn't get what you told me out of my head so I looked in his pockets and I found the watch in there, Carl. He did it." She lowered her voice to a whisper in case Charlie could overhear her. "He killed Jim."

Carl closed his eyes and let out a big, heavy sigh. When he opened them again, they fixed upon her with such an intensity that it made her heart pound hard in her chest. "Eva, I have something to say to you, and I hope you will listen."

Eva felt her hands trembling and she nodded, not trusting her own voice in that moment.

"I never should have done what I did. I regretted even thinking about not letting you stay at the ranch the second you left. And I only did it because I was afraid of just how much I wanted you there. I wanted us to be able to stay that way, Eva. For a long time. I liked the idea of Charlie being my boy, and you being my woman. I wanted it so much that it tore me up inside because I didn't think I could ever deserve something quite that beautiful, you know?"

Eva's mouth fell open in surprise. "You wanted us that way?" She shook her head in astonishment. He was saying everything she had hoped he might feel, and that he might say. It was too good to be true, so she voiced her small voice of doubt. "Carl, it seemed like you wanted us nowhere near you. I thought you were angry with us."

"I was never angry with you, Eva. I was angry with myself for being a man who wasn't worth the kind of love you two had shown me. I was angry with my father, with the world. All of the things I was feeling had nothing to do with you individually and everything to do with me. I couldn't stand the thought of you throwing your future away on a man like me, a man who I didn't think could deserve the love you could so clearly give to me. But I know better now, Eva. I know that was a mistake."

Eva put her shaking hands to her temples as she tried to process Carl's words. "I don't think I quite understand what you're saying, Carl. I just didn't expect this…"

Her hands were suddenly in his and she was looking into the depths of his eyes, lost in them in a way she never wanted to be found from. "I love you, Eva. I've loved you this whole time. I didn't know how to show it, didn't even know if I could feel or deserve it, but I know better now, and I'm so sorry for everything that I've put you through. I'm terrified to lose you and I want you and Charlie to come home with me. I want you to live back at the ranch. But not as my housekeeper. I want you in my life just because you are who you are, and I love you. And Charlie too. I love you both. I want us to be a family."

Eva could hardly believe what she was hearing. It was too good to be true. Every single thought that she had about Carl, he had been having about her. She just didn't know it. "I love you, too, Carl," Eva said, her tears finally falling. Carl smiled gently at her and wiped them away with his strong hands on either side of her face, before cupping her chin in his hands and tilting her head up to press a tender kiss against her lips. Eva closed her eyes and wrapped her arms around his broad shoulders, wishing for this feeling to stay with her for as long as she lived.

The kiss seemed to last a lifetime and they held each other close, letting their bodies speak the words that their hearts were singing so sweetly. Everything she had ever wanted was in this little cabin, and she couldn't have been more elated and at peace.

When they broke from the kiss, Carl took Eva by the hand, then glanced over to where Charlie still lay sleeping. "I'd like to take you both home to the ranch tonight if that's all right. I miss you. Maggie misses you. And I want us to pick up right where we left off. You mean the world to me, Eva. I can't stand the thought of losing you."

"You're not going to lose me, Carl. You mean the world to me, too," Eva whispered. She smiled at him; her heart completely full of the joyous feeling that his confession invoked within her. She touched his cheek and then nodded. "We will come home to the ranch with you, tonight. But please be careful. Clarence is a dangerous man and having us there with you could cause problems. Think about that before you take us in, again. For your own safety."

Carl shook his head, a fire in his dark eyes. "I'm not going to let that man touch a hair on your head. Or Charlie's. And I can protect you better at home. So then. Let's go home."

Eva smiled, overcome once more with emotion. "All right. Let's go home."

# Chapter Twenty-Eight

Charlie was sound asleep in bed, so Eva suggested they wait until morning to take the trip back to the ranch. Carl was okay with this. If Clarence came looking for Eva, he wouldn't be likely to come to this little hunting lodge. Even if he did, Carl would be there and he would be ready for him.

Once Charlie was awake the next morning, his sleepy little eyes widened into giant orbs of excitement. "Carl!" he cried, jumping off the bed and into the man's open arms. Carl's heart filled with joy and warmth and he hugged the little boy close to his body, surprised by just how much he had missed these little affectionate gestures.

"Charlie! I missed you so much!" he exclaimed, lifting the child off the ground, and holding him. Charlie leaned back so he could look Carl in the eye. "I missed you too! I don't like Uncle Clarence; I like you and I want ma to marry you and not him and I told her so but she said she's not going to -"

Eva put a hand on her son's shoulder to silence him, and Carl caught her eye with a teasing grin. "Oh, did she now?" he asked, noting the lovely flush that was making its way across Eva's face. Charlie nodded enthusiastically.

"I like living at the ranch. Can we go back to the ranch with you, Carl? I miss my swing and Maggie. And I miss you lots and lots and lots!"

"I would love it if you two would come home to the ranch with me, Charlie. If it's still okay with your ma, that is?"

Charlie whipped around in Carl's arms to face his mother, who was chuckling at her son's excitement. It was pretty cute, Carl had to admit. "Can we, ma?"

Eva nodded. "Mr. Spencer has invited us back and I think that we should go and stay with him."

Eva left out the part about Carl saying he wanted to be a family, and he felt a pang of guilt. Of course she would want to keep that to herself until she was entirely sure he meant it rather than getting the little boy's hopes up, but Carl was going to make sure she knew that he meant it every day for the rest of their lives.

"Yay!" Charlie cheered wildly in Carl's arms and he chuckled, finally setting the little boy down.

"All right, you two. What do you think? Are you ready to head to the ranch with me now? I need to get Smokey to the barn where he can relax and have some breakfast and water. And I think the two of you could use a nice hot meal too."

"Maggie!" Charlie cheered again. Eva and Carl laughed and Carl helped to gather the few belongings that Eva had managed to bring with her to the lodge. He packed everything up on Smokey, then helped Eva and her son onto the horse's back. They rode back to his house with Carl leading the horse by the rope, not trusting them to go on their own.

Carl was upset to find Clarence waiting on the porch when they arrived. He brought Eva and Charlie to the barn and put Smokey away, then headed to the porch.

"You two get on inside now," Carl said. "I'll keep you safe."

"What's the meaning of this?" Clarence demanded once they were within earshot of each other. He marched from the porch and headed to Eva before she had the chance to escape. "You're meant to be at the boarding house, Eva. Waiting to tell me that you're going to be my wife!"

Clarence made a lunge for Eva and grabbed her by the arm. He made a move as if to drag her off with him and Carl acted quickly, punching Clarence hard in the face. The impact startled the man and he released Eva, who grabbed Charlie and cowered behind Carl.

"She's not going anywhere with you, Clarence. We know about the pocket watch. We know that you killed Jim in cold blood and we're going to tell the sheriff everything! You just wait, you weasel, you're in big trouble!"

Carl made a move to grab Clarence by the shoulders but the man evaded him and took off running. Carl started to go after him but Eva shouted for him to stop. He did, and turned to face her, his adrenaline pumping through his body. "He's getting away, Eva," he complained.

"Yes, and you're going to let him. I'm not going to let that man kill two of my men, do you understand me?" Eva stated. "Let's just go inside and calm down. Then we can go and speak with the sheriff about everything that has happened today."

"Yes, ma'am," Carl said sulkily, eliciting a tolerant grin from Eva. He let himself smile fully at her and she carried Charlie inside. Carl put his arm around her waist to steady her. She was shaking like a leaf. The man terrified her something fierce, and Carl had half a mind to go after him even if she wanted to scold him about it. But he would respect her wishes and try to do things the smart way, even though it made him feel very impatient.

"Eva, Charlie! Carl, thank goodness you're all home!"

"Maggie!" Charlie exclaimed. Charlie wiggled from his ma's grip and took off running to launch himself into Maggie's arms much as he had done with Carl that morning. Eva leaned against Charlie with a soft smile as they watched the scene. The two reunited and shared several smiles before Maggie finally sat the little boy down.

"I bet you could all use some breakfast," she said.

"Yes please!" Charlie exclaimed. "I'm hungry."

"You're a growing boy, of course you're hungry. Let me get something on right away."

Carl and Maggie exchanged a secret look of happiness before she disappeared into the kitchen, and Carl, Eva and Charlie sat down at the table together to wait.

"I can't believe he was waiting here for us," Eva said, shaking her head.

"Did Uncle Clarence really kill daddy?" Charlie asked, turning his eyes to his mother. Eva let out a heavy sigh. It was clear that she had been trying to shelter her son from all of this, but at this point it was too late.

"Yes, sweetheart. I'm afraid he did. And we have to talk with the sheriff after we eat to tell him the whole thing."

"Okay," Charlie said. "He should go to jail!"

"That's right, honey, he should go to jail. We're going to do whatever we can to make sure that happens."

Charlie nodded, not seeming as disturbed by the situation as Carl might have expected him to be. Then again, he was a young boy and didn't fully grasp the complicated emotional nature of the whole thing. He probably missed his pa, but it was likely different for children that young.

"Here you are. Eggs and bacon just how you like them," Maggie said in a sing-song voice, placing a plate in front of Charlie first, then Eva. She went back and got Carl's plate too and they all began to eat quickly.

When they were finished, Carl, Eva, and Charlie got washed up and changed, then he set up his buggy and retrieved Eva and Charlie. It was odd to finally use it for himself. Usually he just took Smokey out with him, but now he had a whole little family he could cart around. He was suddenly grateful that he had it. "We're going to go have a talk with the sheriff now," he said. "Let's get a move on. We don't want Clarence getting too far ahead, now."

Eva nodded in agreement and lifted Charlie to her hip. They got settled in the buggy and Carl drove them toward the sheriff's office.

"Good morning, Sheriff White. I'm afraid I have some big news to talk about," Carl said with a bow of his head.

"Morning, Carl. What's this all about?" the sheriff asked, leaning back on his desk, and watching the group curiously.

"It's to do with what I came in about before, the other day," Carl said. "Eva's husband Jim was killed and we know for sure that Clarence is responsible. Eva found the watch that was missing from Jim's body in his coat."

The sheriff arched a brow and turned to Eva. "Is this true?"

Eva nodded. "Yes. He has been trying to get me to marry him since he got back in town. He found me back at the ranch this morning and tried to man-handle me. Carl stopped him, and told him what we know, then he ran away."

The sheriff was quiet for several long moments before taking his hat off and wiping his brow. "So if we apprehend this Clarence fellow, we're going to find Jim's missing watch?"

Eva nodded. "Yes, it was in his breast pocket, on the inside. It was a family heirloom, and he must have taken it off Jim's body after he killed him. He would be the only person to even know that it's there. I don't think it's worth much outside of the family."

The sheriff nodded. "I remember you saying that when we questioned you after he was killed. I'm sorry to hear he was treating you so poorly. We're going to start an organized search for this man, and don't you worry. Justice is going to be served for you and your late husband."

Eva smiled at the sheriff. "Thank you so much."

"And what about you, little one? Do you like peppermint sticks?" the sheriff asked, looking to Charlie. Charlie gasped and nodded enthusiastically.

"I like them!" he exclaimed.

"Well then it is mighty important that you take this one off my hands. Seems my wife packed me a big lunch this morning and I reckon this is just going to be too much for me to eat along with it. What do you say?"

The sheriff retrieved a peppermint stick and offered it to Charlie, who grabbed it quickly with a bright "Thank you!"

They left the sheriff's office and headed back to the ranch, Charlie pleasantly preoccupied with his treat and Eva staring outside, lost in thought. Carl was thoughtful himself, and when he dropped them all off at home, he put the horse and buggy away and tended to the animals, as his morning ritual had been disrupted by all the excitement.

Finally, he went back into the house. "Eva? Charlie?"

He frowned. It was too quiet inside. He looked in the living room, then the dining room, and when he didn't see them in the bedroom either, he figured they must have been in the kitchen with Maggie. He pushed the door open to check. "Hey Maggie, have you seen-"

Carl froze, his heart dropping to the floor.

In the kitchen, Clarence was standing against the counter with an arm wrapped around Eva's waist. His free hand was pressing a gun against her neck, and her wide, golden eyes were screaming at Carl silently for help.

Maggie and Charlie were nowhere to be seen, and he worried that something may have already happened to them. Carl stood completely still as he took in the scene. He had just gotten his family back home to the ranch after every horrible thing that had transpired. Now was he going to have them taken away again, but permanently?

# Chapter Twenty-Eight

"Clarence, what are you doing?" Carl asked, his voice even.

Eva was frozen in fear. The feeling of the gun barrel pressed against her throat was terrifying. Was she going to die? Was this really going to be the way her life ended? She couldn't stand the thought of it leaving her son all alone in the world as an orphan. Was there something she could do to get out of this? There had to be a way.

The one thing she was grateful for was the fact that Charlie was upstairs sleeping. Maggie had offered to take him up for his nap and Eva had been doing the dishes to thank her for it. She didn't like someone else always having to clean up after herself and her son, and Charlie had missed Maggie fiercely, so she was happy to let them bond for the moment. Now, she felt like God had had a hand in the way this had played out, knowing that Maggie and Charlie were safe from Clarence. At least for now.

"I'm here to take what's mine, rancher," Clarence said, pressing the gun tighter against Eva's neck. She shuddered in fear and it took everything she had not to get sick right there and then. But she needed to maintain her composure. Any wrong move and she could find herself dead.

"You do realize that the lady here isn't property to be bought and sold, Clarence. She can make up her own mind on things and she doesn't want to marry a murderer. Would you blame her for that?" Carl was speaking calmly, trying to reason with Clarence. But it was no use, Eva could already tell there was no reasoning with him. His breath stank of alcohol, and there was the small matter of the gun he was wielding that could very well mean the end of her life. She was terrified and caught Carl's eye from across the room. He sucked in a sharp breath, clearly trying to stay composed despite how concerned he clearly was.

"The 'lady' is raising my nephew, who ought to be raised by his own kin. She knows as well as anyone how important family bonds are."

It took everything Eva had not to make a comment about Clarence being a hypocrite. He had shot and killed his own brother but she chose not to speak on it because it could easily have caused him to shoot her. Still, she fumed at the gall of this man, coming here with a gun, and preaching to her about the values of family bonds. He knew nothing about family and never would. She would rather die than let him take Charlie.

"No one's doubting that kin is important," Carl said. "In fact, I agree with you there. That's why I think you ought to let Eva go and put that gun away. She ain't going anywhere, right? You all can work this out as a family without bringing any violence into this, now can't you?"

Clarence's grip slackened against Eva's neck for a moment, and she felt a strong surge of hope that he might be listening to Carl and she would be freed. But after a pause the gun pressed against her neck again and she felt crushed by the anxiety and discouragement. She was verging on panic. She wanted to watch her son grow up and raise him into the fine young man she knew he could be. And she had so desperately wanted to walk through life side by side with Carl and enjoy a real family. None of that was going to happen if Clarence killed her.

"This isn't some kind of game," Clarence slurred, leaning forward to regard Carl intently. "Jim took something from me and I want it back."

"Clarence, I can give you whatever you want. I'll give you money if you just let her go. You can get on a train and have enough to go off and start a new life somewhere. We won't tell anyone where you went. You'll be a free man."

Of course, this was all a lie to try and get him to unhand Eva, but Clarence didn't need to know that.

Clarence shook his head. "No. Eva was my first and Jim always took what I wanted. It's always been like that! Always. Ever since we were kids he's done this to me and I'm glad he's dead! And the only thing left now is to make Eva mine."

Eva furrowed her brow. She had been Clarence's first? First what? Crush? Love? Was this man even capable of love? And if that were true, she certainly hadn't noticed him. Jim had come to live in Oak Bend and she had met Clarence when they were younger, but he had been awkward and shy and hadn't made a big impression upon her. If he had been coveting her all this time, no wonder he and Jim hadn't gotten along very well. But Jim had never told her anything about it. She'd just assumed he had been keeping Clarence away from his home because he hated his brother and thought he was just going to cause trouble or steal from him if he visited their home.

"Think about this now, Clarence. There's no reason to hurt her when you can have whatever you want. I can give you money if you want to get out of here. Hell, I could even help you get set up with a ranch of your own, eventually, if that's what you would want. Just send a letter once you need to get settled and I'll even throw in some livestock for you," Carl said, stepping carefully forward. "There isn't any use in hurting Eva, you know. You won't be teaching Jim anything. He's already dead."

"You think I don't know that?" Clarence said with a sneer near Eva's cheek. It made her shudder in disgust and she saw Carl tense, keeping himself from moving forward. The way his fists were clenched, Eva could tell he wanted more than anything to intervene and to keep this man away from her, but he was forced to stay still because of the gun. She could see how worried he was, how angry, but he was helpless to do anything. He wouldn't risk hurting her, and she could see the pain and love written all over his face.

The thought of losing the family she had just reunited was agonizing. All Eva could do was pray that Charlie would stay asleep, and Maggie wouldn't come back to the kitchen and find herself in danger too. But what would happen if she were killed? Would Clarence stop there or would he search the house for Charlie? Would he murder everyone he could find? Where was the line with this man?

"My brother was a screwed-up man," Clarence slurred. "He didn't know how to treat no woman, and he didn't know how to treat his kin either. What made him so special that he got to have a pretty wife and a son to bear his name? It ain't fair and nothing is going to stop me until Eva is mine!"

Eva flinched as Clarence swayed on his feet, staggeringly drunk. If his finger pressed against the trigger with just enough pressure, she would be a goner. Her eyes widened frantically as Clarence corrected his posture and repositioned the gun against her throat.

"I don't see what good it is to have a gun to her throat if all you want to do is be with her," Carl said calmly. "A dead woman isn't going to do you any good now, is she?"

Clarence scoffed. "I'm not going to shoot her you ninny," he said. "But you'd have to be crazy to think she might come along with me willingly. She knows I killed Jim. So the gun is just for a little added persuasion."

"I've got to wonder, what good is it going to do you to just up and kidnap a woman who doesn't love you. How would that ever make you happy?" Carl asked, crossing his arms over his chest and eyeing Clarence coolly. "You didn't earn her. She should be able to decide where she goes and with whom."

Clarence grew rigid and the gun tightened against Eva's skin. "Oh, and I suppose you know all about earning a woman, eh boss? That's why you live on this ranch all alone with no kin and no wife."

Carl glared at Clarence but said nothing.

"Wait a minute. I know what this is," Clarence said, his eyes widening. "This ain't just a job. You two are having some kind of sick affair. It's been going on since before Jim died. Hell, y'all were counting down the days 'til you could get rid of him!" Clarence whooped out a laugh, but when he looked at Carl again there was no mirth in his eyes. Only rage.

"You don't know what you're talking about, Clarence," Carl said, shaking his head. "Eva and the boy needed a place to stay and some work. I felt like I owed it to them because I had to fire Jim and it made them lose their house."

Clarence was quiet as he studied Carl, then shook his head. "Naw. You can't fool me, boss. This one here? You're sweet on her, ain't ya?" Clarence put his arm around Eva's shoulders and gave her a little squeeze that made her stomach lurch. "You think you're going to be the big hero who gets her off the streets so she'll marry you and live on the ranch with her little built-in family!"

Eva looked to Carl, curious how he would approach this. Of course he would never admit to his feelings for her while Clarence had a gun to her throat, but she could tell the man had struck a nerve in Carl and he was doing his best to maintain his temper.

"Clarence, nobody's part of any conspiracy to keep Eva for themselves. Like I already said before, she isn't property and you don't have to think of her that way. In fact, you'd get on with her much better if you did."

But there was no consoling Clarence now. He was drunk and irrational and angry and Eva gasped when she felt the cool barrel of the gun detach from her skin. Clarence was holding the gun up now and aiming it at Carl.

"You ain't got no right to tell me how to conduct myself, rancher. This ain't your concern and you're just trying to keep me from doing what needs to be done because you wanna keep Eva for yourself, just like Jim did!"

"Clarence, now, you need to just calm down," Carl said, raising his hands up in front of his chest. "There's no reason to act rash. We can get you whatever it is you want."

"You're a liar," Clarence exclaimed. "And whether you like it or not, Eva is mine!"

Eva shrieked when the deafening gunshot went off in her ear. Pure and blinding panic welled up inside of her and she couldn't even think. Clarence had shot Carl. He'd shot him. Just like he'd shot Jim, and just like he would shoot her. The man was ruthless and evil and oh god, was Carl okay?

Eva forced herself to calm herself down enough to look, even though she was terrified of what she might see. Finally, she gulped in a deep breath of air and felt tears begin to pool in her eyes and stream down her face.

"Carl!" she wailed when she was finally able to clear her blurred vision enough to view the sight before her. "No! Are you all right? Talk to me, Carl, please!"

This couldn't be. Clarence couldn't have just taken Carl out of her life just like that. It was too cruel, too twisted. How on earth was she ever going to survive this without him? She couldn't lose him. "Carl!" she cried again.

Carl didn't answer her. He was slumped on the ground with a pool of blood forming around his body. Eva was still in Clarence's clutches and Clarence was pulling her away so she couldn't look at Carl any longer. She couldn't tell whether he was dead or alive, or where he had been shot. All she knew was that Clarence had shot him, and now she was likely in the biggest trouble of her life.

# Chapter Twenty-Nine

Carl collapsed to the ground, hot, searing pain shooting through his arm. The bullet had hit him in the shoulder, and he could feel the warm blood as it began to pool beneath his hand. He felt overwhelmingly dizzy for a moment and his eyes fluttered closed. Carl tried to fight to keep himself focused, to stay steady, but he just wasn't able to do it. He lost his grip on consciousness for a moment and felt himself grow limp, his vision completely fading as he found himself unable to press forward any longer.

He was disoriented as hell when he came to, and for a moment he felt a spike of fear, worrying that he had been out for an exceptionally long time. He moved his head and forced his eyes open. Once he stirred he realized that it couldn't have been much later from the point where he had been shot to the point where he had just woken up.

He winced, groaning up at the ceiling as he tried to put pressure on the wound. He had never seen so much of his own blood in his life, and he felt like he was swimming in a sea of red. It made him dizzy and he had to look away and try to remember what he had to do next. Although he felt like he might pass back out, he forced himself to suck in a deep breath and try to focus. The next thing to do would be to sit up. He could do that.

Carl managed to sit his head up just in time to see Clarence whisking Eva around and dragging her toward the back door. He felt an icy spike of panic surge through his chest. That bastard had Eva, and who knew what was going to happen to her if someone didn't stop him. He stared at the back door as the screen door bounced from being carelessly slammed shut. Why was there even a door right there for Clarence to use? Of course it would have been his father's idea. It was located in the kitchen so they could access the cellar with more ease, which of course was very practical. But Carl was angry at his father for the door now and realized that it was how Clarence had gotten inside in the first place. He wasn't just angry with his father though, he was angry with himself, too. He cursed himself for not thinning to secure the place before they came inside.

He sat up with tremendous effort. The shock and pain of the gunshot had caused his body to grow stiff, and it still felt like his head was swimming from everything that was happening, but Carl managed to maintain his consciousness. As disoriented as he might be, he wasn't going to let Clarence get away with this. There was no way he was going to run off with Eva.

Carl grunted in pain as he got to his feet, steadying himself against the counter with his bloodied hands. His palm slipped once from the blood but he kept his grip and managed to get himself back to his feet. He took a deep breath to settle his nerves and his stomach and push the pain away as he staggered outside.

He was doing his best not to let the tremendous pain of the wound in his shoulder slow him down. Nothing was more important than getting to Eva and stopping Clarence. Carl was determined to look after Eva, and once he got his mind around exactly what had happened, the anger of knowing that Clarence had her in his grasp was overriding any of the pain he felt in his shoulder. He had to save her. She was his to protect, and he was going to do everything in his power to do just that.

The bleeding didn't slow down, and Carl did his best to speed up his gait once he made it out the door. He caught sight of Clarence and Eva several paces ahead of him. He tried to break into a run, but it was clumsy and loud and

Clarence heard him. He whipped around with his gun aimed right at Carl.

"Carl, no!" Eva shouted. Eva's voice was exactly what Carl needed to dodge out of the way of the second bullet that Clarence had aimed at him. He felt the air of it whiz past his cheek as the gunshot echoed in the air around them.

"Let her go, you stupid son of a..." Carl forced himself to stop speaking. He needed to stay calm, no matter how furious he was. Instead, he glowered at Clarence as he continued forward, and Clarence laughed unkindly at Carl.

"The ranch man is as stubborn as a damned ox," Clarence muttered. Instead of shooting again, he grabbed Eva by the back of the neck and dragged her along with him as he forced his way through the yard. Carl kept after them, trying to speed up but having to force himself to slow down before the dizziness overtook him. His head was pounding and he felt a little bit like he was going to throw up. He could feel himself growing more lightheaded the more blood he lost. He hadn't done anything to treat his wound but he couldn't let Clarence get away, even if it killed him. He would die knowing that he was trying to protect the woman he loved, and there was nothing he would rather die doing than that.

"Let... her... go," Carl grunted as he staggered after them. But Clarence didn't even seem to hear him. He disappeared with Eva and Carl shuffled for it as quickly as he could.

"Carl! You're in rough shape!"

Carl was shocked to see the sheriff riding in on his white steed like some kind of bona fide hero. He felt a rush of relief knowing he had another able-bodied man there to help him to save Eva. He realized that the man must have been searching the property but once he had spotted Carl, he'd steered the horse toward him.

"Sheriff White," Carl gasped, surprised to see the man standing there in front of him. "Thank God you're here."

The sheriff surveyed the scene, a troubled expression on his face.

"I came out here looking for Clarence and heard gunshots," the Sheriff said, frowning. "Looks like he got to you before I got to him. Which way did he go? We have to act fast."

Suddenly, another gunshot fired off. The sheriff's reflexes were like magic. This time the gun wasn't aimed at Carl, and instead the bullet whizzed past them both, narrowly missing Sheriff White. The sheriff must have seen Clarence from the corner of his eye just in time, because he pulled his horse back to avoid the gunshot. "That son of a bitch!" the sheriff exclaimed, urging his horse forward, and glanced at Carl from over his shoulder. "Keep pressure on that wound, Carl," he shouted, riding furiously after Clarence. "I'll get him."

Carl watched helplessly as the pursuit began, feeling frustrated to be stuck on foot, but extremely grateful that the sheriff was there just when they needed him the most. Carl minded the sheriff's words but forced himself to keep moving forward. It didn't matter how many bullet holes found their way in him; Carl wasn't just going to sit idly by while Clarence tried to have his way with Eva. He followed the chase with his eyes as he struggled forward and saw that Clarence was pushing Eva ahead of himself and toward the barn. The sight made him furious, and despite how badly he was bleeding, Carl felt himself pushing on. Sure, he followed the sheriff's advice, but he didn't let it stop him from trying to keep up with them.

"She's mine!" Clarence was shouting. Carl watched with terror in his breast as he shoved Eva forward. She couldn't keep her balance from the force of his shove and she fell to the ground in a heap.

"Ouch!" Eva exclaimed.

"Get up you damned fool of a woman! Come on!" Clarence screamed at Eva.

"Clarence, please…" Eva begged, but Clarence wasn't having it.

He let out a sigh of annoyance before dragging her back to her feet and shoving her forward. A gunshot sounded and for a moment Carl was certain that Eva had been killed for inconveniencing the vile man. His stomach dropped, and he bit back the bile that was rising in his throat. When the wild panic passed, however, he quickly realized that the sheriff was on his horse with his gun drawn, trying to get a shot at Clarence before he did any more damage. He was having a tough time and didn't fire until he had Clarence isolated in his view. Carl jumped at the noise; his eyes focused on Eva. He worried she could be hurt but he trusted the sheriff to have true aim. Eva was alive and Clarence was still handling her in the most disgusting way.

Unfortunately, the shot didn't hit him and instead struck the barn, blasting through it and leaving a bullet hole in the side. For some reason, Carl's first thought was Charlie. But no, Charlie was inside, hopefully still sleeping upstairs undisturbed by the commotion. He wasn't in the barn where he might be injured by a stray bullet, though the gunfire was bound to wake the poor child up. Thank God that Maggie was there with him, keeping him calm and contained during this whole fiasco. Though he was certainly going to notice the bullet hole in the barn next time he came out to play.

The important thing was that Charlie was safe and would remain safe so long as Clarence was stopped before any further damage could be done.

Carl fixed his attention on Eva who, thankfully, was back on her feet again. The fury of seeing the way Clarence was treating the woman he loved made Carl move a little faster, though admittedly he was in bad shape. But it was just his shoulder that was wounded, not his legs, and he forced himself to continue forward. He would do anything for Eva and he fully intended to. He was so furious with his body for not cooperating better, for not being as fast as a horse and as fierce as a wolf. If he were, none of this would be happening because he would have torn Clarence to shreds by now, whether his shoulder was injured or not.

Another gunshot made Carl jump, but once again the sheriff had missed.

"Stop shooting or I'll kill her!" Clarence shouted.

Clarence was dragging Eva behind himself now, using her as a shield, and Carl could hear Sheriff White shouting, "Let the woman go, Clarence!" as he began closing the gap between them on the horse. He slowed and dismounted just as Carl's foot caught on the big roots of one of the old trees. He lunged forward and caught himself with his one good arm, wincing as a sharp pain shot up his wrist. But he didn't let it stop him and he picked himself up with tremendous effort. Once he was on his feet, he kept forward as Sheriff White ran after Clarence and Eva on foot because he was now getting close enough to try and apprehend them. Carl lost sight of them for a moment because of the hay bales, but he had a feeling he knew where they were going.

As if to confirm, he saw Eva being pushed into the barn. The sheriff was close behind, and Carl picked up speed, summoning every last ounce of strength he had. Clarence wasn't going to get away with this, and if the sheriff didn't take care of him before Carl got there, Carl would see to it that the man could never touched Eva again.

# Chapter Thirty

Eva was terrified. The last thing she ever expected was a shootout right in front of the house where her son was sleeping. As soon as Clarence shoved her into the barn, he closed it and latched it from the inside before the sheriff could come in.

"He ain't gonna shoot blind if he's any sort of a man," Clarence said with a sneer. "Once we get out of this mess, we're getting on the road, you an' me, and we're finally going to have the life Jim stole from us. Unless you give me trouble. If you give me trouble you'll be as dead as he is."

Beads of sweat were pooled on his forehead and his eyes were wild. It was frankly terrifying to Eva but she couldn't let on just how scary it all was to her, she needed to be calm and rational if she were going to get out of this, and she needed to try and get Clarence to be calm and rational too.

If he was anything like his brother, the alcohol would make him unpredictable and emotional. If she could get him to feel any kind of sadness or remorse, he would start getting maudlin like Jim had, but she didn't know enough about him to figure out what might get him feeling maudlin. Was a killer like Clarence even capable of being sentimental? She prayed he was, it might be her only shot to get herself out of this.

"Sounds like you know what a good man ought to do," Eva said carefully. "Seems to me people misunderstand you a lot. But I think it would be safer for us both if you just tried to make a getaway now. I'd just slow you down."

Clarence shot a look at her and opened his mouth as if to reply, but he was interrupted by a banging on the outside of the barn door. "Clarence! Come on out here and surrender the woman!"

The sheriff's interruption brought the mania back into Clarence's eyes and he began to pace the barn, shaking his head. "No way! She's mine! My brother may have gotten every other good thing in life but he doesn't get to keep Eva too!"

"Clarence, Jim isn't even alive anymore, remember? He doesn't have me, and frankly he treated me poorly enough that he didn't really have me anymore anyway."

Clarence scowled and shook his head. "That don't mean anything. He had a wife, he had a family, a house, and he looked down on the rest of us. Treated you like you were some kid of a prize to him, something that made him better than the rest of us. But he was always the same rotten man he always was. Nobody can change that, not even marrying a woman like you."

Clarence scowled at the barn as another knock came at it. "Clarence, this is the only chance I'm going to give you to be reasonable. You've already fired at an officer of the law, I ought to hang you for that. But if you just come out and let Eva go, we can be reasonable about all of this," Sheriff White said.

"Horse shit!" Clarence shouted. "You're not going to work with me. You're not going to give me a damned thing. Do you think I'm stupid?"

His pacing grew even more frantic and Eva looked around the barn, hoping she might find some way to get out of there without Clarence noticing. He was distracted, and making a move like that was incredibly risky. She didn't want to upset him, the way he was waving his gun around and acting like a mad man, but her efforts to calm him down were backfiring horribly. Especially with the sheriff outside demanding that he surrender himself.

"He's right, Clarence," Eva said softly. "If you just let this whole thing go, I won't testify against you in court. You and I both know how horrible Jim was, and maybe if things had happened differently, I would have ended up with you and I would have been happier. We both would be. But things happened the way they happened and now we just have to deal with that. We can pick up the pieces and move forward."

Clarence shook his head. "You think they're just going to let me ride off into the sunset after murdering my own brother, Eva? You really are stupider than I thought you would be, aren't you?"

Eva winced as Clarence spoke. It was like having the ghost of her dead husband speaking through this man. They both had the same deep-set eyes, eyes that grew dark and menacing when they felt they had been crossed. Was it possible that Jim may have crossed a line like this one day with her? Was this temperament something inherited?

No, she wouldn't even let herself entertain the thought. Charlie was a sweet, tender-hearted little boy, and if she could just make it through this long enough to be his mother for the rest of his life, she would steer him right. He wouldn't even have to worry about ending up like Jim or Clarence, and if she had any say in it he wouldn't be touching alcohol either. Not if it could make an otherwise sweet man act like this.

"All right, Clarence, you've left me no choice. If you don't come out right now, I'm getting reinforcements. The whole place will be surrounded and you're going to be taken directly to jail. This is your chance to do the right thing. Think hard about the next choices you make."

"Go to hell!" Clarence exclaimed with such vehemence that it made Eva jump.

"Think on it, Clarence. This is your last chance to do the right thing."

The sheriff went quiet suddenly and Eva frowned as Clarence began pacing manically around the barn. After a few minutes, Eva gasped. She saw the sheriff's hands slowly creeping up on the window. He was going to climb through and try to save her, but if Clarence saw him, it would mean certain death for the man. She had to distract Clarence.

"You know... they can say what they want about you, Clarence, but the truth is, I'm glad you killed Jim. You feel like a hero to me, honestly."

The words felt heavy in her mouth but she knew she had to say them. Clarence looked at Eva in surprise.

"You mean that?" he asked, furrowing his brow skeptically.

"I do mean that," Eva said. Clarence began to pace again and Eva stepped forward quickly in a panic. If he turned around he would see Sheriff White at the window and she couldn't allow it. It felt slimy to be lying and manipulative but under the circumstances she had no choice. "He was a terrible husband to me, and a mean drunk. He was even cruel to our son, a poor, innocent boy. I hated him."

Clarence paused and faced Eva; his brow creased. "Nobody seemed to realize just how vile he was," Clarence spat. "He never did no good for no one. Not since we were boys. He's always just been a leech and a coward."

Eva nodded. "It certainly takes a cowardly man to hurt a woman. I didn't know that you were trying to protect me from Jim until recently, though. You'll have to forgive me for not seeing the truth even when it was right in front of my face."

Clarence was quiet for a moment, then squinted at Eva. "This some kind of a trick or something?" His eyes grew hard and he waved the gun in her direction. "You're gonna pay if it's a damned trick. I don't take those sorts of games well, you know."

"No!" Eva said quickly, trying to think of a way to convince him she was being sincere. "It's not a trick. Look at my back if you don't believe me."

"Your back?" Clarence asked, confused.

Eva glanced to the window. The sheriff was halfway through, so she turned around and showed an area where her dress had been torn during the rough handling he had given her after she had fallen. It was torn enough to reveal some of the horrendous scars that Jim had left on her body. Clarence took an unsteady step forward and leaned in to look closely at her skin. It made her skin crawl, and she could smell the strong alcohol wafting from his mouth as he breathed through it heavily. Her stomach churned and she realized she should keep speaking. If she could keep him distracted then maybe the sheriff would come in before Clarence spotted him and she would be saved. She would have to choose her words carefully though.

"Jim did this to me. There are more, of course, but it would be improper to show you since, well, we haven't been wed yet and all." She grimaced as she said the words, grateful that Clarence couldn't see her face. He was still gazing at her back, and she would let him until the Sheriff was inside safely. "This is the kind of man he was and I mean it when I tell you that I'm glad he's dead."

Of course she wasn't glad he was dead, but there was a little bit of truth in what she was saying. If Jim hadn't been killed, she would never know what it was like to be with a man like Carl. A man who wanted to take care of her and protect her, who would risk life and limb to keep anything like this from happening to her again. Her stomach sank when she thought of the way he had been shot. She didn't know if he were dead or alive at this point, and she was eager for the Sheriff to come and rid her of this horrible man so that she could check on him and know what had happened. But she couldn't let herself get lost in the what ifs right now. Not when her life was at stake. Whether Carl was okay or not, she still had to take care of her son.

"I'm mighty glad I killed him too. I'd have never done that to you. Jim knew I fancied you before he ever got with you, you know. He saw me looking at you and that's when he started paying attention. It ain't right what he done to us and he got what he had coming to him."

Eva's hands were trembling against the fabric of her dress, and she nodded slowly. "It wasn't right. You did me a big favor, Clarence. You gave me my life back, you know. I'm free of him now."

Eva glanced subtly over her shoulder and looked to the window. She saw that the sheriff was making his way through. It wouldn't be long now, as long as she could keep Clarence occupied.

Clarence grunted and Eva winced when she felt his touch on the exposed skin of her shoulder. She tried not to flinch away, but it startled her badly. Clarence didn't even notice though, and he leaned in closer to her. "We can be together now, proper, you know."

Eva recoiled inwardly at the thought but again, forced herself to nod. "Yes, you've made quite sure of that, haven't you?" Eva kept her voice light, though there was a passive aggressive undertone to the statement that she was hoping he wouldn't notice.

"You shouldn't have run away from me you know? Otherwise none of this would even be happening right now.

That stupid sheriff has it in for me, but he's going to get what's coming to him too, just like Jim did." Clarence stroked Eva's shoulder and she sucked in a deep breath.

"You're a powerful man," she said, her voice quavering despite her tremendous effort to stay composed. "And I'm sorry for running away. I was scared and I didn't know what to believe. I didn't understand why you did what you did. I'm glad you told me."

"Yeah, well I did it all to have you and to teach that no good brother of mine a lesson about taking what ain't his. I saw you first, you know. I saw you and said how pretty you were when we was in town together, but Jim went and stole you before I even had a chance, the bastard."

"Yeah…" Why Clarence had held onto this vendetta so long, Eva couldn't say, but she was getting the feeling that he wasn't all there. It made him even scarier and more unpredictable, and she closed her eyes in a silent prayer for her safety.

The probing fingers on her skin made Eva want to cry, but she held it together just in time to finally hear Clarence exclaim, "What the hell?"

His hands dropped from her shoulders and Eva whipped around just in time to see the Sheriff's face as he tackled Clarence to the ground.

"Get off me you no good son of a bitch!" Clarence yelped, struggling against the sheriff's strength. The man had Clarence pinned on the ground with a knee on the arm that was holding the gun, and he wrestled it away from Clarence and tossed it aside, within reach of Eva. She ran to it and picked it up, surprised with how heavy it was for a small firearm. She'd only ever held and fired the rifle.

"You made a lot of mistakes today, Clarence," the sheriff said, unrelentingly grappling with Clarence. "And you're going to pay for every single one of them."

"Like hell!"

But the drunk man was already disarmed, and although he was tall and wily, he was no match for Sheriff White. He finally got Clarence onto his stomach and forced his hands behind his back, then pulled the handcuffs from his belt and secured them around his wrists. "You're under arrest for the murder of your brother, Jim, and several other idiotic things that came to pass today."

Sheriff White stood up and forced Clarence onto his feet. Clarence scowled at them both and the sheriff pushed him forward. "We're locking you up for good."

Eva hurried to the barn doors to unlatch them so the sheriff could escort Clarence out. Now that he had been apprehended, all she could think about was finding Carl. Once the sheriff was leading Clarence away, she ran out and found him leaning against the side of the barn where the sheriff had climbed through the window.

"It worked," he said, his voice labored. "I wasn't sure it would but it did. Thank God you're all right, Eva."

Carl bowed his head, his face pale and full of sweat. Eva ran to him and threw her arms around him, covering his face with kisses. "I'm all right, darling," she murmured. "Are you all right?"

Carl nodded. "I am now that I know you're safe, Eva. I told the sheriff to try the window but I was so scared it might get you both killed. I helped him through but I couldn't be much use otherwise, you know."

"You were perfect," Eva murmured, holding Carl close. "I love you so much. I'm so glad you're all right."

Carl nodded, pressing a quick kiss to Eva's lips. "I love you, Eva. More than... anything..."

Eva frowned as she felt his weight grow heavier against her. "Carl?"

But he didn't answer. His grip slipped from around her and she watched helplessly as he began to crumple in on himself. He collapsed to the ground and Eva cried out in a panic, doing her best to brace his fall with her body so he wouldn't hit the ground too hard, but it was a losing fight. She was a small woman, and he was a large, heavy man. Her body crumpled against his like paper and they both ended up on the ground together. "No! Carl!"

Her mind raced with thoughts but the sudden realization crashed upon her. Carl wasn't all right at all. A single word kept racing through her mind. Dead. Was he dead? He couldn't be dead. She had just found him. They were going to be a family. He was everything that she had ever wanted in a man, the promise of a fresh start and a beautiful new life for all of them. So much love unexplored, left without nurturing. Even though Clarence was gone now and had been brought to justice, he might have cost her everything. She couldn't picture her life without Carl.

"Sheriff, help!" she screamed, cupping Carl's face in her hands and pressing her forehead against his, tears of grief and turmoil cascading down her cheeks. "Help him!"

The world went by her in a daze before she felt a pair of strong arms lifting her up off the ground where she had collapsed against Carl's body, and Jeff's face was before her.

"Eva, you gotta be strong now," he gently said. "Come on, now. Think of your boy. That's a girl."

Eva followed Jeff's advice numbly and managed to support her own weight, but she didn't even feel like a real person anymore. All she could do was watch, an observer in her own life during one of the most critical moments she had ever experienced, wringing her hands and sobbing. She had never felt so helpless as she stood there uselessly, watching the Jeff and the sheriff's deputy carrying Carl's limp body away from her.

## Chapter Thirty-One

Carl stirred and opened his eyes, looking around himself in confusion. There was a small stream of light hitting him from his window. He tried to sit up and hissed in pain. He glanced down to his shoulder and memories of everything that had happened came rushing over him.

"Carl! You're awake!"

Eva's voice felt angelic and he turned his head to find her standing in the doorway. She rushed over to him and threw her arms around him as gently as she could despite her enthusiasm. "I was so worried I was going to lose you."

Carl's body forgot what pain was when her soft lips pressed against his. He relaxed in her embrace, allowing himself to kiss her back. He lifted his good arm and draped it around her slight waist in a firm hug as they kissed one another. When they broke apart, Eva's eyes were filled with tears and she touched his cheek gently. He offered her a smile that he felt throughout his whole being. "You're never going to lose me, Eva. I love you and whether Clarence likes it or not, I'm here to stay. How's Charlie?"

"I'm sure he's fine, Carl."

Eva smiled and stroked his hair, and Carl thought that it might be the best thing he had ever felt in his life. The woman's hands were like magic. Hell, everything about her was like magic to him. He had never been so enamored with a woman in his whole life, and all he wanted was to make her happy. Being around her was the best thing he had ever felt.

"Well, I'm really happy to hear that, Carl. I don't know what I would do without you. I was lost when I thought that you might..." Eva trailed off, her beautiful golden eyes troubled with the thought. Carl put his hand against her cheek.

"No, I'm here for you and I don't ever plan for that to change. I'm yours for as long as you want me."

Eva's eyes pooled with tears, but she was smiling at him with such adoration that he felt himself lost in her gaze, never wanting to be found again.

"Ma?"

Carl grinned at the tentative little voice. He had been so worried about Charlie when Clarence was there, but it brought him so much joy to hear the little boy there with them now.

"Hey there, sweetheart. How was your nap?" Eva said, turning from Carl to smile to her son.

"I couldn't sleep, ma. Is Carl better yet?" Charlie asked, stepping shyly into the room. When Carl turned to look at Charlie, the little boy's face lit up with the biggest smile he had ever seen on the child's face. "Carl!"

Charlie ran to the bed and paused. It looked like he wanted to jump right into the bed with Carl but instead he gave him the most gentle, precious hug on the side that wasn't wounded. Carl hugged him back, a deep tenderness filling him. He genuinely loved the little boy, and the little boy genuinely loved him, too. He was emotional for a moment but cleared his throat so that he could speak, knowing that the boy would be reassured if he could sound more like his old self.

"Hey there, buckaroo! It's good to see you!" Carl meant the words with everything he had in himself. The house had felt so empty without Eva and Charlie when they were gone, and he had barely had a chance to enjoy them again before

Clarence had done his best to put a stop to their happiness together.

"You feel better now, Carl?" Charlie asked, pulling back to examine Carl's face carefully. "You were sick for a long time and I was scared."

Eva put a hand on her son's shoulder, then looked to Carl meaningfully as if to say that Charlie had been worried sick about him, which Carl could already tell.

"I'm feeling so much better now, Charlie. Don't you worry about that. Nothing's going to keep me down," Carl said in a soft, reassuring tone. He didn't want the poor child to worry about him, and knowing that he had made Carl's heart lurch.

"I think I want to take my nap with you," Charlie said decidedly. He crawled carefully into the bed and curled up next to Carl, making sure to lie on Carl's uninjured side. He gathered the blankets over himself and rested his head on the man's chest. "I think if I have my nap here, I won't have any more bad dreams about you getting hurt."

Carl frowned and looked down at the little boy, tousling his hair. "You had bad dreams about me getting hurt?"

"Yeah! That man who wanted to marry ma came back and shot you all up and then I couldn't play with you again." Charlie's eyes watered and he looked at Carl with the type of sincerity that can only be witnessed in the purity of a youth. "I never want you to get hurt like that again."

"I won't, Charlie," Carl said, wrapping his arm around the boy's small body comfortingly. Charlie nodded and rested his head against Carl's chest, letting his eyes flutter closed. "That whole thing is over and done with and that silly man is locked up because he made a lot of bad choices."

"I want to be a sheriff when I grow up," Charlie said. "To make sure no one ever hurts you or my ma ever again."

Carl chuckled. "I think you would be a fine sheriff," he said.

"Do you think I'd be a good rancher?" Charlie asked, his voice sounding tired and far away now.

"I think you'd be good at whatever you want to do, Charlie. You just focus on growing up and learning the things you care about, then you'll know what would make you happiest."

"Okay Carl," Charlie said, fully asleep now. "I love you."

"I love you too," Carl said, smiling down at the boy. His little face was entirely peaceful with sleep, and Carl looked up at Eva in amazement. He had never experienced what it felt like to have a child fall asleep on him like this, and it was one of the purest, most peaceful things in the entire world. Eva understood exactly how he was feeling because she smiled knowingly at him.

"Go ahead and get some rest, Carl," she murmured, running another blissful hand through his hair again. "I'll stay here and keep an eye on you both."

Carl nodded with a smile and found himself pulled easily into a sound sleep, quickly deciding that falling asleep with Charlie was one of the coziest things in the entire world.

"Is he awake?"

Carl opened his eyes to Maggie's voice, and he looked to her with a smile, noticing that Charlie must have crawled out of bed before he had woken up. He wasn't in the room anymore, but that was okay. It had been nice to share that moment with him.

"Maggie!"

"Carl! My heavens, you don't know how good it is to hear your voice!" Maggie came to the bedside and hugged him carefully before stepping back with a bright smile on her face, even though her eyes were rimmed red with unshed tears. Everyone had been struggling with the thought of losing him. Fortunately though, Clarence hadn't done enough damage for that to happen.

"It's good to hear you too, Maggie. How are you?"

"Much better knowing you're awake!" she exclaimed. "I just wanted to see how you were doing. Eva mentioned you had woken up briefly earlier but I missed it, so I put some soup on for you. It's ready now. I'm going to bring you up a bowl. And don't even think about rejecting it!"

Carl chuckled at Maggie's maternal scolding and smiled at her. "I won't. Thank you."

"Eva hasn't left your side for hardly a moment since it all happened. She's a good woman."

Carl smiled at Maggie for telling him that, and honestly, he wasn't surprised that Eva had been with him. He was touched, but something in him just knew that she was devoted enough to him to stay like that. Still, his eyes found Eva's as Maggie left and he reached for her hand.

"Is that true?" he asked, already knowing that it was. But he wanted her to know he recognized it, appreciated it, and appreciated her so much.

"Yes, Carl, it's true," Eva said. "I've tended to Charlie, of course, but other than that I haven't been able to step away for any longer than a moment. It was terrifying when they took you off like that, you know. Lucky for us the doc was nearby when the shots were fired and came just as soon as he knew you were hurt. Jeff and Sheriff White brought you up to your room and did what they could to stop the bleeding until he could get here to fix you up."

"It feels an awful lot like people round these parts might actually care for me," Carl teased with a chuckle. He was making light of it but the truth was that he was extremely touched. He had never really felt the intensity of caring the way he had that day. Between Eva, Charlie, and Maggie, then learning how much other people had done just to try and save his life... well, he was a little bit overwhelmed by it all. But he wasn't going to let himself get too sappy over it. Not with Eva right there.

"People love you, Carl. I love you. Charlie loves you. Maggie loves you. We all care an awful lot if you want to know the truth."

Carl smiled. "I suppose that's true. And I love you all too. I truly do."

Eva's pretty face lit up just as a soft knock came at the door. "Is it true what Maggie told me, ma'am? Is Mr. Spencer awake?"

"Sheriff White, hello. It's really good to see you," Eva said. "And yes, Carl is awake now."

"Is it all right if I come in, Carl? I just wanted to give you all an update on everything that's happening."

"Of course, sheriff, come on in," Carl said, waving the sheriff inside with his good arm.

The sheriff removed his hat and nodded first to Eva, then to Carl. "It's good to see you looking better, Carl. You had us all a bit worried."

Carl smiled. "I'm fine, sheriff White, but it's good to see you too. I've been meaning to thank you properly for everything you did to help us and to save Eva. I don't think this town has ever had a finer sheriff and won't have another one." Carl paused. "Well, that is unless Charlie decides to accept the position. Then you all might be tied."

Sheriff White laughed. "Oh Carl, you don't need to thank me for that. And as for saving Eva, that was as much you as me. It was your idea for me to climb through the window and go after Clarence that way. I don't think things would have worked out quite so well if it weren't for your quick thinking."

"Either way, Sheriff, you were there right when we needed you and I'll always feel indebted to you for that." Carl offered his hand to Sheriff White, who took it and gave it a firm pump.

"You're a fine man, Carl. And I wanted you to know you were right about everything. Of course he had admitted to it before I arrived, but we got a full confession from Clarence. But that isn't even the wildest thing. He admitted to things we didn't even know he had done."

Carl looked to Eva, who looked just as surprised as he felt.

"What sorts of things?" Eva asked, stepping forward in interest.

"Well, it turns out that his brother isn't the first man he's killed. There were a few boys out in Tennessee that he got into a brawl with a few years back and he shot all of them dead before running back to Great Bend. And some other... well... less savory things that wouldn't be proper to discuss in front of a woman. Suffice it to say, you're lucky that you found his pocket watch, Eva. Even if he didn't want to shoot you, being with him might have been a fate worse than death, if you catch my meaning."

Eva went pale and she looked to Carl. "I wouldn't have found the pocket watch if Carl hadn't told me about it. I hadn't thought about it being missing in so long, I never would have connected Clarence with that. I can't believe I was really thinking about marrying him."

Eva sighed, sitting down shakily on the end of the bed. Carl frowned.

"Eva, you can't blame yourself for that. You were doing what anyone might have done. You had to look after yourself and Charlie after what was going on at the ranch. I was unfair to you and it's actually all my fault that he even found you and had a chance to try and weasel his way into your life."

Eva sighed and shook her head. "Carl, as much as I know you love to blame yourself for every possible thing that could go wrong with me and Charlie, none of that was your fault." Eva said.

"That's right," the sheriff agreed. "Clarence had it in his head for a long time that he wanted Eva and that he was going to make Jim pay for getting to her before he had a chance. He felt like he stole her from him and it has been stewing under the surface for years. He was bound to act out on it one way or another eventually, whether she was living at the ranch or not. The important thing is that everything worked out the way it did. Clarence is in custody and the world is a lot safer for it. And that wouldn't be possible if you hadn't gotten involved, Carl."

Carl was quiet as he thought about the sheriff's words. That was true. He hadn't been able to catch Clarence himself, but he had learned about the pocket watch and he had warned Eva about it. If that hadn't happened, he might never have been caught.

"I guess everything did work out for the best," Carl said. "I don't think I'll ever be able to understand men like Clarence."

"Me either," the sheriff said. "That's why I became a sheriff, actually. Knowing there are people out there who do senseless things to good people. It's important to protect people and uphold the law."

Carl smiled at the man and nodded approvingly. "Well, you do a mighty excellent job of it, Sheriff White. We owe you a lot."

"I'm just glad you're all okay," the sheriff replied with a grin. "Has the doc been back by yet?"

Eva shook her head. "He had to check on someone but he'll be back soon to give us an update. I think he will be pleased that Carl is awake now, though. I know I am!"

The sheriff grinned. "I think it is safe to say we all are happy about that, Eva," he replied. "Clarence isn't going to get away with what he's done. We're going to give him the harshest sentence possible for the trouble he's caused the lot of you, and many other women."

"Thank you for stopping by, Sheriff. I really appreciate the update," Carl said, struggling to sit up to give the man a proper goodbye. He winced in pain, unable to fully manage it, and Eva was immediately at his side, pressing a gentle hand against his shoulder and allowing him to relax against his pillows.

"My pleasure, Carl! Ma'am," the sheriff said, regarding them both with the tip of his hat before leaving the room.

Once he was gone, Eva shook her head at Carl and narrowed her eyes at him in a teasing attempt at scolding. "You're not well enough for that yet, mister," she said, running her hand from his shoulder to his chest and giving it a soft, affectionate rub. "You stay put before you go and hurt yourself more."

"All right, all right," Carl said, hating how much he was loving the attention. He might have to get hurt more often just to bring out this side of her. But of course he would never actually do that. It was just nice to be coddled, in a funny way.

"Good."

"Soup, Carl!"

"Oh, Maggie, I forgot about that."

Maggie chuckled. "Well, I thought I ought to wait to bring it to you until you were done visiting with the sheriff. I didn't want to make you uncomfortable or have the soup be cold by the time you could eat it. I know how fussy you are about your soup."

Carl grinned sheepishly. "Boiling hot or it's not worth eating."

Maggie rolled her eyes and sat a tray down in front of Carl with the steaming bowl of soup sitting on it. He smiled at her gratefully. Before she pulled her hand fully from the tray, Carl caught it in his own and held it for a moment. "I love you, you know," he said, looking up at her sincerely. "You're my family as much as anyone and I'm so glad you're here."

"Carl!" Maggie was caught so off-guard that she began to cry. "Now why did you have to go and say that? Making me cry and look like a foolish old woman."

"You're not foolish, Maggie. I just needed you to know that. You've never been just a cook to me. You've been like my family, looking after me for so long. Understanding me and being patient with me like no one else ever would. And I need you to know I love you like family."

Maggie shook her head. "I love you too, Carl Spencer. Of course I do." She chuckled. "Now if you'll excuse me, I've got a very impatient little boy who has been waiting for me to bake some cookies with him. Oh drat, that was meant to be a surprise for you. He was excited to make you something nice to eat and insisted we make you some cookies. Please pretend to be surprised when he brings them to you, I'd hate to ruin that for him."

Carl laughed. "Consider this conversation forgotten."

"Thank you," Maggie said with a laugh. "I'll check in on you soon and see to your bowl."

"Okay, Maggie, thank you."

"Of course," Maggie said with a smile before disappearing outside.

"She really needed to hear that, Carl. It was really sweet of you to say it aloud."

Carl grinned. "Yeah, well, she was scared that I'd died and I was thinking about what it might have been like if I had. All the things that I wouldn't have had a chance to say to the people I care about the most. I would hate not to be here, or for her not to be here, without me telling her that. We know it in our hearts, but I think there's something special about being able to say it aloud, too, even if we don't do it that often."

Eva smiled. "I agree with that."

"Well I thought you might," Carl said with a laugh.

Another knock sounded at the door and Carl looked to Eva with wide, perplexed eyes. "Who now?" he whispered. Eva laughed.

"It's the doc. We should let him in."

"Oh. I guess so. But it's starting to feel like I will never get another moment alone with you again."

Eva laughed brightly and shook her head. "There will be time enough for that when you're not laid up in bed with half the town worried about you."

Carl sighed dramatically and Eva went to answer the door. "Doc! Welcome back. Come in, come in."

Carl squirmed a little at the mention of the doc. He didn't like doctors, never had. Being poked and prodded and harped at over his health had always made him uncomfortable. But he supposed he had needed the doc after what had happened, and he was grateful that he was there at all. "Hey, Doc. Thank you, you know. For patching me all up the way you did."

The doc smiled. "Don't mention it, Carl. I've just come to check on you. Make sure things are healing up the way they're meant to. No infections and whatnot, you see."

Carl nodded. "Right. Just... you know. Go easy on me, would ya?"

The doc laughed brightly. "Of course, Carl. I know your wound is tender. I won't do anything unnecessary."

Carl squirmed. "Thanks. I appreciate that."

After a quick examination, the doc smiled at Carl. "You're doing just fine, but you are going to need to stay on bedrest for a while just to be on the safe side. Do you think you can manage that?"

Carl frowned. "How long is a while?"

"A few weeks at least. I'll come and check on you frequently and clear you to get back to work once I'm comfortable with your condition. All right?"

Carl sighed heavily. The last thing he wanted was to be confined to bedrest, but he supposed he could manage that if he had no other choice. "All right."

When the doc left, Eva sat down beside him and held his hand. "I know this is going to be tough for you, but you'll get through it. Before you know it, you'll be back on your feet and getting work done just like always."

Carl gazed at Eva tenderly and took her hand in his own. "I think there's only one way I'm going to get through this in one piece."

Eva looked at him curiously. "Oh? What's that?"

"If you're my wife."

Eva's mouth dropped open and she gazed at Carl in shock. "Do you really mean that?"

"I really mean it, Eva. Here, do me a favor and look on top of my dresser.."

"All right..." Eva did as she was asked and soon carried the little piece of lace over to Carl. He hadn't found a suitable time to give it to her, but now he knew exactly what he wanted to do with it. "Is this what you meant?"

"Yes. I know it won't quite do for a ring, but the thing is, I love you, Eva, and this is the best I've got right now. If you take those scissors on the bedside table, let's cut a strip of this, all right?"

Eva nodded, though she looked confused. She took the scissors and took a strip of the lace. Carl took it from her and grinned before continuing. "Marry me. Marry me and be my wife. Live with me on the ranch, you, me, and Charlie. Be my family officially. I don't want to go another day without you as my wife. Please say you will."

Carl poured his heart out to Eva, and finally looked to her when he was done, feeling anxious that she might, for some reason, reject him or need more time. But she was beaming from ear to ear. "Oh Carl... I will. I'll marry you."

She laughed and he took her hand, struggling to wrap the lace around it and tie it with just his one good working hand. She took one end of the lace and helped him to secure it, and they smiled at each other, each thrilled by their decision.

"I want you to be mine as soon as possible, Eva. I know what it's like to be on death's door now, and I don't want to wait another second. Unless you prefer a long engagement, of course."

Eva laughed. "No. I'd like to be yours just as soon as I can, too."

"Perfect," Carl said, leaning in for a gentle kiss that brought a blush to Eva's cheeks.

The next few days went by quickly as Eva and Carl planned their wedding, and by the end of the week, the minister was standing at the end of Carl's bed. The bedroom was crammed full of people, mostly the ranch hands. The sheriff and the doc were there, and Maggie was standing with Charlie, who had the job of holding the rings for his parents. When his part came, he walked up to them dutifully and presented the rings to them with the biggest smile Carl had ever seen. Carl grinned and took the ring he'd had Maggie go out and buy for Eva on his behalf, then slipped it on her slender finger. She placed a simple golden band on his, and then they joined hands as the ceremony proceeded. Carl was so excited that it all went by in a blur, until his heart leapt to hear the closing words.

"I now pronounce you man and wife," the minister said in closing. "You may kiss the bride."

Carl and Eva locked eyes, their hearts brimming with love and joy. He took her lips against his, and shared the first kiss of many with the woman he knew would be the love of his life, forever and always.

The room erupted in cheers, and Carl and Eva laughed together as Charlie jumped onto the bed to embrace them both. "We're a family now?" he asked excitedly.

"That's right, son," Carl replied.

# Epilogue

*Two Years Later*

"Do you think he'll like it?" Carl asked in a hushed voice, looking at Eva with wide eyes. She chuckled at him and pressed a gentle hand against his cheek, leaning in to plant a kiss against his lips. She would never tire of kissing this man.

"He's going to love it. Trust me," Eva said with a smile. "He's going to feel just like his pa, and that's all he ever really talks about."

Carl thought for a moment. "Yeah, I guess he does talk a lot about that lately. He gave up on that sheriff idea pretty quickly."

"He kept it in his mind for at least a year. He may always be drawn to upholding the law, you know. But he wants to be just like you," Eva replied, laughing at the long phase that Charlie had gone through of wanting to bring in the bad guys. It had been two years since Clarence had been arrested and the excitement of it all had left Charlie a changed boy.

"I think he'll be even better than me. He's got a way with animals, you know? It comes in handy on a ranch," Carl said.

"He does. He's always been an empathetic boy. He bonds with animals pretty easily."

"Oh really? Remember the first time we almost kissed and he ruined the moment by torturing the cat?"

Eva laughed. "He was just a baby, then. And still learning how to manage animals. He'll be starting school in the fall and your gift is going to make him the happiest boy in Kansas."

Carl smiled. "I sure hope so."

Eva nodded. "It will. And soon you will be able to give this one their birthday gift, too."

She gestured to her belly, which was swollen with pregnancy. She was seven months along now, and soon Charlie was going to have a new baby brother or sister. Carl had been working tirelessly on the nursery for the new baby and had whittled many toys for it already.

"I can't wait to meet our baby," Carl said, wrapping his arms around Eva's waist. He nestled his face into her neck, pressing a series of soft kisses against it that sent shivers all throughout her body. "Do you think it will be a boy or a girl?"

"I think that it won't matter either way because we will love them the same. But if I had to guess, I think you're going to have a daughter."

Carl beamed. "A little girl?"

Eva nodded. "I'm carrying her differently than I carried Charlie. Plus there's this mother's intuition that people talk about and I really just feel like it's a girl."

Carl pressed a hand to Eva's belly gingerly and gave it a gentle rub. "A baby girl. What would you like to name her?"

"Maybe Rose. What about you? What names do you like?"

Carl thought for a moment. "I was always partial to the name Violet."

"What if we named her Violet Rose?" Eva suggested. Carl crinkled his nose.

"Two flowers in one name?"

"Well, one is also a color. It could just sound like a purple rose," Eva pointed out.

"I do like that..."

"Besides, no one would need to know her middle name unless they asked. It's mostly just for us anyway. And for her." Eva smiled down at her belly where Carl was caressing the little baby mound.

"You're right. I like that idea. We'll see how you feel about it once she gets here. If she fits the name then we can keep it if you like it," Carl said, pressing a kiss against Eva's temple. He didn't even question whether or not it would be a boy. He trusted her intuition, and Eva loved him even more for it. He was perfect in so many ways. Some days, she couldn't even believe he was truly hers.

A soft knock came at their door and Eva parted from Carl's embrace to open it. Maggie was standing outside beaming. "The guests are starting to arrive, and Charlie is beside himself with excitement. He said it's the best day of his whole life, and he hasn't even seen his gift from Carl yet."

They all laughed with fondness at the little boy's excitable nature. Carl put his arm around Eva's shoulders. "Well, I guess we had better get down there then. We just have to grab another gift. The one you made for him."

"Oh, I almost forgot that was why we came up here," Eva said with a laugh. "You know, I get so forgetful when I'm pregnant."

"That's all right, sweetheart. That's why you have me around." Carl winked and went to the closet to retrieve the wrapped parcel that Eva had made for Charlie. He held it under his arm and guided her carefully down the stairs and outside, where sure enough, the yard was becoming littered with people.

Charlie ran around greeting them all, excited for his big day. He had been making friends around town and was beloved by many for his outgoing and caring nature. Before long, he was pulling two of Carter's children with him to the swing, where Carl had set it back up outside on the big tree where it had been originally.

"It's so good to see you, everyone. Thanks for coming," Carl said loudly, making his rounds to greet each guest personally. It felt like the entire town had shown up to celebrate her son's special day, and Eva felt blessed. A group of local women flocked to her and began asking her questions about the baby, how it was coming along, when it was due, if they had chosen any names for it. Carl overheard the name question and caught her eye, giving her a slight nod as if to silently tell her it was okay with him if she told them the name they had come up with just that day. She smiled brightly at him and did tell them what they were thinking about and enjoyed the chorus of oohs and aahs that it elicited.

"Pa! Come push me!" Charlie shouted from the tire swing. Carl laughed.

"Excuse me gentlemen, my son is beckoning me. If I don't push him on his birthday, what kind of father would I be?"

Everyone laughed and Carl made his way over to Charlie. Eva watched fondly, remembering the very first time that Carl had pushed Charlie on the swing. It had been disastrous, in a way, but at the same time, it had shown her depths to the man that she never would have expected. He had taken it so hard when he felt like he let Charlie down, and she had seen just how badly he wanted to be a good man, a man who could be a good father. The shame of it was that he had always been that man, he just didn't know it yet.

"Higher!" Charlie cried, his loud laughter carrying over the crowd. Many people gathered to watch and chuckle at the sight, and Eva smiled to herself, rubbing the bump of her belly where the baby was resting. Would she like the swing too, once she was old enough for it? Likely so. And Charlie would be an amazing big brother, she already knew that much. He had drawn several pictures of their family since he found out about the pregnancy, always including the baby even though he didn't know whether it would be a brother or a sister. He sometimes made baby boys, sometimes baby girls. He had two that were his favorites that he kept in his dresser, and he'd whispered to her one night that when the baby came, he would pick the picture of whatever the baby turned out to be and gift it to them the first day they met, so they would always know that Charlie was happy they were there.

"Me next, me next!" shouted every single child attending the party. Carl laughed but agreed to push several other children, and Eva admired how far he had come from the man who had taken the swing down in shame so many years ago. She was proud of her husband and hoped that he would always know it to be the case.

Eventually, other adults were enlisted for swing pushing duty, and Carl returned to Eva with beads of sweat forming on his forehead. She pulled the handkerchief from his pocket and wiped his forehead for him before folding it and tucking it back away. He laughed and kissed the top of her head.

"Boy, he sure loves that thing, doesn't he?" Carl said with a chuckle.

"He sure does," Eva agreed. "I think it's special to him, you know. He was really young when you set it up and I don't think he remembers everything very clearly, but he knows that it's there because you love him. That's the kind of thing he will never forget."

Carl looked away for a moment, overtaken by the words. "I don't think I could ask for a better son. I love him just like he's my own."

"I know you do. Because he is, in his own way. I think us finding each other made all of us whole."

Carl nodded in agreement, putting an arm around Eva's waist as they watched the children playing. Eventually Maggie emerged from the house and rang a bell.

"Lunch is served!" she exclaimed, gesturing to the big table and benches that Jeff had set up for them outside that morning. Maggie had been cooking all day long, and even into the night the night before, and the whole surface of one of the tables was covered with an exquisite feast. Soon the guests were all filing over to the food and they sat down to eat.

"You take a seat here, my darling, and I will get you a plate," Carl said, leading Eva to a spot in the shade where she could sit. "Charlie, come get some lunch!"

"Okay, pa!"

Charlie ran from the swing and went with Carl to the table, where they both filled up plates full of food and then returned to where Eva was sitting so they could eat together.

"How are you liking your party, sweetheart?" Eva asked, grinning at her son, who was eating ravenously.

"It's so fun!" he cried. "I want a party like this every year!"

Carl chuckled. "That can be arranged," he said. "When you're done eating, I think we should start with your gifts. What do you say?"

"Yeah!" Charlie exclaimed. "I can't wait for my gifts!"

The promise of opening his presents caused Charlie to eat even faster, which made Eva sigh. "Slow down, honey. I don't want you to choke. Everyone else will still be eating by the time you're done so be mindful, okay?"

Charlie sighed but did as he was told. Eva smiled at him and patted his hand. "Good boy," she said. Even though he wasn't happy about it, he ate like a normal five, well, six as of that day, year old, and smiled at his mother when he was finished.

He was well behaved enough to wait until Carl and Eva were done to ask if they could do the presents, and Eva smiled.

"This one first," she said, sliding the little parcel over to her son. He looked at Carl as if to get his go ahead, and when Carl nodded he ripped the paper open. His mouth curled into a pleased smile and he looked at his mom in shock.

"You made this for me, ma?" he asked, standing up to put the gift on.

"I did, sweetheart. What do you think?"

It fit him perfectly and Charlie jumped in the air. "I love it! It's just like Pa's!"

Eva smiled, pleased with her son's reaction. He was right. She had modeled the leather jacket after Carl's, knowing how much Charlie admired it. She had made it just a little bit big so that he could grow into it and hopefully get use out of it for more than a year. Either way though, it was a perfect replica and Charlie was thrilled with it.

"Pa, I look like you now! Do you like it?" Charlie exclaimed.

"I love it, son," Charlie said, placing a hand on Charlie's head. "Now come with me. We've got one more thing for you and I think you'll like that just as much."

"Okay."

Eva followed Carl and Charlie as Carl led their son to the barn. Charlie looked at his pain confusion before Carl opened the doors up. Standing inside was Jeff, holding the reigns of a gorgeous horse.

"That little beauty is for you, son. I'm going to teach you to ride with me this year. Your ma said she thinks you're old enough now."

Charlie stared at the horse in shock. He was a dark, chestnut brown with soulful, brown eyes and a white muzzle. His mane was long and well kept, and his hooves each had white tufts of fur at the bottom. "He's mine?"

"All yours, son. Bought him especially for you. What do you think?"

Instead of speaking, Charlie ran to Carl's side and hugged him tightly, squeezing his eyes shut. It looked like he was trying not to cry. Carl laughed and held the boy in a tight squeeze before finally releasing him.

"I love him, pa. What's his name?" Charlie finally asked, his voice quavering. But he had managed to compose himself enough not to cry.

"Well that's up to you, Charlie. I'm not going to name another man's horse."

Charlie walked up to the horse tentatively and gave his muzzle a gentle stroke. The two seemed to form an instant connection, and Eva watched with a full heart as Carl approached the boy and the horse with a smile on his face.

"He reminds me of the chocolate cakes Maggie makes," Charlie said, rubbing the horse behind the ears. "And he's sweet like them, too. I might name him Chocolate."

Carl grinned. "A mighty fine name," he said with a nod. "You get to decide it all, you know. And once you two have gotten to know one another a little, I'm going to show you how to saddle him up so we can take him for a ride together."

Charlie beamed at Carl. "I love him, Pa. I feel like we're going to be really good friends!"

"I'm glad, son," Carl said with a grin. "I'm going to get the saddle. You two keep getting to know each other. I'll be right back."

Eva approached as Carl disappeared and placed a hand on her son's shoulder. "Who is your new friend?" she asked with a gentle smile.

"I think I'm naming him Chocolate," Charlie said. "But I'm not sure. Do you think it's a good name?"

Eva smiled at her son. "Charlie and Chocolate. It has a nice ring to it. I think you should ask the horse though, not me, and decide what he thinks."

"Oh, okay!" Charlie rubbed the pony's muzzle and smiled up into his eyes. "Do you like the name Chocolate?"

To everyone's surprise, the horse nuzzled Charlie's hand as if to say he did, and Charlie turned to Eva with the biggest smile she had ever seen on his face. "I think he likes it, ma!"

"Then Chocolate is the perfect name for him!"

Charlie laughed and hugged the pony just as Carl returned with the saddle. "Now, I'm going to set this up for you and I just want you to watch me for now. I'll explain what I'm doing but don't worry too much if you don't remember how. I'll show you properly later, all right?"

"All right, pa."

"Good."

Carl began to secure the saddle, explaining carefully what he was doing with every step. Charlie watched in awe and finally, when Carl finished, Charlie bounced in excitement. "Can I ride him now, Pa?"

"Yes, son, but not alone. It's your first time so I want to stay with you and talk you through it. How does that sound?" Carl glanced to Eva from over Charlie's head and gave her a little wink of reassurance. He knew she would kill him if he let their son ride by himself for the first time, and he wasn't going to let anything bad happen to the boy. It was just nicer to make it sound like it was Charlie's idea to be guided and not something the adults were imposing upon him, and Eva felt her heart grow more in love with Carl with every passing minute. He always knew just how to talk to Charlie, and the two of them had a closer bond than she ever would have imagined.

"Yeah, Pa, I'm ready!"

"Great. Now come here and I'll help you up on the saddle, all right?"

Charlie nodded and went to Carl, who hoisted him up on the saddle. "Now make sure you're comfortable and keep your feet in the stirrups. Hold on here, to the reign, just like this, you see?"

Charlie listened intently to everything his father said and when Carl was content that Charlie was stable on the pony, he shot Eva a grin before looking back at the boy. "Now, we're going to go out and walk Chocolate to the pasture where we can be alone with him. We don't want anything spooking him and right now the other horses are out in their field. Hold on tight but stay relaxed. If the pony thinks you're afraid, it's more prone to get spooked himself or feel uncomfortable with you. They're sensitive creatures and they need to know we're confident and we know what they're doing. We're the leader so they have to trust us not to get them into any trouble. But if they think you doubt yourself, they're going to be anxious. Does that make sense?"

Charlie nodded. "I'm not scared, Pa. Chocolate can trust me."

Carl smiled at the boy and then led them off, walking with the pony and keeping an eye on Charlie to see that he stayed stable on the pony. Eva watched, her heart growing fuller every second.

"When can we gallop, pa? I want to ride like you and Smokey!" Charlie exclaimed with a laugh. He was clearly in his element and seemed to have a natural ability to be comfortable in the saddle.

"We're not going to run yet. It takes a bit of time and practice before we do that. We can trot though. Stay steady, now," Carl said, jogging with the pony to speed it up a little bit.

Charlie whooped in excitement, and for a moment Eva was afraid that the pony would be afraid of the sudden noises her son made. But he was a docile little creature and didn't seem bothered at all. Carl had picked the perfect pony for their son. He was a better father than she ever would have imagined. A better father than *he* ever would have imagined himself to be.

And she was so excited to be the mother of his biological child now as well. Their family would truly feel complete once the baby was born.

Before long, all of the guests were gathered around, watching as Charlie and Carl broke in the pony. Eva laughed at their antics, completely in love with her family. Charlie was really having fun, and she could tell that his father was too.

"That boy of yours is a natural, Eva," Carter exclaimed with a bright chuckle. "Look at the way he sits. He's completely at home up there."

"And that jacket! The two of them match. It's just the cutest thing I've ever seen," Maggie said. Eva hadn't noticed her come up beside her, but she smiled warmly at Maggie.

"Charlie wants to be just like his father, so I thought I would try and do something for him to make him feel a little bit closer. I didn't know whether he would be excited for clothes for his birthday, but it looked like it really touched him," Eva said, smiling fondly.

"Oh, bless his heart," Maggie exclaimed. "The two of them really make quite a pair, don't they?"

"They really do," Eva agreed.

"Charlie took to him straight away, do you remember? Carl had to warm up to the idea but look at them now. They're practically inseparable!"

Eva laughed at the memory. Charlie had certainly grown attached to Carl quickly, and he had given Carl no choice but to love him right back. She never would have imagined then just how perfect their lives would grow to be together. It was the biggest blessing of her life and every day she felt so lucky to be where she was.

"I don't know if you heard me say to the ladies earlier, but I think that we're having a girl next," Eva said, lowering her voice. "And we've thought of a name for her that we think we might like."

Maggie gasped and looked to Eva. "Did you?"

"Yes, we just spoke about it today. Violet Rose Spencer."

Maggie squealed in excitement and hugged Eva. "A beautiful name! Goodness, I'm trying to picture Carl with a daughter. He's going to be so protective of her."

Eva laughed. "He will, just like he is protective of the rest of us. I don't know about you, but I can't imagine a better father for any child, girl or boy. He's just... so wonderful."

Maggie nodded in agreement and smiled wistfully as she turned her attention back to Carl and Charlie. "You certainly are a beautiful family," she said.

"You're just as much a part of it as the rest of us, Maggie," Eva said, draping an arm around the woman in a half hug. "I don't know where we would be if it weren't for you. I'd like to ask you if you would like to be the godmother to our children."

Maggie gasped. "Do you really mean that?"

"I really mean that. Carl and I have spoken a lot about it. We want you to be part of their lives for as long as we all have each other. And there's no one else I would ever want to trust my babies with if something were ever to happen to us."

"Oh, Eva!" Maggie's eyes filled with tears and she hugged Eva tightly. "I'd be so honored to be their godmother!"

Eva was elated to hear it and she couldn't wait to tell Carl the news. Finally, he returned with Charlie, lifted the boy off the pony, and handed him to his mother. Eva held him and went to Carl, draping her free arm around him in a hug. Charlie was growing a lot, and it was a bit harder to hold him now that she was pregnant, but right now, it wasn't a strain at all. It was the most natural thing in the world for her to hug her family.

"We have one more piece of good news for you, Charlie," Eva said, gesturing Maggie over. "Maggie is going to be your godmother. Yours and the baby's."

Charlie's eyes widened and he smiled in excitement, looking between all of the adults. "Really? Another ma?"

Maggie laughed. "Like that, yes, Charlie. It means you're always going to have someone to look after you, no matter what happens. Someone who loves you just as much as your own ma."

Charlie reached for Maggie and she scooped him up into a big hug. Carl's arms found their way around her waist and she leaned into him, feeling safe and secure in the broad, masculine form as it surrounded her.

"I would say this is shaping up to be a pretty good sixth birthday," he murmured to Eva as Charlie chattered excitedly to Maggie about her new status as his godmother.

"I would say that you're right," Eva replied with a grin, pressing a kiss against Carl's bearded cheek. "He looks like just about the happiest boy on earth."

"That's because he was lucky enough to be born with you as his ma," Carl teased, although she knew that he meant the words with a deep sincerity.

"Well he was lucky enough that you didn't send for the sheriff when you found her rummaging through your cellar all those years ago," Eva teased back. "And he was lucky enough that you took pity on us and learned to love us."

"Nothing I have ever done in my life has been easier than loving you two," Carl said firmly, pulling Eva to face him. "Not a day goes by that I don't know how lucky I am. And although I always feel like I can't love you any more than I already do, the morning comes and I realize I was wrong. Somehow I love you more every day."

"Carl..." Eva felt overcome with emotion and she rested her forehead against Carl's chest. He held her close in an intimate embrace. The rest of the world melted away and for a moment, the only thing that existed was the island of love that she and Carl had made together. "I feel the exact same way," she whispered. "You're so perfect, the perfect father, the perfect husband... and I love you. So much."

"I love you, too, Eva darling," Carl murmured. He kissed her then, a kiss so unabashed that she was tempted to take him right to the bedroom. But, of course, that wasn't an option, and soon he was pulling away from her and the rest of the world came back into focus. Charlie was tugging on Carl's hand and laughing, and Eva watched the two loves of her life as they went back toward the swing where it had all begun.

## THE END

## Also by Lydia Olson

Thank you for reading "**The Mountain Man's Unexpected Family**"!

I hope you enjoyed it! If you did, here are some of my other books!

**Some of my Best-Selling Books**

**Check my previous Stand-Alone Best Sellers:**

**#1** The Wrong Letter for the Suitable Bride

**#2** An Unforgettable Love by a Twist of Fate

**#3** Two Scared Souls Finding Redemption

**#4** The Mountains Between their Hearts

**#5** A Western Lottery to Find his Bride

Also, if you liked this book, you can also check out **my full Amazon Book Catalogue at:**
https://go.lydiaolson.com/bc-authorpage

**Thank you for allowing me to keep doing what I love!** ♥